THE ALTERED WAKE

The Sentinel Quartet
Book One

D1295394

MEGAN MORGAN

Clickworks Press · Baltimore, MD

First publication: Clickworks Press, 2018
Release: CWP-ALT1-INT-E.M-1.0

Sign up for updates, deals, and exclusive sneak peeks at clickworkspress.com/join.

ISBN-10: 1-943383-41-3
ISBN-13: 978-1-943383-41-2

"Stars hide your fires

    For these here are my desires

    And I won't give them up to you this time around

    And so I'll be found

    With my stake stuck in this ground

    Marking the territory of this newly impassioned soul."

— Mumford And Sons
"Roll Away Your Stone"

001

CAMERON TOOK THE curve too fast. A shiver ran through the motorcycle, up into her hands. She shifted down, her eyes on the next bend, this one so sharp it almost became a circle. Each twist and turn meant time lost. The fool who chose motorcycles as the vehicle for patrols must have been more concerned with fuel costs than the schedule.

Snow tires gripped the asphalt of the curve. Cameron's revolver lifted away from her hip, and her blade slid a few centimeters against her back. The shell of the bike rattled, and the battery buzzed in the cold air.

Wind knifed into the gaps between her gloves and jacket and under the edge of her helmet when she rounded the next turn. Cameron shuddered. She remembered the long, straight roads of Cotarion's southern plains, and the summer sun that had warmed her back when her patrol began. Now her bike's brilliant scarlet lay under a coat of gray winter dust. Some of the Low Crescent Mountain villagers did not even recognize her as a Sentinel until they saw the golden eyes embroidered on the shoulders of her jacket.

Cameron glanced at her odometer. Not far. She dropped down another gear.

A town sprang up out of the mountainside. She drove between the steep roofs and tiny shuttered windows common in the Low Crescents. The light was fading, and they had just reached Palisade. At least they hadn't fallen further behind.

A few houses flashed by, then a pub, a small hotel, a mechanic's shop, all showing signs of salvage in their construction. There was a Remnant somewhere nearby, visible in pieces of pale metal cut into roof tiles, a gleaming post where a log would normally be, a series of perfectly smooth glass windows. The few people on the street looked up at the hum of her engine, and their eyes followed her progress.

Posters plastered every building, and from every poster a child gazed.

Cameron slowed, enough to glimpse a few words, and then she slowed more, enough for the second motorcycle to catch up. When her patrol partner was near enough, she made a few hand signals, and though she couldn't see Captain Fletcher's face behind the dark glass of his visor, she did see his shoulders stiffen. He was going to argue.

He followed her to the scarlet flag that flapped over the Public Safety Office. They pulled their bikes into the small gravel lot in front of the PSO. In this, at least, Palisade was lucky. In many towns, the PSO was a blocky building, cheaply made. Palisade's was older, and it looked like an arrowhead of stone and wood from the front, pointing into the sky. No salvage, either.

They both pulled off their helmets. Captain Fletcher's mouth, usually curved in a pleasant smile, was marred by a frown.

"Are you stopping over some missing posters, Kardell?"

"You could go on alone while I look into it, Sir. I know catching up to our schedule is important."

The frown deepened. A breeze ruffled his thick hair, which was unaffected by hours under a helmet. "It's against regulations for us to split up."

"Yes, Captain Fletcher. It is also against regulations to ignore a call for help."

"I don't need lectures from a Unibrow on regulations. When you've been Sentinel more than four months, then maybe you can form an opinion."

"Sir, I've been a Sentinel for six months."

Captain Fletcher cursed. "You know what I mean." He held up his helmet, and stared down his own reflection in the visor, though it looked like he was communing with the head of some aerodynamic insect, shiny black except for the slashes of red that might have been eyebrows.

"It's at least five kids, Sir."

"I guess you're right. If we don't do something, there'll be hell to pay." He gave her one of the aggrieved looks that he seemed to reserve just for her. "You're staying out here."

Captain Fletcher swung off his bike, and his boots thudded on the worn planks of the stairs. The door slammed shut behind him. Cam dismounted, tucked strands of dark hair behind her ears, smoothed out the heavy black field uniform. The horizontal bar for which fresh Lieutenants had earned the 'Unibrow' nickname was stitched into the collar of the jacket. The field uniform bore no medals or honors beyond rank. She pulled out her blade and checked that it was clean. It had been her grandmother's, so it was a little too short, and she'd never liked how much it curved, but it was clean and sharp. The pistol was loaded, but who knew how much of the ammunition would actually discharge properly?

Cam watched the wind turbines spin on a ridge far above, slicing unceasingly at clouds heavy with snow. All the while she counted off the passing seconds in her head.

When enough time had passed, she went up the front stairs, her footsteps almost silent, even in the heavy boots. A bell rang over the door when she walked in, and Cam bit back a curse. A woman sat behind a desk at the far end of a room more hunting lodge than office, her redfish-pink cardigan and matching glasses glowing against the paneled walls.

The woman looked startled at first, but her welcoming smile covered it quickly. "Hello, I'm Mrs. Lenka."

"Lieutenant Kardell. I'm with Captain Fletcher."

Cam must have spoken a little too sharply, because Mrs. Lenka's smile faded a couple of degrees. Still, she rallied well enough.

"The coffee is about done. If you don't mind waiting a minute, I'll show you back when I take it in."

Cam limited her response to a nod and didn't say anything else until Mrs. Lenka placed a hot ceramic cup in her hands. The coffee was weak, but at least it was fresh. Mrs. Lenka picked up two more mugs, and Cam followed her just a few steps down a hallway to the left.

A brass placard on the door bore the name 'Sheriff Manning'. Balancing both mugs in one hand, Mrs. Lenka knocked, and a man called, "Come in."

Mrs. Lenka delivered the coffee to Captain Fletcher, who was all smiles and effusive thanks. Mrs. Lenka returned the smile, and Cam knew she'd never believe for a moment that Captain Fletcher had argued against stopping. When Fletcher turned his attention back to the sheriff, Cam slipped through the door and stood back near the wall. Sheriff Manning glanced up at her just once, but otherwise Captain Fletcher held his attention.

Sheriff Manning's office was tidy, but the papers on his desk were in disarray. On the nearest shelf stood a set of nature guidebooks, all brand new, with notes sticking out of the tops of some pages. Wedged between the bookshelf and the wall, almost out of sight, was a sleeping cot. Manning himself was a tall, middle-aged man. He held himself too straight, perhaps to compensate for weariness. His dark skin was even darker under his eyes.

As soon as the door closed behind Mrs. Lenka, the sheriff picked up the story he'd been telling before the interruption. "The next one was a week later. This time it climbed in through an open window, grabbed Maple Knowles out of her bed, and carried her off. Her family just saw a dark shape running into the woods behind their house.

"That's when we called up the neighboring Safety Offices and started patrols of the town at night. When it came again, my son saw it creeping around the Whitley's place. He called for help; he was afraid to shoot at it so near the houses. I was out, along with a couple of the townspeople, and we ran to him.

"It was on him when we got there. He stabbed it a couple of times, but the knife he had wasn't big enough to do much. When the rest of us showed up, it tore off. Fastest I've ever seen anything move."

He looked at Fletcher, and his pause was heavy while he measured the Captain. He decided against whatever he wanted to add. Smart man.

"Well. Kai died that night, and the thing got away. Since then it's taken two more kids out of their beds, always at dusk or in the middle of the night."

The sheriff sat back in his chair, rubbing his neck. Captain Fletcher said, "Did you search the woods?"

"We've had the whole town out there more than once."

"Have there been any attacks in nearby towns?"

"Some smoke-houses ransacked and livestock missing, but nothing like here."

Captain Fletcher stood. "I'm sure you heard that we're under a lot of pressure to finish patrols quickly. Some of the budget got pulled from us to build more turbines, so we can stay for a couple of days to look around, try to find the bear. If we don't, I'll put in a request for some experts to come and deal with it."

Officer Manning nodded, all expression gone from his face. Of course he had hoped for more. "We'll take any help we can get. Would you like me to show you around?"

"I don't want to deplete your resources, thank you. But if you have an extra map . . . "

Cam stayed where she was when Captain Fletcher left the room, just out of his sight. Samuel Manning looked at her, his eyebrows raised. She strode to his bookshelf, and took down one of the new guidebooks. A thick piece of paper was tucked inside, the kind used for drawing. She unfolded it, looked for a moment at the hulking shape sketched in pencil.

"Is this what you saw the night your son died?"

Manning just barely nodded, as if half afraid to admit it. "Kai had this book when he was a kid, a story about a man who turned into a bear, went around helping forest animals. He loved it. For months, we read it every night. That thing, it's like it came straight out of the book, halfway between man and bear. Only it wasn't nice. It tore Kai apart."

Cam folded the paper, tucked it back in the book. "I'll do everything I can, Officer Manning."

"Thank you, Lieutenant."

Captain Fletcher poked his head around the door. "Move it, Kardell. Sorry, Officer Manning, she's got a streak of insubordination in her a mile wide."

Cam followed Fletcher out of the building before Manning had a chance to defend her. The temperature outside had dropped several degrees, and flakes of snow swirled through the air, while the sky threatened more. Street lamps flickered on, barely pressing back against the gloom. Fletcher's cheery expression vanished, and he turned on Cam. "I told you to stay out here."

"It was cold, Sir."

"You got us into a real mess, Kardell. How are we going to find a bear in the mountains? One specific bear? We could have been at Camp Hastings, having beef and potatoes and carrots, sleeping in rooms that don't smell like cat piss, talking to real people."

Cam didn't mention that her rooms at the camps usually smelled like cat piss, and she didn't see much difference between talking to fellow Sentinels and the people of a place like Palisade. The beef, though, would have been nice.

"We have two days. I can search south of the town, if you don't mind, sir."

Fletcher's lips compressed until they nearly vanished. Clearly, he wasn't ready for her to start making suggestions about search tactics. A brilliant red rose up his neck, his jaw, and into his face. Cam braced herself for the shouting, which, once started, could go on for quite a while.

He'd just parted his lips to begin his lecture when a scream broke Palisade's watchful silence.

Cam's hand went up to the hilt of her sword, as did Fletcher's. They both turned their faces toward the sound, straining for more.

At the second scream, they pulled on their helmets, swung their legs over their bikes—and Captain Fletcher put his hand on Cameron's shoulder, signaled for her to stay behind. She ground her teeth together. If he'd bothered to look at Sheriff Manning's drawing, he wouldn't dare go alone, even if it meant having her as backup.

She let him pull out of the parking lot, his tires spitting gravel at her, and then she followed. He'd write her up after. There were worse things.

A few citizens of Palisade gathered out on the main road, hunting rifles in hand. They saw the bikes coming, and pointed south. Fletcher turned down a narrow lane, and Cam followed. A gun went off, not far away, and its echo guided them forward, even over the hum of the engines, even through the helmets. The lane brought them out into one of Palisade's side-streets.

The window of one house exploded into the road. A shape leapt out in a spray of glass.

Fletcher and Cam both stopped, and drew their silent blades.

The creature crouched in a circle of gleaming glass, a vaguely simian shape with a broad chest. It supported some weight on one front arm, and in the other clutched a screeching, struggling child. Light gleamed on folds of skin on the face and chest, while coarse hair sprouted from every other part of the body, running long and thick from the top of the head and down the spine.

Its head whipped around as it searched for an escape. Its small eyes locked on Fletcher. Lips peeled back to display long teeth, and then it leapt up onto the roofs, the crying child grasped to its chest.

Fletcher rode after it, and Cam kept right behind. Their bikes scraped through the alley between the houses, blasted across another side street, and then cut back through another narrow gap. The creature dropped from the roof, scurried over the ground, and then leapt back up on the next roof without pause.

The next alley put them out in a muddy garden, and their bikes churned up dirt as they accelerated across the open space and into the wood line where the creature almost vanished. The sky still held just enough light for them to make out its black shape through the trees.

Cam's bike bucked and rattled under her hands, its tires sliding over rocks slick with fresh snowfall. Somehow, Captain Fletcher managed to find a path through, and he sliced between trees, hardly swerving. He neared the giant creature, his blade in one gloved hand.

The creature dropped out of sight, and then so did the ground. Fletcher turned sharply to the right, but on the snowy earth his bike kept sliding forward. He hopped off, and he and Cam watched it slide over the ledge. It hit the ground a moment later with a metallic crunch.

Captain Fletcher groaned, but even as Cam pulled up to him, he had already climbed back to his feet. Without pausing to check for injuries, he walked to the edge of the bank, then slid down the steep ledge of rock, cursing the whole way. Cam hopped off her bike and followed him. The child still screamed, and that guided them forward.

They ran. Snow and branches struck Cam's face; her lungs drew frigid air. Again and again her shins banged into fallen saplings. Screams twisted through the shadow trees, and they followed.

The terrain steepened as they went. The beast's flight straightened, the sound of its escape going out ahead of them without deviating to the left or the right. It was getting away. The shouts of the child became muffled, and then stopped. A few steps later, Cam and Captain Fletcher nearly collided with another rock outcropping. It stretched up, a wall of sandstone almost six meters high.

They stopped, quieted their breathing, and listened. Cam heard nothing except the pounding of blood in her ears and the soft hiss of falling snow.

She pulled the flashlight from her belt, clicked it on, and swept the beam of light along the pitted and fissured rock face. Captain Fletcher did the same. A few feet to their left was a deep line of shadow where the outcropping was split. Holding the flashlight high with her left hand and her blade forward in her right, Cam eased around the edge. The gap was a steep-sided "V", the sides high and remarkably straight, as if the massive rock had been split by an equally massive axe. Saplings grew up from the bottom, which was just wide enough to walk through. Their lights caught a reflective surface a few yards in. They went forward, while seconds slipped past.

A metal object became clear, a door lying on the ground. A vacant frame gaped in the rock face to their right, leading to a staircase that descended into shadows. The smell wafting from the dark space was a mix of stagnant air, damp fur, and decay.

"You'll stay here," Captain Fletcher said.

"Sir—"

His eyes glittered dangerously in the glow of flashlights. "You should still be in town. I'm going to kill this thing, and then I'm going to have some damn awful dinner, and then I'm going to write you up. Stay. Here."

He vanished down the flight of stairs. The darkness seemed to swallow even the light he carried with him. Cam stood between the rock walls, shaking with cold and fury.

She heard a rumbling growl from below, a noise that seemed to fill the air around her. She went through the opening and down the short flight of stairs strewn with detritus.

The smell rose up to meet her and grew increasingly pungent with every step down into the dark. Cameron swallowed, but it didn't help, so she inhaled through her mouth. Captain Fletcher whispered, "Come on, you bastard."

Cam gripped the wrappings on her hilt tighter, the woven ropes digging into her fingers. The narrow beam of light in her hands stayed steady, though the hairs on her arms prickled. Feet scuffled. Captain Fletcher grunted, then shouted, and Cam heard him hit the ground. His yell was cut off.

Cam reached the bottom of the stairs. Shapes mounded up along the base of walls, broken curves of shadow and light. Sticks with knobbed ends and orbs with holes and jagged edges. All gnawed.

Then, in the corner, a glitter of eyes, and Captain Fletcher on the floor under the beast's grip. Cam stepped back in front of the stairs. Her heel caught on something, and it clattered across the floor, hollow, spinning randomly. When it stopped rolling, the room was silent.

Dark, cramped quarters. An inhuman opponent: fast, strong, and from the glint in those eyes, intelligent. She'd seen worse in exams.

The rangy mound of fur rose up, and in the beam of Cameron's light its arms unfolded, its shoulders shifting, roiling. Teeth flashed, not in warning this time, but in promise. This was the monster's lair, where she was just more potential meat.

The creature stepped forward, huffing. Like a laugh almost, but of course it wasn't.

Cameron couldn't grip her sword any tighter. She needed both hands, but she couldn't spare the light. The thing huffed again.

Then it leapt.

Cameron met it, her blade sweeping forward. It dodged, faster than she'd expected, but she nicked its chest and shoulder. Then it barreled into her.

Cameron just slipped between the grasping claws, but her foot came down on another odd-shaped object that twisted under her weight. She cursed as she went down, her hip and back scraping the wall. The beast was a mountain above her, a whir of teeth, claw, fur, and shining eyes.

She kept her sword up, a thin barrier. Fetid air brushed her face. She cut the first reaching hand. Scrabbled for footing as hard shapes on the floor punched through her jacket. Kicked her heel into its shin.

The creature withdrew, long enough for her to regain her feet. It roared, washing her again in hot, rancid breath.

Then it went low and charged on all four limbs. It looked to overwhelm her, and she had no room to escape on either side.

She made a short sweep, and still the tip of her sword scraped the wall. The edge bit into the vulnerable flesh at the neck. The creature shrieked, but didn't stop. It gripped the front of her jacket. Only the padded leather stopped claws from piercing her skin.

Every one of its teeth showed as its face pressed close. The wall pushed at Cameron's back, the monstrous claws at her chest, and the thing's blood fell hot on her hand, her hilt. She worked the blade deeper. The beast did not relent. Its lips pulled back in a snarl that was almost a smile.

Cameron writhed, leveraged for some room with her hips and shoulders even as the beast leaned in. The bristled fur on its hands prickled against her neck. At last, she managed to get her left shoulder free enough.

She twisted and slammed the flashlight into the side of the creature's head, cracking the bony ridge over its eye. Glass shattered, and the room plunged into darkness, howls reverberating through Cameron's skull. She swept the flashlight out again and connected. The claws released her, and the stench pulled back ever so slightly.

With both hands freed, she swept her sword through the dark, and connected with flesh.

An agonized roar guided her next strike. After that, a thud, and then everything was still.

002

CAM STOOD WITH her blade at ready once more. The smell of blood pricked at the back of her throat.

She steadied her breathing, swallowed, and swiped the blood from her blade before returning it to the scabbard. Her hands swept against her pockets and found everything intact. She allowed herself a small smile.

"Captain Fletcher?"

"Find the kid." His voice floated out of the darkness, rough and a little vague.

Cam fumbled in the dark, her hands brushing things she was glad were invisible. Finally, she found the small, warm shape hunkered down in the corner where the monster had been, his body pressed against the wall as if he could burrow through to safety. He recoiled when her hand brushed his shoulder. Eventually she coaxed him into wrapping his arms around her neck so she could carry him on her back.

Captain Fletcher finally found his flashlight, and light cut through the darkness. Cam blinked in its beam, until Fletcher was satisfied that she wasn't hurt. When he lowered the beam out of her face, she saw that blood ran down one side of his head, and the back of his jacket was torn. His hair was even ruffled.

"Well . . . that was not a bear."

"No, Sir."

He stared at her for several long moments, his expression unreadable. Then he turned and started up the stairs. Cam followed, and the boy clutching at her neck found his voice.

"What was that thing?"

Captain Fletcher remained silent, so Cam finally said, "I don't know."

"Why not?"

"Because I've never seen anything like that before."

"Was it going to eat me? Do you fight monsters like that all the time?"

"No." She reached the top of the stairs. Captain Fletcher most definitely smiled, even though they now faced a forest nearly as dark as the lair. The trip back was going to be slow. Cam's knees trembled as adrenaline drained away. The cuts she had accumulated during her run through the forest stung.

"You killed it really fast," the boy said.

"Yes." She followed Fletcher over the rocky ground. Snow tumbled in fat, wet flakes. The air quickly cleared her sinuses of the lair's fetid odor.

He sniffled. "It wasn't very exciting."

"Maybe we should go find another one, and I can take my time. How does that sound?"

The boy shuddered.

"No?" Cam said. "Good."

They tramped along until lances of light cut through the trees, sweeping back and forth, turning the forest into a broken geometry of shifting shadows. Captain Fletcher stopped and whistled between thumb and forefinger. The searchlights swung to them, and shouts rose.

Cam lowered the boy to the ground and rolled her shoulders, easing some stiffness from the muscles. He shivered, and she draped her jacket over him.

"Next time a monster snatches you from your house in the middle of the night, don't forget your coat."

He stuck out his tongue and smiled when she returned the expression.

The boy's mother thrashed through the trees first, her face and arms livid with scratches. She scooped up the boy. They clasped one another, both weeping. Cam averted her eyes, picked up her jacket, and brushed off every obvious scrap of muck.

Officer Manning appeared next. He stared at the boy, and smiled.

"It's dead?" he asked Captain Fletcher.

"Yes, Officer Manning." He paused for several seconds, and added, "Thanks to Lieutenant Kardell."

Manning looked to her. "I want to see it. You aren't hurt?"

"Nothing that can't wait," Fletcher said. "Kardell could use a flashlight, though."

One of the rescuers lent Cam a flashlight, and minutes later she led Officer Manning and Captain Fletcher back through the forest. Her stomach growled for a meal past due as she descended the stairs, even as the reek of the lair brought on a wave of nausea. The borrowed flashlight cut deep, unfriendly shadows.

The room was a perfect cube, with the stairs ending in the center of one wall. Every surface was smooth concrete. Metal doors stood in the walls to the left and right, also centered. They had no handles. The wall directly across from the stairs was smooth and blank. Other than the former inhabitant's gruesome leavings and the doors, the room was empty.

Cam glanced at Officer Manning. "You didn't know about this place?" The hairs prickled along the back of her neck as they had when the monster shrieked. How long had the door above been in place? Had the monster torn it from its fittings?

"I've never seen it in my life. When I was a kid, I climbed that rock up there a hundred times. My friends and I called it The Canyon. That door must have been covered, made to look just like the rock."

If this place had been built in Samuel Manning's lifetime, he would have known. The supplies would have had to pass through Palisade, the machinery would have been noisy. The concrete might look freshly poured, but it had to be very old.

Cam crouched next to the beast's corpse, her flashlight moving over the mound of flesh and hair and bone. No guidebook had a place for this thing. As it lay on the ground, Cam could see the patterns underlying the strange shape of it; the beastly features rose up from the otherwise human framework, like rock outcroppings rising from a flat prairie. Officer Manning's description of a thing halfway between bear and man was close, but the word in her mind was *monster*.

Captain Fletcher picked a scrap of fabric off the ground. It was a saturated purple, printed with pink hearts. He handed it to Manning, who took it with a stony expression but gentle fingers.

Cam went back to her own work.

She pulled two plastic bags from one of her pockets, her notebook from another, and a pen from her sleeve. She flipped through sketches of the local terrain until she found a blank page. She dated the top, described the location, and then yanked out a tuft of the creature's coarse hair, which she dropped in a bag.

When she turned her focus to the creature's head, she noticed a black tattoo on the hairless skin inside the left ear, very small. It might have gone entirely unnoticed if it had been tucked into the cat-like fold of the front edge, but instead it ran along the flat outer edge. The letters were crisp, the characters evenly formed. *715–2.1*

Somewhere there was a person who could subdue the beast, long enough to tattoo it. Someone who wanted to track this thing.

Cam heard air moving, like a small gasp. She looked up to Manning, but the sound hadn't come from him. It had come from behind her.

She heard a growl, and it was strange, because it was too far away. It wasn't inside the room.

Cam swung her flashlight to the door in the wall. It stood open, and in its frame crouched a creature, much like the one lying on the floor, yet not like it. This one was smaller, its shape unsymmetrical. Its eyes were glassy, sickly.

Captain Fletcher cursed, and fumbled for his pistol, his flashlight swinging wildly. The creature shuffled forward; the door hissed shut behind it. Cam rose to her feet, drawing her sword. Before she could move, the tiny room exploded with sound. She ducked, late.

The creature slumped to the ground, keening softly as it died. Cam, heart racing, looked back to Manning, who smiled grimly as he lowered his pistol. He deserved a larger portion of justice, but at least it was something.

"Good shot, Sheriff," she said.

"Thank you."

Captain Fletcher let out a long breath. "How many of those things could there be?"

"There can't be many," Cameron said. "No other towns have reported attacks or sightings. Let's check to see if one of these was stabbed by Kai, though, just to be sure." The logic sounded good, but Cam was unsettled. What was the point of numbering the creatures if there were only two?

They wrestled with the larger beast's body, gripping rolls of greasy skin and hair until it rolled. Cam held the flashlight's beam on the chest while Manning spread the fur and located the half-healed cuts inflicted by his son. "It's the same one."

Cam pulled a knife from her belt, along with another plastic bag, and gestured at the creature's ear. "You don't mind if I take this?" Samuel Manning shook his head. She sliced through rubbery cartilage, then dropped the ear into a second bag.

"Where did this one come from, though?" Captain Fletcher asked, nudging the body of the second creature with his boot.

"It came through that door," Cam said.

Manning frowned. "I thought it must have crept around behind us."

Cam went to the door. She ran her hands around the edge of the frame. The join between metal and concrete was smooth, without cracks or crumbles. The seal between the frame and the door itself showed no gaps. She rapped her knuckles against the metal. The responding thuds were solid.

"I'm sure it was standing just in front of that wall, Kardell," Captain Fletcher said.

Cam had seen it crouching within the frame, a dark space stretching out behind it. She pushed her shoulder against the door, her hands splayed against the cold, smooth surface. Even with her full weight thrown into it and her boots skidding against the floor, it stood immobile. She tried again, pressing the door in the other direction, with exactly the same result.

"Maybe the other side is caved in," Officer Manning said.

"Look, there's no way of opening it," Captain Fletcher said. He pointed, rather insultingly, at the blank wall around the frame. "That thing would have had to go both in and out. There's no way of doing that."

Cam stepped back and gave the door one mighty kick. It still did not budge, did not even vibrate in the frame. The nerves in her foot and up her leg sparked in protest.

She breathed deeply a few times and thought about ocean waves, the steady beat of a pelican's wings, the slow opening of a lotus flower, but those images just made her want to kick the door again. It was like being presented with a plate of cookies hot from the oven, and then being told not to eat any.

Thinking about dessert made her stomach rumble.

"We'll try the other one," Officer Manning said, "and if we can't move it we should head back to town. I've confirmed the remains of all the missing, and there's nothing more we can do here tonight."

The second door was equally unrelenting, and Cam knew kicking the door had looked childish, so she didn't push. She picked up her broken flashlight, glad to find the only damage was some marring on the case and a shattered bulb. The Quartermaster might yell at her for the damage, but at least she wouldn't have to file for a new one.

She followed Officer Manning and Captain Fletcher back to town, silently mulling over the door the whole way.

Supper at the town's diner was stew, made with winter vegetables that had been in storage too long and bland canned foods. Cameron cleared two bowls without caring. As she scraped the last remnants of broth for the second time, Captain Fletcher cleared his throat and said, "Kardell—we're a bit of a mess, you know."

Cam looked down and saw clothing stained with dirt, muck, and splashes of blood. Captain Fletcher had smoothed down his hair, but he hardly looked better. The way he held his hastily-bandaged shoulder, he'd probably been hurt worse than he was letting on. Cam wrapped leftover rolls in a napkin, slid them in a pocket, and left more than enough money on the table.

She and Fletcher checked into the town's only motel and unloaded what few personal items they carried on their bikes— Fletcher's now very dirty and dinged. Cam pulled out a field dressing kit.

"I thought you weren't hurt, Kardell."

"I'm not, Sir. But you are."

He rolled his eyes. "It's nothing."

Cam pinned him with her gaze, and he met it well, right up until he shifted his pack on his shoulder and winced. "Fine. But I hope your stitches are pretty. I don't want to live with a jagged scar for the rest of my life."

Captain Fletcher led her into his room, threw his pack into a corner, pulled a flimsy chair into the center of the room, and sat. Cam pulled off her filthy jacket, rolled up her sleeves, and washed her hands and arms in the bathroom sink, scrubbing until her skin was raw. When she'd returned, Fletcher had his shirt off, and the cut was visible in full for the first time. It ran from the center of his left shoulder blade up to the base of his neck, about a hands-width long, and deep enough to warrant the stitch kit Cam opened.

"You should have said something," Cam said. "Was it a claw that did this?"

"Just clean it and stitch it, Kardell."

She clamped her teeth together and laid out all the supplies on a shoddy table. Captain Fletcher scarcely flinched while she cleaned the wound, though his knuckles were white where he gripped his legs. It wasn't his first field-dressing. His back bore several wicked scars, and the one on his opposite shoulder looked like it had been especially deep.

"Most of that's from bandits down south," he said. "Spent a few years trying to solidify Armel I's legacy. You'd think after two hundred years we'd have that figured out."

Cam opened the package containing the needle and surgical thread. She pinched the cut closed with her fingers and drew the thread through both sides of skin.

"Kardell—would you please talk about something?"

"Like what?"

He winced as she drew the stitch tight and made the knot. "Anything."

"How many times have you patrolled the Ring?"

"Two full patrols, a few partials."

She snipped the excess string and moved on to the next stitch. "Those animals. Have you ever seen anything like them before?"

"I've seen some weird shit, but not like that."

Cam started another stitch, drawing the slice closed a quarter inch at a time.

"There's all kinds of things out there that shouldn't be. Stuff from a different time. You don't notice until you've run the Ring a few times."

"What kinds of things?" She asked not only because he flinched less while he talked, but also because she was interested. The ear in the plastic bag kept rising up in the back of her mind. A creature from a different time?

"Wolves that don't quite look like wolves. Animals that look almost right. Once I stopped in the low hills to have a piss, and this white thing flew right over my head, landed in a tree about twenty yards away. It was a bird, this huge eagle, and every feather on it was white. Its talons were white. Its eyes were white. Even where the pupils should have been."

Cam repressed a sigh. A wild imagination and superstition. Nothing useful.

"There's a lot of strangeness out there beyond just Remnants. By the way—you did well today."

"Thank you, Captain Fletcher." She snipped the string from the last knot and stepped back to check her work. It was even enough.

"It's no good, you know, trying to figure out what those things were. People smarter than you have tried. And some of the things we lost aren't worth getting back."

Cam gathered up the remains of the stitch kit while Fletcher threw himself down on his bed. He snored within seconds, even though he still wore his boots and filthy pants. Cam gathered her things and left.

She washed her hair twice and scoured every inch of skin but still found bits of unidentifiable gore under her fingernails. She remembered picking up the dead beast's head, remembered the grit caught in the fur, and she shivered. Better not to think about it.

That scrap of a little girl's nightgown was hard to dismiss.

She picked up the bag of dirty clothes on the bathroom floor and dressed in what clean items remained. She walked outside and down to the tiny room where a washer and dryer shared space with a vending machine and a cooler. She poured more than the usual amount of detergent into the washer and filled a bucket with ice.

Back in her room, Cam pulled the tattooed ear out of her jacket pocket and buried it under the ice. She loaded her bags, leaving space for the clothes sloshing around in the washer, then inspected and cleaned her weapon until even her most fastidious weapon masters would have nodded. Her jacket would need to be replaced at their next checkpoint. The creature's claws had punctured through more of the padding than she'd realized, and little specks of blood had been left on too long to buff out.

She made a second trip down the sidewalk to move her laundry from the washer to the dryer, and then found her thoughts turning back to the faces on the posters.

Had it taken kids because they were easier to carry?

It didn't matter why, at this point. What mattered was where it had come from, and she wouldn't learn that from the government lab. They were neither specialized nor interested enough.

But her friend Erika had a brother who studied biology. Cam could have it sent to him once the Sentinels were done with it. From her brief meetings with him, he seemed like exactly the kind of person to plow enthusiastically and heedlessly into an investigation.

She picked up the phone to call Erika and had dialed half the numbers when she realized that it was extremely late. And a Friday night. Even if Erika was around to pick up the phone, she wouldn't be very interested in answering questions.

That meant Armel would be out, too, and Cam was alone in trying to drive out unpleasant thoughts of what had happened to all those kids down in the dark.

003

Erika struggled to focus. Three hours of sleep were not nearly enough when someone was whacking at her with a wood practice blade, especially with nothing but coffee swishing in her belly.

"Wake up, Harfield, or we'll all have the pleasure of watching you run the perimeter another twenty times! I thought Travers might wet himself when he disarmed you. Best day of his life!"

The man across from Erika turned a brilliant red. She made an apologetic face, and when the instructor turned away, made a mildly rude gesture at his back. Travers grinned and forgave Erika when she beat him soundly the next round.

The clacks of training swords filled the cavernous sparring room, punctuated by the occasional shout of a Sentinel too slow to halt a strike. Usually Erika enjoyed the once-a-week sparring practice, but today she was having too much trouble staying awake.

Damn Armel, and his streams, and his fish.

"Attention!"

That slightly panicked shout came from the Major, who stood by the door observing his underlings. Erika was the first to take position. She suppressed a smile.

As everyone fell in on either side of her, she looked to the door that led into the training room from the observation hall. She recognized the visitor right away. He featured prominently in her father's lectures on important people in Cotarion.

General Sean Ellis walked across the room with all the snappy assurance of someone who had commanded thousands of troops and would not mind commanding thousands more. Erika had seen those heavy eyebrows, that slightly quirked lip, and those dark eyes glowering out of flash cards and newspapers. He surveyed the line of officers. Erika did not need to touch him to see the thoughts that hovered in the front of his mind.

All this is mine.

As the others realized that the High General's nephew stood in front of them, the sloppy edges of their salutes stiffened. Major Kent said, "Whatever it is you need, I will be more than happy to—"

"Of course you will." General Ellis stopped in front of the line, a couple of feet to Erika's left. "Which of you is Lieutenant Harfield?"

Her fingers tingling, Erika stepped forward, hoping she looked sharp enough. "I am, General Ellis, sir." Had she really been tired a minute ago?

"If you can spare her, Major Kent, I want to speak with Harfield in the hall."

He turned away, and Erika followed him, even though the Major had not given his consent. She had no idea what to think. This summons was either a very good sign, or a very bad one, and either possibility made her palms sweat. She wished she weren't wearing a practice uniform, which was misshapen and baggy compared to Ellis' red coat with all its gleaming medals.

In the hall, with the door shut behind them, General Ellis turned to face the windows that looked into the practice room. Erika remained at a respectful distance, her arms folded behind her back.

"Your performance reviews are impressive. Consistently the best of your year group," he said.

"Thank you, sir."

"You know Lieutenant Cameron Kardell."

"Yes, sir."

"Her reviews are less consistent. Her patrol partner has regularly referred to her as uncooperative. The sheriff of Palisade thinks she ought to have a medal, but the Sentinel examiners believe that the creature she killed must be fake. The weapon instructors consider her a prodigy. I'm curious to know your opinion."

Of course General Ellis hadn't come to compliment her on good reviews. He'd come to ask about Cam. Cam, who could scarcely speak beyond a monosyllable when faced with a superior. It was her ability to end a match faster than any other Sentinel in the Cotarion Armed Forces that garnered her so much attention. It would probably get her killed someday, too.

"She takes her duties seriously, although sometimes she interprets them a little differently than her commanding officers. I believe she stopped in that town because an animal had killed several children. She was able to hunt it down, even though the local Safety Officers had not."

Sean Ellis turned and stared at her. "You believe her story, then? Monstrous beast and all?"

"Yes, sir. Without question."

The general's lips turned up again. "Interesting. I appreciate your information. When she gets back, I want to meet her."

Erika shook his extended hand, surprised that he would make so humble a gesture. She could not resist the opportunity it gave her to learn more.

As their palms made contact, she concentrated and brought to bear the skill she had always kept secret. She scooped up the thoughts floating on the surface of his mind.

I'll get there; I'm just steps away. I could change things, show my strength, make things better. And I'll be safe, finally safe, because who would dare to kill the High General . . .

Before she could pick up anything more distinct, he removed his hand. His smile was unpleasant, knowing, and he held her gaze for several moments. Finally, he strode away, leaving Erika uneasy. It was almost as if he knew what she had done.

Impossible. Sometimes even she didn't believe.

Erika returned to practice, fully awake. She might never beat Cameron, but at least she could speak to the High General's nephew without looking foolish.

Armel had the good grace to bring Erika hot coffee from Three Sides around mid-morning. He grinned as he presented it, looking like a friendly bear. He was the only Sentinel in the room with unkempt hair. Did it grow that way, or did he let it get untidy because he could get away with it?

"Sorry we got back so late last night. I really thought that drive was shorter," he said.

"No more fishing trips until Cam gets back," Erika said.

"But that could be months, and none of my other friends will go. You can't do that to me."

"I can. Unlike you, I have an actual job, which involves actual work. Your cousin came to see me this morning, by the way."

Armel's eyebrows shot up. "You mean Sean? What the hell did he want?"

"He was asking about Cam."

"That can't be good."

Erika kept her eyes on her work while Armel considered the implications. It took a while.

"If the rumors are true . . . and he's looking at Dad's job . . . if I were him, I'd want someone like Cam for the Guard. She'd be my first pick."

Erika had heard whispers that General Ellis was in Advon because he wanted the High General's job, but he was not the only person eying it. Still, if people had been talking about it where even Armel could hear, that gave Ellis an edge.

Cam for the Guard, though? She had skill, but it hadn't been tested outside of training matches. Armel might think she was good enough for the job, but the Guard required a lot more than raw talent.

Erika didn't ask whether Armel knew his father's intentions. If the High General decided to step down, the son who had already refused to take his place probably would not be among the first to know. Information like that couldn't be allowed to leak.

"Things are changing," Armel said.

"Yes, they are." One of Erika's soldiers walked up behind Armel to speak with her, but as soon as he recognized the High General's son, he scurried back to his desk.

Once, Armel would have been a good person to know. Now his crowd of politically-minded friends was vanishing faster than a flotilla of ducks when an eagle passed over. Maybe they were foolish. Who knew which way the eagle might circle next?

Her phone rang. "Go back to work, Armel. I'll talk to you later." He grinned one more time before leaving. "Hello, Lieutenant Harfield speaking."

She recognized the lilting, pleasant tones of her father's receptionist at once. "Hello, Sentinel Harfield. Seat Member Harfield would like you to attend a family dinner tonight—"

"Of course he would. Put me down as a 'yes', George. The usual time?"

"Yes, ma'am. I'll let him know that you'll be there. You have a wonderful day."

Erika dropped the phone, cursing. Her father asked questions, ones she would rather not answer.

Erika stopped at the statue of Armel I, Bandit-Killer and City-Builder, after she'd finished work. It was considered good luck for a Sentinel to visit the bronze likeness at some point during the day, or at least bad luck not to. He knelt, as if a humble servant. He held his blade, but with the point digging into the ground, which made Erika shudder. So many scratches. He looked down into her face, and she looked up into his. He wasn't a handsome man, having too much mouth and jaw and not enough forehead, but he did seem thoughtful, if not noble.

Not *every* High General had been an Armel. She'd get there, eventually.

She brushed his foot and left the Military Quarter.

Erika was second to arrive at her father's apartment. Her younger brother William sat at the dining table, tapping a pen on the blank page of a notebook and staring into the flames of a candle flickering in front of him. He appeared worn and listless, which was a pity because the looks they had both inherited from their father suited him so much better. She ruffled his light auburn hair and sat next to him, a smile appearing effortlessly on her face.

"What's up kid, having a rough week?"

He rubbed his face and sighed, a sound that seemed to well up from the very depths of his soul. "Just more project rejections. In a couple weeks I'm going to end up assisting Doctor Spears over the summer, and she's hated me ever since I disproved her theory on the genetically transferred behavior of leopard frogs."

"When you were eighteen."

"It's not my fault she was wrong! Of course, now they all just think I'm insane."

She patted his shoulder. "It's all going to be okay, Will. You've just hit your first little rough patch." She leaned back in her chair and looked around at the place settings. "Do you think Tristan is the fourth? I haven't seen him in a while." Unless she counted the occasional glance on the streets of Advon before he slipped out of sight. He often came to her seeking advice, but not recently. That probably meant he'd been getting assignments he couldn't dodge.

William cleared his throat. It was no wonder the other geniuses liked him so little, when what he thought appeared so plainly on his face. "I think Dad's been keeping him busy."

So rapidly and silently that Erika jumped, Tristan slid into the chair across from William and lounged as if he'd been there for hours. "You could say that. Don't look so grim about it, cuz'. Information is so much more valuable than lives." He flashed his white teeth. "Most of the time."

"Let's not talk about it," William said.

"You're the one who brought it up."

"Now boys, let's not fight," Erika said. "I think we should save our strength for the real enemy. Any idea what's going on, Tris?"

"Not a clue. Things are stirring, though, that's for sure. Lots of messages being delivered, high level stuff."

"You really savor creeping around and spying on people, don't you?" William said.

"If you want him doing better work, maybe you should hire him to find you a steady girlfriend," Erika said. When William blushed and Tristan laughed, she rounded on her cousin as well. "Of course, you probably aren't the right man for the job if he wants someone longer than a night."

It was low, but the wounded pride of both temporarily united them. William was still muttering about "societal over-emphasis on a lasting relationship as a sign of personal worth" when Conrad Harfield arrived.

Erika sat straighter. Her father was clearly thriving on the current political chaos. His green eyes were bright, his suit and hair impeccable, his step lively. That meant trouble for the rest of them.

William stood and Conrad pulled his son into a close embrace. He laid a hand on Tristan's shoulder, then hugged Erika as well. He turned back to his nephew and asked he notify the kitchen that they were ready to eat. He handed his jacket to William. Erika was tasked with pouring the wine, and finally she, Tristan, and William returned to their seats.

He looked to William first. "How are things at Gates?"

"About the same," William responded, attempting an off-handed tone that fooled no one. Clearly, he hoped their father would move on quickly, and on this rare occasion, Conrad didn't even comment.

The first course came out, a tiny plate bearing a fried leaf smattered with delicately chopped redfish. As Erika gazed at the pink flesh cupped in the dark green curve, cold sweat prickled on her back. The fish wasn't easy to come by in Advon, but on the northern coast where they'd grown up, it was plentiful. Such expense for a first course, the reminder of home—whatever her father wanted to talk about must be life-altering.

William, oblivious to the implications, ate happily and relaxed. Erika's nerves soured the food, but Tristan savored it like a man enjoying his last meal. He was next.

"What about you, Tristan? Has your business been operating smoothly?"

"I'm still waiting for an interesting assignment. I spend an awful lot of time listening to people argue with their spouses and children." How did Tristan get away with that tone?

"You will be getting more interesting jobs very soon." Then the green eyes turned on Erika. "I heard you had a visit from Sean Ellis this morning. Why did he come to you?"

The first course was cleared, and the second, a cold soup of spring vegetables, arrived. Spirals of roasted fern garnished the surface. Erika looked at Tristan, who pointedly avoided her gaze. There weren't many ways that her father could have learned about her conversation with Ellis so quickly. "He asked me about Cameron Kardell."

Her father frowned. "The girl who scowls? Who is close to Armel VII?"

Erika nodded. William was crunching the croutons atop the soup with abandon, no longer paying attention to the conversation.

"Tell me more about her."

"She comes from a long line of Sentinels, was never good at anything involving book-work, but her skills with a sword are incredible. I've seen her beat Master Reese more than once. She's almost as fast as Tris, great instincts."

Erika stopped, sipped a spoonful of soup. No one was as fast as Tristan. Erika had never questioned Cameron's skill during training. Her friend worked harder than any other Sentinel, and her focus never wavered. But maybe there was more to it than that. Maybe Cameron was special, gifted, like them.

Erika had never believed that she, William, and Tristan alone had inhuman abilities, and she considered this alongside Cameron's skill. Quickly she pushed this to the back of her mind, but already she had paused long enough to make her father notice.

"There's something else?"

"I've been thinking about it all day, and I can't figure out why General Ellis would ask about her. There are plenty of people who are good with a sword, and Cam's social skills are—well, people don't like her enough that it offsets all of that." Nice cover.

"Then it should be easy for you to prove that you're more suited to whatever he has in mind. That man could be a powerful ally for us to have. Get as close as you can, whatever it takes."

Erika raised her eyebrows. "*Whatever* it takes?"

"I trust you to use your own judgment and to be cautious. If using your more unusual skills helps, then yes, I encourage you to do so. Now is the time to be bold."

William rejoined the conversation, several steps behind. "Isn't Cameron the one who sat in the corner and talked to me during all those parties you dragged me to? She seemed okay. She didn't mind when I talked about physics. She actually read one of the books I lent her; nobody *ever* does that."

Their father knotted his hands together as the second course vanished and the main dish, a choice cut of some unfortunate elk, arrived. Tristan set about carving it, and Father launched into a lecture about paying attention to what was happening, a talk William had received so many times his eyes glazed over, and he inserted the appropriate responses automatically.

So, Sean Ellis really was angling for High General. If her father was asking about Cameron, he might really want her for the Guard.

She's so fast—inhumanly quick. She is one of us.

Erika hadn't been favored with any extraordinary physical skills, so Cameron probably couldn't read minds. William was even less dexterous, so she probably couldn't do all that energy transferal stuff, either. She was fast like Tristan, but not to the same degree.

Maybe Cameron was something else, unlike any of them.

Maybe it was nothing, after all.

Erika returned her attention to the conversation at hand. William still tolerated the lecture, but barely, and flickers of his annoyance began to show. When their father took a breath, Erika stepped in.

"I know you didn't make this nice dinner to talk about Sean Ellis. What else is going on?"

William cast her a grateful glance, and she smiled as their father changed course.

"I wanted to work up to this, but if you really must hear it at once, then that will suit me as well." He took a drink of wine, set the glass down carefully, and folded his hands on the table. "You are beginning to reach an age, Erika, where I think you should consider a strategic marriage. Armel VII is an excellent candidate. With your help, he can pull through the current turmoil. He is well-liked in spite of his father."

Erika suppressed a laugh. She had known this would come eventually; her father was a great proponent of arranged marriages. It was an antiquated tactic, but all the more effective when two families wanted to consolidate power. "I have a boyfriend, Dad. And Armel wants to get as far away from all this political stuff as possible."

"I'm sure you could persuade him of the good he can do, especially allied with someone like you. He seems like a sincere young man. The slightest change of mind is all it would take."

William did not miss this suggestion that Erika use her skill, and he took an audible breath. "Dad, what you're suggesting—it's wrong. After all this time of hiding what we can do, now you're telling Erika to get into the people's heads and change things! What if it goes wrong? What if she hurts someone!"

Their father sighed. "How much longer do you think we have to get back the Harfield Estate? We're running out of time and options. Keep in mind that I have a list for you as well. A woman from an important family in Varcove is in the city right now, and the access to ammunition and firearms—"

"Never."

"If you ever want to get your home back, you will."

The air in the room cooled, the candles flickered, and William's face flushed. Erika exchanged a look with Tristan, and her cousin altered his position in preparation.

"I will not be married off to someone I don't love. I've spent all my life watching how that works, and I will not do it."

"We all have to make sacrifices to get what we want. You can always marry and keep some girl on the side; it's practically expected in these arrangements."

William leapt up, the candles flared, and Erika's next breath puffed out in a fine mist.

"Tris, do it," she said. Her cousin blurred. When William yelped, his voice was muffled by the carpet. Tristan had a gentle but very firm knee in the middle of his back. The candle flames settled, and the air warmed.

Tristan looked up to Erika. She nodded. He released Will, and she stood to help her brother up. He avoided her eye as he took her hand.

"I would like to be excused," he said. Their father nodded, trying and failing to hide the tremor in his hands as he took another drink. William left.

"He can't handle it, Dad. You know that."

"He must. Between your mother's decline and the loss of the estate, the Harfield name is not what it used to be. It will require drastic action to recover."

Erika returned to her seat and tried to eat, but the elk stuck in her throat. She saw her father's point, but she didn't want to get married any more than William. "I don't know how far I can go with this. But I'll try."

If she could get Armel, maybe William would be spared. Something like that was sure to destroy him, and they all knew it. Erika remembered the year he had taken off after getting his first doctorate, when their parents were debating a divorce. He had walked around, a twitchy, nervous shell of his former self, until their father decided that keeping the family intact was essential to his career.

"That's all I'm asking."

The rest of the meal passed in a restrained way. Erika picked at a dessert which seemed to have been spun out of sugar, air, and Char Fruit. Conrad Harfield discussed details of political discourse, and Tristan threw in the occasional snarky comment.

Erika excused herself as soon as her father would consider polite, and then went to the library. William was there, pacing and flipping a lighter open and shut over and over. He looked up when she entered, then turned away quickly.

"You can't let that happen, Will."

He stopped moving, and shut his eyes. "Believe me, I know. But he can't really ask me to live like that, either."

"People are going to make you angry. If you keep losing control, someone will get hurt, and I know you don't want that."

He paced some more, his eyes still troubled. She didn't know how to help him, except by distraction. Her own agenda could provide that.

"Remember two summers ago, when you found the genes that give us our abilities? Can you see them in someone else?"

This stopped him, and he looked at her, his eyebrows creeping up his forehead. "What, you mean outside of the family? First of all, it's entirely theoretical, and secondly, I'd want some privacy at the lab, which means I'd have to wait until the end of the semester. You think there are more? Who?"

"I'm not ready to say who yet, not until I'm sure. But we can't be the only ones." Finally, maybe they would find out they weren't so alone after all. And others had been hiding right next to them for years. "It sounds like it will be easier if I just take a peek."

William frowned. "I'm not comfortable with you throwing your ability around. It's not a toy, and we don't know much about it."

"You're one to talk. Besides, I'll be very careful. Just think, though, if there are other people out there who can do what we do."

If Cameron did have an ability, it would give them a place to start looking for answers, after so many years of having nothing but questions.

004

WILLIAM READ THE newspaper while he poured his second cup of coffee, yet another article about the expense and complications of wind turbines. The dark liquid came up to the edge of his mug, curved slightly with surface tension, and then spilled over. It soaked into the paper before he noticed.

He watched the puddle spread across the print, the curve moving out in a fuzzy, fractured line, evidence of the pressed tree pulp from which the surface was made. Strange, how it moved like frost. He shook his head and mopped up the mess with a towel.

William glanced at his watch. He had papers to grade before his first class. He scratched Cesar behind his golden ears, picked up a stack of reference books and his keys, then set off for Gates University.

The walk was long, but William could hardly complain. His apartment was inherited from his grandfather, so he didn't pay rent, which was very good in light of his slim paychecks. He spent the eight-tenths of a mile observing the behavior of Advon's wildlife, which was particularly active during late spring. On the corner of Second Street and Miller Road, he heard the song of a warbler he hadn't seen since the autumn migration.

He was strolling along Maple Road, which was lined with ornamental pear trees rather than maples, when his mind wandered off course. A breeze swept down the street, and to William's eyes, the moving air glowed.

William stepped under the awning of the closest shop, his pulse thumping. He closed his eyes. The bands of light still moved in the darkness. He saw the street as a negative image, the glow appearing like a mold around cars, leaves, and light-posts.

Clutching his books, he reviewed the bones in his body. Phalanges, metatarsal, tarsals, talus, tibia, fibula . . .

After bones he reviewed skeletal muscles, the process of cell division, and basic physics. By the time he finished the equation for electric potential, the ribbons of light had faded.

He opened his eyes. No one was staring, thankfully.

He had to keep control. For years it had been easy to retreat to his books and suppress the glow. That outburst at his father's house made clear that he was losing his grip on the emotions that made his powers so volatile.

William stepped back into the flow of people on their way to work. He focused his thoughts on his first lecture. It was an introductory biology course, and the students rarely appreciated any attempts to enliven the material, but the basics of nonvascular plants were a safe place for his mind to rest.

The stack of papers on his desk was taller than he remembered. He swallowed a sigh. Better to be buried in papers than have the energy floating in his vision, tempting him.

The piles of graded and ungraded papers were even when someone knocked on his door. William looked up into the frowning face of Dean Higgs. She had a copy of *Sciences Quarterly* clutched in her hands.

She dropped the magazine on his desk and flipped to the page with his article. She leaned much too far over his desk, and the Remnant she wore on a long chain around her neck brushed the tops of the paper stacks. It was green, and covered in a scrawl of aged copper threads, intricate geometric lines.

"I thought we discussed this. 'The Inheritence of Personality'? It's ridiculous."

"But my research suggests—"

"Your sample sizes are a joke," she said.

"If I had more funding, access to the equipment—"

"Until I see a paper that doesn't make Gates look like a university of fools, you aren't getting anything. Learn the game, Doctor Harfield." She took the magazine and left.

He stared at the doorway until a professor from a couple of doors down walked by and waved at him. William flapped his hand in response, then bent back over the papers.

His morning lecture went as expected. The students grumbled when they received their grades, and he met the flood of objections at the end of class.

It seemed a small eternity later that he reached his office. The place was about as much protection as a blanket fort, but at least it was his.

When someone knocked at the door again, he expected another dissatisfied student. Instead, he saw Erika, and his eyebrows shot up. She carried a cooler with clamps securing the lid. It thudded onto his desk, and she tossed a thin red folder of papers in front of him, right between his pen and the tests he was grading.

"I need you to sign the line on the top sheet. Everything else is all yours."

He put down his swooping signature and passed the paper back to her. She sighed and shook her head as she folded it and stuck it in her jacket pocket. "You didn't even read it."

"You told me to sign it. What is this, anyway?"

"You just took custody of samples Cameron Kardell collected from a monster in the Low Crescents. Now you get to prove it's not some standard woodland critter. The Patrol Coordinator thinks the whole thing is fake, which sure, I could see if she was some jumped-up Sentinel looking for glory, but she's not. Her reputation is in your hands. By the way, who's that cute professor down at the end of the hall?"

William blinked. "I'm sorry, who?"

"Short hair, neon green headphones around her neck, she guessed that I was your sister and said hello to me."

He waved his hand, already scanning the documents in the folder. "She's a biologist. Don't remember her name, haven't talked to her much."

Erika pulled the folder away from him, and then held it up out of his reach. "Learn her name. Ask her out."

He didn't bother trying to jump for the file. He knew very well that he would not get it away from her. "I don't know her. She probably despises me just like everybody else around here."

"You won't know if you don't talk to her. You might as well try. Dad can't exactly marry you off if you beat him to it." She held out a hand to his swift objections. "I'm not saying that you're going to ask her out for that purpose, but it's not bad to keep that in mind. Now, get to work!" Then she threw the folder back down and dashed away.

William perused the papers in the folder, but Sentinel Kardell hadn't written much. There was a photocopied map with some notes on it about the creature's lair and where victims had disappeared and a dry description of the animal's behavior and physical features. William didn't even realize that he was reading an account of how she'd killed the thing until he was halfway through. In someone else's hands, it would have been a hair-raising story.

At the end were a set of photographs. William leaned over them, squinting.

There was a close-up of the creature's teeth. William counted, impressed that whoever took the photo pulled the lips far enough back to get the molars in the picture. He counted thirty-two, and then recounted to be certain.

He ran his tongue across his own teeth, pulled a fresh notebook from a drawer, and his pen flew over the paper.

Within half an hour, the grading lay forgotten, and stacks of reference books perched on every available surface. A few minutes later, he rushed down the hall and stopped in the first occupied office. He convinced the colleague there to look at the information.

Not long after that, every professor on the floor gathered in the Biology conference room, packed around the cooler as William prepared to open it for the first time. It was the most attention he had endured since his last graduation ceremony, and he felt a conflicting mixture of elation and anxiety. The latches on the lid popped, and a wisp of carbon dioxide gas drifted out. He shifted the dry ice aside with metal tongs and lifted out the vacuum-packed sample.

The scientists leaned forward, none of them speaking for quite some time. A few looked from the ear to the photos and back several times, while others just stared at the object William held up. A whisper of "hmmmm's" ran among them. Glasses were wiped and replaced.

The biologist his sister had pointed out said, "Well, that's definitely not from a deer or a mountain cat."

An older man said, "I would say it appears to be canid, if I might be so bold."

"If anything it's feline," said Doctor Sherman, head of the Biology Department, "but not exactly like any species I know."

"What do you think, Doctor Harfield?"

This question came from the biologist whose name William still could not remember. She looked at him over the top of her glasses, which were framed with the same vibrant green as the headphones still around her neck. Her eyes were light brown, and she kept them on his face. He swallowed.

"The animal's overall appearance resists categorization. I'd like to run a genetic profile before I decide anything. Doctor Sherman, are there any openings?"

"If you meet me outside the building early tomorrow morning you can start the test right away. I suggest you draw up a proposal for the project this afternoon. Something like this will definitely get the Dean's approval." The old man raised his silver eyebrows. "Doctor Paige might be able to assist you, if you ask nicely."

Ah, yes, her name was Doctor Dakota Paige. She smiled while every other person in the room objected. They all had concluded that if Doctor Sherman thought the project worthwhile, they should try to get involved. Over the clamor, William asked Doctor Paige if she was interested.

"Investigate a potentially new species of this magnitude? Is that *really* a question?"

William would need to call Erika and thank her. She could not have guessed the importance of Sentinel Kardell's discovery.

William slept restlessly that night, and the next morning he launched himself out of bed before the sun rose. He dressed in his gray slacks, a collared shirt, a tie, and an overcoat. He promised Cesar a walk at lunch, then rushed to campus.

He puffed through the cool, quiet city and quaked to think about the physical training that his sister was probably already engaged in at this early hour. Still, walking through Advon when all lay so still wasn't entirely bad. At some of the intersections with roads leading south, he could hear the dock workers over in the Wharf District unloading the goods that made Advon what it was: crops, Remnants to research and shape into new products, charged batteries from the turbines. And the smell of fresh food wafted up and down every street.

The department head and William met at a side door to the biology building just as the clock tower chimed. Doctor Sherman's hair drifted over the top of his head like snow streaking away from a mountaintop. He blinked at William through thick glasses, but his eyes were still sharp.

"Very exciting stuff. Hopefully Whir will tell you something today. You know she's been getting a little imbalanced in her old age. And she was ancient when I was but a student in these halls." As he spoke he rifled through his pockets for the keys to the side door. Finally, it creaked open. "Of course, back then we called her Drone. The sound she made was a bit different, you see. Soon we might be calling her Wheeze." He chuckled at his own joke, and William joined in as they entered a stairwell and started down. Doctor Sherman went slowly, but William didn't mind the opportunity to chat.

"What do you suspect we're going to find, Doctor?"

"Something very strange, Doctor Harfield. I have seen many creatures, of all shapes and sizes, in my lifetime. I even travelled across the mountains a few times when the east was more peaceful. Very informative. I ate those crustaceans with all those legs, surprisingly tasty. I've never seen anything like this."

William switched on the lights at the bottom of the stairs, and they buzzed to life. "I was thinking last night—either this must be a new species, or something that was believed to be extinct. It could even be a remnant of The Wars."

"That would be unlikely, but I'll admit the idea is exciting. There we are." The door to the basement lab swung out into the hallway, and William flicked on another set of lights.

Whir sat on a table in the middle of the room. At its heart was a small machine, a simple metal box with a slot on one side for depositing a sample, and a slot on the other where the printed result slid out. Over the years, a variety of life-support systems had been connected, and now Whir sprouted wires from every side, which snaked away to power sources and much less elegant computers that kept the genetic profiler running. The box was a Remnant of the rarest kind, and no one knew quite how it worked. The machine had been in the biology department for as long as the university had existed.

William had used Whir for his own purposes once, though his name was not in the logbook. Two summers before, someone had left the door unlocked and ajar. William had seen it, realized that Whir was unattended, and he had snatched the opportunity.

The sample size needed was small. William had pricked his own finger, had watched the metal flap close over the slide. Then he had called Erika and Tristan. It had taken almost a day and a half for Whir to finish all three profiles.

He had spent the rest of the summer studying the results. Some of the similarities were, of course, attributable to shared lineage. But there were a few places where the alignment of the markers was unexpected. At last he had at least a potential answer. Tristan's extraordinary physical skills, Erika's telepathy, William's power to manipulate energy, had left on each of them the same set of genetic markings.

Doctor Sherman coughed, and William returned to the present.

As he turned the machine on, his fingers tingled with fear as much as excitement. Some answers weren't answers at all. Sometimes the whole world cracked open and out poured questions.

He slid in the animal's sample on its little glass slide. The metal door slapped shut. The box whirred and clicked rhythmically.

Doctor Sherman patted William on the shoulder. "This will take a while. Let's go get breakfast."

005

CAM AND CAPTAIN Fletcher drove into Advon from the east. They had travelled almost a full circuit of The Ring. Just fifty miles short. Cameron cursed the early recall. The loop wasn't finished, and there would always be that fifty-mile stretch, between one spoke of The Ring and the next, left undone.

The buildings grew as she drove up to the center of the city. All the shops and cars looked just as they had when she left, but the people were different. They glanced at her motorcycle, saw its distinctive shade of scarlet, and quickly looked away.

Maybe she should read the newspaper more often.

Cam and Captain Fletcher turned down West Court Avenue, a broad street that ran alongside the Military Quarter's outer wall. Parts of the city had been built with Remnants, and the Arts District wore the ancient materials like a badge of honor, but nothing salvaged showed on these streets. The stone wall towered on her right, while shops and offices, with all their cornices and columns, stood to the left. The fresh leaves of redbud trees created a canopy over the road, supported by a network of thin, dark branches. The sound of the motorcycle engines echoed back and forth between the wall and the buildings. After so long on open roads, Advon was like a cave.

Cam pulled up to the front gate, handed her identification to the guards, and registered her weapon. She rumbled through narrow archways and courtyards to the garage, where she handed off the vehicle to a mechanic for an extensive tune-up.

Captain Fletcher separated from her there, for the first time in almost a year. He shook her hand just before going to his apartment. "You're a pain in the ass, Kardell, but I think I might miss you."

"You've complained about me every day for the past eleven months, sir."

He rolled his eyes. "Well, I was trying."

He left, and Cam crossed the Military Quarter at a brisk pace. She didn't have time to savor her homecoming. She could admire the stately architecture and flowerbeds in bloom later.

Cam arrived at the meeting hall with a mere ten minutes to spare. The weather was fine, so crowds of Lieutenants and Cadets stood outside. She wove through them and caught snatches of speculation.

"I was on leave for another week. Never heard of someone getting pulled off leave unless there was war."

"Shut up, Halan. We aren't going to war. Who would we be fighting?"

"Everyone knows the Low Crescents want to secede. No way would we let them go without a fight. All the power turbines are up there."

"I'm telling you, it won't happen. Kardell, you were just up there, tell Halan here there isn't about to be a secession." The request came from Gordon Palmroy, a young man from Cameron's class.

"I didn't see anything imminent."

Halan wandered off to exchange rumors with someone more interested in her theories.

"And yet you didn't even change out of your road uniform. Or shower, from the smell of it," Palmroy said when Halan was out of earshot.

"I was just told not to be late. And I did shower, this morning." Cameron ran a hand over her hair, feeling for loose pieces to pin back. Everyone around her, she realized, was much crisper. She'd grown lax in keeping her appearance up to regulation out on Patrol, and it didn't help that her jacket was black with scarlet trimmings, while all around her Sentinels and Cadets wore brilliant red. She stood out, and she was untidy. She cursed.

"It's not that bad, Kardell. And unless you have a spare uniform in that bag, there's nothing to do about it, either."

"Later, Palmroy."

Cam went inside. The meeting hall was cool, dimly lit, and buzzing with conversation. She stood at the top of the tiers and scanned for a couple of seconds before she spotted the back of Armel's head at the front right corner of the room, alone. It took a moment to find Erika, because she sat very close to where Cam had entered. Cam went down the near-empty row in front of her friend's seat.

"Cam, good to see you," Erika said as she approached. "Welcome home to the city of chaos."

"I didn't expect things to be so different."

Erika shrugged. "To those of us who've been here in the city, the change probably hasn't been so noticeable."

Cam looked down at where Armel sat and raised her eyebrows. Erika winced and leaned forward so she could speak more quietly, her auburn braid falling over her shoulder. "My father suggested I arrange a mutually beneficial marriage with Armel. I'm just glad he didn't punch me when I brought it up. I've been letting him cool off for a while."

"Wow, I'm glad I wasn't here to see that."

"There was shouting, but nothing I haven't heard before. My brother doesn't recognize the value in a strategic marriage, either. I assume you're going to go sit with Armel."

"Yes. Something tells me he needs my company more than you do."

"Armel is lucky you're on his side. Just—be careful," Erika said.

Cam frowned. "I'm always careful."

"You went running through the mountains in the middle of the night, chasing a monster."

"My sword was sharp," Cam said.

"Yes, I'm sure it was. Someday I'll be engraving those words on your tombstone. 'My sword was sharp.'" Erika's laughter was chased by a sigh. "I hope you know what I mean, though."

So it was something political. Erika always worried about things like that; who was liked; who had influence. Cam was more worried about who she could trust.

"I'll do my best," Cam said.

"Good. Go, comfort the lonely outcast."

Cam went down the steps, weaving around stalled groups of Sentinels. The room was filling, but Armel was still alone. He looked like he was trying to escape notice, but his stature made that impossible. He was tall by nature, training had made his shoulders broad, and he had a voice that could fill up a room. Armel, no matter how he tried, could not vanish.

When Cam slid into the seat next to him, he leapt out of his doze and stared. "You scared the hell out of me, Kardell; you can't sneak up on people like that." Then the surprise turned into a relieved smile. "Damn, it's good to see you. I haven't had many friends the past couple of weeks."

She finished arranging her sword, a job she always took extra care with when she was with Armel. There hadn't been any attempts on his life in years, but tensions were high. "What's going on around here?"

"How much of the news have you been getting?"

"I know that things aren't great, but I don't pay much attention to the papers. You can't count on anything but the puzzles, and to be honest, I think the answer to the math question from a few days ago is wrong."

Armel scowled at her attempted levity. "Well, there have been serious threats against my father, and a lot of people can't seem to decide if they want him deposed or dead. The Seat, of course, wants to keep him as their scapegoat. Then it turns out most of my friends were only there as long as I was the heir apparent. You might want to consider sitting with someone else, by the way; apparently I will kill your career."

"You sound like a fourteen-year-old who didn't get invited to the cool kid's party." She elbowed him in the ribs.

"That hurt! Please remind me why I let you sit next to me."

"Because nobody else will. Stop being such a baby."

"I seriously think this is going to bruise," he said.

"Now that you aren't next in line for High General, nobody cares if you get hurt."

He shook his head, but he was grinning. "You, my friend, are a jerk."

For the first time in weeks, she was able to smile without trying. "There's that winning personality."

Before he could respond, a door at the front of the room swung open. A general, her jacket gleaming with medals and pins, strode in, accompanied by an aide. The conversation petered out. Sentinels broke from their groups to find seats, even though the meeting wasn't set to start for another five minutes.

At last, the clock tower outside struck three o' clock, and the general took her place behind the podium.

"Good afternoon, Sentinels. I am General Holing. You have been called here today so that you might begin preparations for the great changes ahead of us. This morning, in a closed meeting with his generals, his advisors, and select members of The Seat, High General Armel VI announced his decision to resign from his position as leader of Cotarion and its armed forces." She paused, as if she had expected uproar at the announcement, but no one had anything to say. Armel sat up, his face a shade lighter.

"In order to provide additional security during the transition, all Lieutenants are being assigned to either Commander's Corps or the Guard." She did not pause, even though this time a few people exclaimed aloud, and Cam's stomach dropped. She had her application in for Intelligence Corps. She wouldn't mind the Commander's Corps, but she knew her one-on-one combat scores were far above anything she had achieved in large group tactics. On paper, she was a perfect candidate for the Guard, which was the last place she wanted to be. "The Cotarion Armed Forces would like to congratulate you on your placements, and extends its apologies that for now we will have to delay the promotion ceremonies. Speed is necessary in these circumstances, and in order to have you prepared for the challenges that will arise when High General Armel VI makes his announcement, we must put a hold on any pomp and circumstance."

General Holing looked up from her notes. The muttering stopped. Cam struggled to stifle her disappointment as the general turned her notes face-down.

"I understand that many of you had goals different from the assignments you are about to receive. You wouldn't be Sentinels if you weren't ambitious. But you would not be Sentinels if you didn't understand the importance of sacrifice, either. Today, Cotarion needs you to put aside your own interests. *This* is what you have trained for. This is what unites us all, from the High General to the lowest Cadet. For Cotarion."

A small echo came back from the room. "For Cotarion."

"For Cotarion," Holing said, more fiercely.

"For Cotarion," the room echoed, loudly enough now to satisfy her. She turned back to her notes.

"At this time, you are going to receive the paperwork you must fill out, which will be processed this evening. Tomorrow morning you will be sworn into your branches and begin your work. Those who've agreed to assist, please come forward."

Seats squeaked as twenty or so Sentinels rose and made their way to the front of the room, all young men and women three to five years out of the Academy, with exemplary careers since graduation. Erika was among them, and she caught Cam's eye as she raised her pile of envelopes and winked.

"Your packets are in alphabetical order. Line up, minimal conversation."

Cam was one of the first to rise, and Erika had her packet on top of the pile, ready to slide into her hands. "Congratulations, Cam," Erika whispered, winking again, but there was tension on her face. They exchanged salutes, and Cam returned to her seat, curious about what assignment might have inspired such jealousy in her friend.

Cam opened the envelope, scanned its contents, then looked up to Erika and mouthed, *Is this a joke?* Erika shook her head.

She had expected the Guard, but her form said High Guard. The position claimed to be a "special, temporary assignment, to be renewed as the High General wishes every six months."

For at least six months, she could look forward to standing around, staring at a wall or the guard across from her, keeping watch. She would follow every command without question, could be summoned at any hour of the day or night, and she would be expected to die in the High General's defense if necessary. She had heard rumors that when Armel III was assassinated, the members of the High Guard who failed him had been executed within hours. All of her history instructors insisted they had merely been dismissed.

Armel sat next to her, leaned over to read her assignment, and then gave a low whistle. "Cam. You'll be the youngest member of the High Guard, ever. I'm pretty sure. I mean, Dad would know for certain."

"What did you get?" she asked. She didn't want him to know she was disappointed with the assignment when he was so awed by it.

He turned his form to her. Commander's Corps. Cameron nodded. Armel needed the responsibility of an assignment like that.

They both turned to their forms. Cam filled in every line, read through the agreement a couple of times, signed her name at the bottom, and tucked all the papers back inside the envelope.

When it was closed, her doubts settled. This was her assignment, and though it might not have been her first choice, or even her second or third, she knew she could do well. High Guard would look very good on her packet, and might mean a better place for her with the Intelligence Corps when all this was over.

She went to Erika and turned in the papers. "Thank you, Sentinel Kardell. I'll see you at the swearing-in at oh-six-hundred tomorrow morning. I've been bumped into the High Guard, too."

"I look forward to serving with you, Sentinel Harfield."

"Yeah, I'm sure it's going to be all kinds of fun. You should go see my brother while you still have any free time. That thing you killed has turned out to be a big deal over at Gates, and starting tomorrow our lives are not our own."

Cameron did want to know what Doctor Harfield had found, but she hadn't even dropped by her dorm yet. There was still dirt on her boots from some town five hundred miles away. Erika saw her hesitate.

"Stop at Three Sides, get some good coffee and take some to Will, bring me your receipt, and I'll reimburse you."

Cam sighed. "You don't need to do that; I'll go see him. He better not give me any more books to read, though."

006

WILLIAM SAT IN front of the hundreds of students in his introductory class, watching them struggle through the final exam. A teaching assistant circled the room, watching for cheating, and occasionally summoning William to answer a question. Gradually, the room emptied out, sometimes in clusters as large groups finished the test at about the same time. A few, mostly students who were majoring in Biology, stopped to thank William for a good semester. Some of the expressions of gratitude might even have been genuine.

Finally, the room was empty, and William was free to walk back across campus. He hummed as he went, a bouncy tune he'd learned from his grandfather. It brought back to him misty forests and rocky shores.

The air smelled *green*, as if all the delicate new leaves were scrubbing the air. It was a beautiful day, he was finished teaching for the summer, and he had his own research project to work on.

Then he clutched the box of test papers tighter. There it was, that treacherous golden glow. The once-pleasant breeze prickled against his face. He walked as fast as he could across the quiet campus, until he reached the biology building. There, he took a side door and ducked into a stairwell.

William closed his eyes and thought about the amount of lift required to keep a song sparrow aloft. He considered the current barometric pressure, wind speed and direction, temperature, and cloud patterns in an attempt to predict tomorrow's weather.

It was easier, in the quiet stairwell, to turn his mind away from the energy. It still took longer than usual. The light was getting harder to ignore. He had thought the new project and time with Doctor Paige would decrease the frequency of his lapses—

"Doctor Harfield? You okay?"

William opened his eyes. A woman stood in front of him. She had dark hair, dark eyes, and sturdy clothing that had seen rough use. Her boots alone would have been enough to attract attention at Gates. Had she just come from hiking the Greatfalls Trail?

She stared at his face with an intensity that, in his world, was reserved for the fighting that commenced when a retiring professor left a corner office vacant.

"I'm fine. Ah, Sentinel Kardell, right?"

"You looked upset a minute ago."

William shifted his grip on the box. "Really, I'm good. Working too much, probably. So . . . did Erika send you?"

The woman's expression changed. Her dark eyes warmed, she smiled, and William no longer felt like she was trying to see right through him. She held up two coffee cups stamped with the triangular logo of Three Sides.

"Erika suggested we discuss my monster."

William breathed again. "Of course. My office is on the second floor."

She followed him up the stairs but moved around him to open doors before he had a chance to try.

At his office, William fumbled to put his class things away and get the appropriate notes out. He hadn't reviewed the results enough yet to be completely confident in his conclusions, and he was unaccustomed to presenting anything to people outside the scientific community. Sentinel Kardell settled in, leaned her weapon in its scabbard against his desk, found a small clearing in the stacks of books to place his coffee cup, and sat, all done in such a smooth motion that he felt foolish for taking so long. He could feel her eyes, first on him and then scanning the mess that was his office.

Finally, he sat across from her with everything arranged, and he paused to take a drink of the coffee. He nodded approvingly, and then launched into his presentation.

"First of all, you should know that we haven't completed our tests, and these are the most preliminary of findings, but what we have so far—"

She stopped him with a raised palm. "Please don't take this the wrong way, but I really need the shortest possible version for now."

"Oh—yes, of course, I heard there's a lot going on, so—the short version. Well, from all the tests we've run, I can say with confidence that this creature is closer to being a human than an animal."

His declaration, which should have been the shocking culmination of his presentation, was met with a nod, as if this was no more than she had expected. It was he who was thrown off when she plowed ahead with a question.

"Do you know anything about the tattoo?"

"The analysis of the ink is still pending, and the tattoo artists I've consulted can't be sure about the type of tools used to make it. I can say that the biologists at Gates don't often use them to identify animals. Leg bands, plastic ear tags, and even embedded chips are more common."

The Sentinel's eyebrows drew down, her eyes darkening. "Where do you think this thing came from?"

William leaned back in his chair, struck the top of his desk with a pen a couple of times. None of the results could answer her question, none had even come close, so it was something he had pushed into the back of his mind. It had been days since it had risen to the surface of his thoughts.

"I don't need anything definite. Just give me your gut reaction," she said.

How often had his teachers lectured that he should never make judgments based on anything but explicit evidence? It was a creed he had struggled to live by when sometimes his mind jumped from one point to another without consulting him much on the way. And yet Sentinel Kardell leaned forward, the eyes that had been dark a moment ago now bright with interest.

"Someone out in the mountains is mucking around with genetics. I don't know how, maybe some Remnant. And he or she made this monster, and it got out of control. That sounds ridiculous, but it's the only thing I can think of."

She didn't laugh. "What we're dealing with isn't sane or simple, Doctor Harfield."

He leaned forward. It was rare that someone listened. "You should see the code on this thing; in most places it's no different than mine would be from yours, but where it *is* different, it's like hodgepodges of patches are just thrown on. Whole strings of code slapped in. Someone had an idea of what they wanted it to be, but they got it wrong somehow."

"There were doors down in that room where I killed it; they could have been hiding anything. I should have pushed to stay and get them open. No one has been able to do a thing since I left. Now I won't have the time." She lapsed into silence for a moment.

He sipped from his coffee, hoping she would start talking again, because he had no idea what to say next. That glower made it hard for him to think. Then her expression cleared, and she focused on him again.

"Did Erika give you the paperwork for the government lab?"

"Yes, I sent it in a few weeks ago."

"Good. Is there anything else I should know?"

"I do have some questions that weren't answered by your report."

Her face didn't change, and she didn't look at her watch, but he had the feeling that she wanted to. She levelled her shoulders. "I can do that. You've helped me just as much as I've helped you."

He rummaged through his piles for a notebook. "I'm sorry, things are a bit of a mess here."

"A bit? Doctor Harfield, there is mold in this coffee cup."

William snatched the mug off the desk. She was right. His neck warmed, and when he realized he was blushing, the heat moved up into his face. How long had that been there?

She laughed at him, not unkindly, but still, at him.

"So, right, what I was going to ask you—"

His office door opened, and he was suddenly conscious of the fact that his forehead was inches from the Sentinel's. Kardell turned as Doctor Paige stepped in. Dakota paused, her eyes going from William's still red face, to the two coffees on his desk, to the Sentinel sitting across from him. Her smile froze in place.

"I'm sorry, Doctor Harfield, I didn't know you had a meeting. I'll just come back later."

In the midst of William's spluttering, Kardell stood and extended her hand to the biologist. "I'm Sentinel Kardell. Doctor Harfield was just telling me about the research he's been doing on the animal I found in the Low Crescents."

"I'm Doctor Paige. I've been assisting with the research."

"This has become an important project," Kardell said, and she reached for her blade. "I'll leave you to your work."

"I really have just a few questions," William said. The Sentinel turned back to him, raised her eyes to the ceiling, but nodded. William glanced over to Dakota, who definitely looked annoyed. "No more than half an hour," he said, not sure which of them he was trying to appease.

Doctor Paige closed the office door behind her. The Sentinel returned to her chair, looking at him with raised eyebrows. Kardell's rapid retraction and then renewal of her agreement to answer his questions made no sense.

She sighed. "I thought you were really smart."

"Really smart is an understatement," he said.

"Doctor Paige likes you. She wasn't very happy to find me sitting here having coffee with you. I was trying to leave quickly so she wouldn't get more upset, but now it's going to take some work to convince her I wasn't here socially."

William tapped his pen against his notebook again. "How do you know she likes me?"

"Observation is part of my job."

William sat back in his chair with the coffee cup clutched against his chest. Kardell's eyes darkened again.

"Just ask your questions, and I'll get out of here."

William rallied. "Did the creature make a broad range of vocalizations, or were the sounds it produced limited?"

"Mostly it was quiet, especially while I was chasing it. But all the sounds it did make were different."

He tried not to glance up at her much while making his notes. Every time he did look at her, she stared hard at him. Sentinel Kardell had clearly spent too much time in the wilderness. He rushed through his questions, looking forward to getting her out of his office.

She answered his questions, and when he closed his notebook, she pressed her lips together.

"I didn't mean to upset you. It's been a long day, and this meeting went pretty much like the first one. At least this time there was coffee."

William tried to muster a smile. "It wasn't that bad."

The Sentinel laughed. "Doctor Harfield, you are a terrible liar. You know, I'm just going to leave now." She stuck out her hand, and he shook it. Her skin was hard with calluses and her fingers gripped with a force that took him by surprise. "Thank you for your help. Good luck with your research."

She picked up her weapon and her coffee. When she was gone he was finally able to breathe again.

He'd met Kardell before. Erika liked forcing William to go to parties, hoping to "break him out of his bubble." Kardell was usually there too, looking just as uncertain as William had felt. She hadn't talked much, except to ask William about his classes.

Erika liked her, which must count for something. His sister wasn't friends with many people who weren't well-connected.

But even now he felt off-kilter, like someone had pushed him over.

Doctor Paige knocked on the door while he was lost in his thoughts.

"What was all that about?" Dakota asked.

"She just wanted to know more about the creature she found," William said, though he wondered why, if it was that simple, he had felt like he was being held under a powerful microscope. Maybe the Sentinel was just bad with people, an affliction he could understand.

He could do better, though. "Do you like The Legitimate Daughters? They have a show in the Arts District right now. We could go together, if you want."

"Maybe," Dakota said. "As long as we go to Jake's Conundrum first."

"That's a deal."

William wondered, a few moments too late, if that had been the right thing to do.

007

ERIKA'S SLEEVES WERE too short, but by the end of the week, she would have her own tailored jacket, rather than a set of haphazardly assembled hand-me-downs. She had to arrange the High Guard uniform several times before it was correct. It was radically different from the standard Sentinel uniform. The fabrics were softer, cut to allow for free motion. Fewer medals were allowed, but the uniform itself said all anyone needed to know, didn't it?

She couldn't help smiling even as she walked through the dark, rainy city. She had never imagined that she would make it as far as the High Guard so early in her career. Had her chats with Sean Ellis convinced him, or did he have her in mind from the beginning? Even her father had to admit that this was an enormous leap..

She arrived at Braydon Hall very early, but found Cameron already standing outside of the Map Room, looking dour. She smiled as Erika approached, but her heart wasn't in it.

"You know, most Sentinels would *kill* to serve in the High Guard. You should at least try to look happy about it."

Cameron nodded. "I guess you're right."

"Your father would be very proud."

As always, Cameron shrugged off mention of her biological father as if she didn't care much what he would have thought. "Mom is freaking out, and Dad says it's an honor, but dangerous. He's mostly worried that I'll be too busy for family dinners. Your dad must be thrilled, though."

Erika made a face to demonstrate her opinion of her father's joy and bounced on the balls of her feet. It wasn't just the swearing in. She still thought that Cameron might have an ability, and she didn't know how to proceed.

Cameron didn't look like much, was in fact plainer than Erika remembered. Her stare was harder, her silences emptier, her face a little leaner since the patrol. Yet Erika didn't know anyone else with such extraordinary focus.

Erika compared her with Tristan. Cameron was not quite so quick, but there was a similarity in the way she moved. She had the same control over her limbs, the same smooth walk, like a prowling predator.

Erika stopped the bouncing, but then rapped her fingers on her scabbard.

"Master Reese would assign you to stand in tree for an hour if he saw you fidgeting like that." Cameron made a face. "Your brother nearly drove me insane with that pen tapping thing he does; it must run in your family."

"I'm just nervous." Erika lifted one foot, bound it around the opposite leg above her knee. "There, tree for Master Reese. Tell me when my hour is up."

Cameron smiled, but her eyes remained cool and analytical. That look always made Erika feel very small. Which was annoying, because it was hard to explain why it would make her feel that way. It was just a hard stare.

The three other new members of the High Guard arrived, and Erika greeted each one, while Cameron grew quiet and watchful. Erika talked and made the rest comfortable. If these handpicked men and women saw her as a leader she would have an edge, probably more valuable than all of Cameron's skill.

Finally, General Holing arrived, looking rushed and sleep-deprived. She commanded them to line up alphabetically, which they managed with some quiet muttering. Cameron and Erika stood next to one another, Kardell and Harfield having few letters between them. Then the doors to the Map Room swung open from the inside, and General Holing lead them in.

In the center of the room was a massive round table, painted with an intricate map of Cotarion. The glass on top was marked with roads, borders, and cities. The carpet was soft under their boots, the light was warm, the domed ceiling and walls detailed with dark wood.

High General Armel VI stood in front of the windows, his posture that of someone who had trained as a Sentinel, though his body showed he had long been out of practice. He was a small man who had put on weight in the last few years and lost a great swath of hair around his temples. There was no doubt that Armel VII, tall, broad, and brown, had inherited all his looks from his mother.

The High General spoke with two older members of the High Guard, his hands behind his back. Erika's father always complained that the Armel VI was too congenial with his inferiors, that he inspired no fear or obedience in anyone around him. He looked up as the new High Guards entered, his brow lined from years of worry.

Sean Ellis prowled around the map of the country he was about to lead, his eyes gleaming, his fingers reaching out here and there to brush a city or a landmark. This man had been tested by years quelling trouble along the borders. Would a clear head in combat make him a better leader of Cotarion?

General Holing lined the new Guards up in front of the table, approached High General Armel, saluted, then turned to Sean Ellis and repeated the gesture.

Erika stood tall, and tried to look as if she belonged. General Holing next went to a cabinet and brought out a fabric-lined tray bearing five shiny pins in the shape of two crossed blades. It was a simple badge, but rare.

High General Armel VI led them in the vow, and then Sean Ellis went down the line, pinning the new rank to their uniforms. He paused in front of Cameron. "You know, you are the youngest Sentinel ever to wear the Crossed Blades. I expect great things from you."

Cameron's face paled. Erika knew her friend had never prepared for this, never meant to end up face-to-face with the High General and the man who would soon be High General as the latter spoke to her in such an off-handed manner. Sean Ellis watched her. Finally, Cameron bowed, swallowed hard, and responded, "Thank you, sir."

"It's a good thing I didn't pick you for speeches," Sean Ellis said. Cameron flushed.

"She just needs time," said Armel VI. "Now, let's move on, we still have much to accomplish." Ellis scowled. So, probably not the sort of family that sent cheerful Winter Solstice cards and knit sweaters.

General Holing lead out the brand new High Guard hastily, and didn't stop until they were out of the building and safely in the classroom where they would be reviewing procedure for the day's ceremony.

As the doors shut, General Holing said, "Kardell!"

Cameron's voice was clear and steady, her face now showing nothing at all. "Yes, ma'am."

"How should you have responded to Incumbent High General Sean Ellis's remark?"

"I do not know, ma'am."

General Holing turned to Erika. "Harfield, please explain to High Guard Kardell what she should have done."

Erika knew that all of this was unfair. Cameron had done as well as could be expected. Erika also knew what General Holing was asking for.

"One should always respond to the High General as pleasantly and as rapidly as possible, keeping in mind that he or she is deserving of the utmost respect. I would have said, 'Thank you, sir. It is an honor to be chosen to serve you.'"

Cameron could never have pulled it off. For years she had been instructed in etiquette classes to say as little as possible. False flattery from Cam sounded, well, false.

General Holing nodded, and Erika wished she were somewhere, anywhere else.

"At least one of you is ready. If the rest of you are still wearing Crossed Blades by the end of the week, I'll be shocked. Master of the High Guard West, they're yours now. Good luck."

General Holing stormed off to her next task while the new High Guard took up chairs at the front of the room. A High Guard, his Crossed Blades bearing a star supported by the blade points, stood there with diagrams propped up on easels. His shaved scalp gleamed.

When he spoke, his voice was clipped and quick, his accent distinctively Southeast.

"I don't know what happened back there, and I don't care. You're High Guards now, and you're sworn to defend the High General with your lives. I don't expect you to bow and scrape in time, I expect you to get the bloody job done. If I dismiss you, it will be for any lapse that endangers the life of the High General. So, pay attention, and get it right."

For the rest of the morning they drilled, and reviewed, and sparred. After lunch they regrouped with Sean Ellis, High General Armel, and the senior members of the High Guard to review some more. Then they moved to the southern wall of the Military Quarter, where a set of ornate stairs would serve as the backdrop for the ceremony.

Cameron seemed more interested in the work as she and High Guard Anais went over their vantage point on a rooftop across the street from the platform. Erika kept up better than most of the other new members, but the older High Guards buzzed with impatience.

The drizzle continued throughout the day. Erika and High Guard Lin, a woman ten years her senior who seemed unlikely to ever smile, stood at the end of the block and watched the crowd for signs of trouble. Erika didn't see the ceremony, but she heard speeches about unity, and the people, and service to their country. Armel VI seemed relieved to give up his power, and Sean Ellis more than happy to relieve him of it.

Small flags waved all around, and pins with golden stars flashed from coat lapels. High Guard Lin snapped about vigilance and scanning sectors, even though Erika knew she had both covered.

The High Guard reconvened when the ceremony ended. The new members shivered in their cold, wet uniforms while they were assigned a schedule full of training and light on guard duty. They were also given binders packed with instructional material, and told to learn every word.

Sean Ellis congratulated them all on a job well done, and Armel VI exchanged goodbyes with the older High Guards. How much was he giving up, besides his power? He wouldn't live in the High General's Quarters, of course, or have a whole team of people cleaning and cooking for him. Erika doubted, after ruling all of Cotarion, that he would be able to sit and write history books as his son suggested.

After their dismissal, Erika walked with Cameron across the Military Quarter to the dormitories. The grounds were quiet.

"I'm sorry about all that," Erika said, knowing Cameron would understand what she meant.

"I already forgot about it. So, where do you think I should start looking for an apartment? If I'll be here in Advon for a while, I might as well find a place to live."

"Based on the hours in this schedule, I'd say closer to the Military Quarter is better."

Cameron was quiet for a moment. "Everyone they picked is unmarried. None of the Guards have families. I knew they wanted commitment, but I didn't realize just how much."

Cam seemed to struggle for more, but ultimately gave up, perhaps afraid of saying something a High Guard should not. There was something on her face that Erika would have called loneliness on anyone else.

Then Cameron lifted her chin and her expression cleared, her voice brightened. "It's definitely going to be interesting work, and I get to spend almost this whole week sparring. I've missed that."

"I think I'm going to come down with a serious case of head to toe bruises. You never pull your blows enough."

Cameron argued fiercely for this strategy, pointing out that a hard hit with a training sword was nothing to a soft tap with an edged weapon. Erika let her make the case until they arrived at the dorms, where they parted. Erika walked the rest of the way home in the chill rain.

Cameron beat High Guard Anais in less than a minute. The second bout took longer, and Cameron had a couple of close calls, but in the end, she won with a tap to the back of the senior High Guard's neck, delivered with delicacy before she turned to Erika with raised eyebrows, as if to point out that she could spar without beating her partner half to death.

It looked so simple when Cameron fought. For Erika, sparring was pure terror, moment after moment of struggling to guess what would come next, wondering who was faster, who would get lucky. Get it wrong, and the result was a painful blow. How many times had Erika walked away from a match with stinging fingers, a ringing head, or a blackened eye?

Cameron didn't appear to be afraid of those things.

Erika won half of her matches. The other junior High Guards were lucky to win one or two, so her rate seemed good, as long as she didn't compare herself with Cameron. The senior High Guards became more cautious as the sparring practice went on, but Cameron still walked away with twelve wins to five losses. Her blunder with Sean Ellis the day before seemed to be forgotten.

At the end of the sparring, the Master of the High Guard assigned them areas to work on in individual practice, and then their time was free, for at least a few hours. Afternoon had passed into evening, and the High Guards packed up quickly to get to dinner. Erika collected her convictions.

Cameron stood beside her as she lingered putting away her practice gear. "Are you finally going to talk about what's been bothering you?"

Erika sighed. If she wanted to get answers, it had to happen sometime. "I'm going to warn you, it's complicated."

"More complicated than trying to get Armel to marry you?"

"A bit." Erika finished tying her boots. "It might be easiest if I just show you, honestly."

She looked up at Cameron, who regarded her with narrowed eyes. Oh good. So they would begin with skepticism.

"Before you went to Palisade, would you have believed it if someone told you there were monsters in the Low Crescents?"

"I guess not."

"Well, this is going to be like that. Think of something very specific, all right? Hold it very firmly in your mind. Then give me your hand." Cameron opened her mouth to object, and Erika opened her hands to show they were empty. "It's not a trick, okay? Just trust me, for ten seconds."

"Ten seconds is a lot." But Cameron's brow furrowed with concentration, and then she held out her hand. Erika took it, keeping her touch clinical.

She heard the ocean waves, first, and then an image floated up in her mind of the seashore, rocky and wild. There was a boy beside her, laughing. What was his name, Jacob? He was in Cameron's year. This must be from several years before, when they were still Cadets, training in Brook's Cove with Master Reese.

"You're so weird, Kardell," he said.

Erika felt an upwelling of frustration, not her own. Then Jacob leaned over, still laughing, to kiss her.

Erika jerked her hand away. "Cameron! That's disgusting. I don't want to make out with that twerp, even if it is second-hand and hazy. Ugh." She shuddered, the scent of salt water still lingering, even though the image had thankfully evaporated.

Cameron's eyebrows were raised, which was as close to an expression of surprise as she ever got. "What twerp, exactly?"

"Jake, whatever his name is. I tell you to think of something specific and that's what you go for?"

"Can you do it again?"

"Only if you promise to pick something way less gross." She hadn't been wrong the day before, when she'd thought Cameron looked lonely. Strange. Cameron had a long-standing reputation for keeping people at a distance, but maybe her run of the Ring had been more solitary than even she could stand.

Cameron closed her eyes, apparently concentrating. When they opened again, their look was sharper, more attentive. Erika took her extended hand.

She sat in a dim room, her knees pulled up to her chest. She watched a man with silver hair and dark eyes sitting across from her, a child on his lap, a book in his hands, a candle burning on a rough-hewn table beside him. The child was 'cousin', the man 'Grandpa'.

His hands were rough, and there was dirt under his fingernails. But his voice was smooth, deep, and as he read it rose and fell like waves. The language Erika didn't understand, but the meaning was there in Cameron's memory. He read a well-known fable about a child who tried to steal an eagle's egg, and was knocked from the aerie when the adults returned suddenly. The child fell to his death.

Erika had always thought the conclusion of the tale horrible. But Cameron rested her chin on her knees and thought, 'No one is safe from death. So why do they always try to frighten us into obedience with these stories? Why do they encourage us not to try? It's not our fault that they worry.'

Erika pulled her hand away again. "I saw a man telling a story. I think you must have been very young. With your grandparents in Varcove?"

Cameron looked at her a long time, and after watching her cool thoughts in the memory, Erika imagined for the first time that she could see some of the calculations happening behind those dark eyes.

"You're telepathic."

Cameron's words were so certain that Erika had to suppress a shiver. It was supposed to be a lot harder than that.

"Yes."

Cameron grinned. "That's an excellent secret. So, why are you showing me this now?"

"Because I think that you can do something like it, but I'm not sure what."

"Is it because I'm so good at fighting?" The furrows between her eyebrows were back, and her voice was slow and thoughtful.

"That and—other things." Erika watched Cameron's face. Her friend seemed deep in thought. She had always felt different, because she had always been different. It was why she had just a handful of friends. "It might be nothing, honestly."

"In which case you've revealed your secret for no reason. So I'm guessing all this is leading up to some kind of a test?"

"Something like that. There's sort of a place in the mind of everyone I know who's—special. And I'd like to see if you have a place like that in your brain, if that's okay with you."

Cameron nodded. Her curiosity had to have been great for her to acquiesce.

Erika, with shaking hands, locked the door of the sparring room, and then sat on the floor in the middle of the room. Cameron sat across from her, with their knees almost touching. Erika rubbed her hands together and considered. Besides the occasional prod at the thoughts that sat on the surface, she had never used her telepathy on anyone but her brother and cousin. This was something entirely different. There was no way to plan when she didn't know what she was looking for.

"All of our abilities come with, let's call it a guidebook. It's a set of instincts and mental visualizations that allow us to do things that most people can't. My brain can follow the electric impulses through another person's mind, and interpret them as thoughts and images, or I can send out signals, and that's what I'm going to try with you."

"Look, I don't need the whole 101 course right now. I'm starting to get hungry."

Erika put a hand on either side of Cameron's head, closed her eyes, and concentrated.

She started at the surface. Cameron's thoughts flashed by quickly and cleanly, one following the other in rapid order. Then she went farther, down into the part of the mind that made little sense without the images she received to interpret the tangled pathways. There was a flash, and then the world of Cameron's mind resolved around her.

008

SHE STOOD IN a bright hallway, the floors, ceilings, and walls of which were white. There was no specific light source, but every surface glowed a little. Doors and new halls marched off in either direction, collapsing down to a point at the horizon line. Cameron stood next to her.

"Where are we?"

"Inside your head. It's just a visual. The brain is too complicated to explore without a lens that the conscious mind can understand. Yours is kind of boring, to be honest. William's head is this huge forest; I always get lost there. So, do you know where to go?"

Cameron had her arms crossed. Funny, how uncomfortable people always looked when confronted with the interior of their own brains. "I think that this is probably your area of expertise."

Erika usually landed at least close to her goal, so she scanned up and down the hall for anything that might guide her. She saw a hallway that was not so brightly lit, so she went toward it. "You're very, um, organized." She peeked down a corridor as they passed by its entrance, and saw yet another long avenue lined with doors, marching on into nothing. She shuddered, and then carried on.

The dim hallway was, in fact, pitch black just a few feet down. However, way down at the end, Erika saw a light. She hadn't thought it would be quite that easy.

"I don't like it," Cameron said quietly.

"It's your head. Of course you don't like it." Erika laughed. "Come on, let's go make sure and then we'll get out of here."

Together they walked through the blackness, the light at the end of the dark hallway resolving into yet another white door. Erika reached out and tried to turn the handle, but it wouldn't move.

"Is this what it looks like?" Cameron asked as Erika jiggled the knob.

Erika lifted up one shoulder in a shrug. "It's usually tucked back, out of the way. It looks different in William's mind and my cousin's, I know that much. I haven't been this far into any minds besides theirs." Erika pressed the door knob up and then down while trying to twist it, like on a real door when the wood had swollen and moved the latch out of alignment.

But the door wasn't real. It just represented a mental block of some kind. There was something here even Cameron wasn't supposed to know. Was it wise to keep going? William could easily run a blood test to confirm the ability. Still, she was so close, and so certain that the answer was there, burning just out of reach.

"What is it, Erika?"

"I'm not sure. But there's always a path from one place to another. Usually, more than one." Erika turned back down the hall, her hands sliding against either wall, until her right hand found empty space. She went into the empty space, Cameron behind her. The hall twisted and turned, forcing Erika to go slowly in the complete darkness.

She emerged back into the light, so suddenly that she was blinded for a long time. At last, she blinked the stars from her eyes and saw she stood in a room just as plain and white as the hallways she had walked. Cameron stood in front of her.

She was different. Slightly so, but enough. Erika turned around to look down the corridor she had just travelled. Cameron was there, too, standing with her hand pressed up against a barrier that she had not been able to cross. Erika looked back to the other Cameron and thought she might understand.

"A second consciousness? That's new."

"You really shouldn't be here." This Cameron's voice was frigid cold and her eyes were more than just dark, they were black. Ice water seemed to trickle down the back of Erika's neck.

"What are you?"

"I am the infinite possibility of humanity, untempered by humanity." Erika might have laughed at such a statement, had it not been spoken in such hollow, ringing tones. She stepped back.

"You're like us, then."

The black-eyed Cameron tilted her head and stepped closer. "Yes and no. You are toys. I am a tool. A weapon."

Erika's feet itched to run, but she hadn't expected this, and she needed to understand. She gestured back to Cameron as she knew her, still in the dark hallway. "Your own mind doesn't know you're here. Why?"

"Weapons are dangerous. So I am hidden, even from her. For now." The black-eyed Cameron smiled, reached out, and took Erika's wrist in an iron grip. "But here you are, and there she is."

Erika didn't know what happened next, but her vision split and fractured, and then she was shoved backwards, into the hallway by which she had entered. Her friend stood waiting and caught her. The images were breaking, coming apart, and she felt that her head was, too.

Erika gasped as she returned to the physical world, and the pain in her skull increased. She dropped her hands from Cameron's temples, and tried to concentrate on her breath. Let the throbbing meld into her awareness just like the air moving in and out of her lungs, to become nothing, but she had never been very good at that trick.

"I didn't see what happened. What's wrong?" Cameron's voice shook.

Erika heard, overlaid on the spoken words, what Cameron was thinking, even though she wasn't touching her anymore. She had never been able to snatch thoughts out of the air. She had tried, so many times, knowing that would make her talent really useful, but never succeeded.

Now she heard Cameron race to reconcile what she had just seen with her knowledge of how the world worked. She went fast, ideas clicking into place one after the other, order rising up from chaos. Erika had often thought Cameron's cool exterior was an act, a shield between her real thoughts and the world. Now she heard her friend move through the incredible facts, explain each one, and accept it. All in a few seconds. Erika tried to tune it out, but the rushing thoughts went on without break or pause.

Something is wrong, those lines on her face, that is pain. Is that normal, is that the price of what she can do? But no, she's surprised.

What did she see, what did she find? What did she see while I was in the dark?

"Erika! What happened?" *What, what, what—*

"Nothing. I must have been wrong. I just pushed myself too far. I'm going to go get some rest." She left, ignoring Cameron's questions, both spoken and silent.

She had to find her brother.

009

WILLIAM STROLLED BACK to his apartment. Summer approached. Tree frogs chirped in the park, joined by the throaty croaks of a bullfrog. The air was warm, but not humid.

The memory of Dakota's gentle kiss lingered on his cheek. He hadn't expected it, since they had struggled to talk about anything besides work. Finding common ground elsewhere had been disconcertingly difficult.

There were so many things he could never say. Tristan's career as a thief and a killer was just a footnote in the book of family secrets he wanted to keep hidden. Dakota had been full of questions. Could he blame her for being frustrated at his reticence?

Yet she had kissed him. Maybe their conversation about the music had salvaged the evening. He did tend to overemphasize negative social interactions.

William hummed as he stepped up to his front door, and then hunted through his jangling keys to find the right one. His keyring was heavier now that he had full-time access to the equipment in the Biology building's basement.

If there had ever been a good time to find someone like them, it was now. He thought about saying so to Erika every time he went to the biology basement, and subsequently forgot in the excitement of new results.

Cesar trotted up when he opened the front door, paws skidding across the hardwood floor, his tail swishing hard in the air. William scratched behind his flopped ears, and Cesar panted. A walk around the park might be in order. It was a nice evening, and besides, he was in too good a mood to sleep easily.

He went to the small desk in the entry that served as a place to pile, and lose, all the things that he most needed on his way out of the house. He pulled open the drawer where he kept the leash. He couldn't find it, no matter how many papers or bags of dog biscuits he shoved aside.

"William?"

The voice was behind him. He spun, his hand fumbling for the light. Who would be here at this hour? Finally, his fingers found the switch, and he flicked it up.

Erika stood in his living room, just off the foyer. She rocked back and forth, from the front of her foot to the heel, and back again. One of her weapons masters had trained her out of that habit a few years ago. It was strange to see it again. There was a feverish brightness in her eyes that he did not like.

"Why were you standing in the dark? How did you get in?" His heart raced, and seemed to be trying to leap up his throat and out of his mouth.

Erika held up his spare house key between two fingers. Her hand was shaking. "I told you not to keep it over the door. And I forgot to turn on the light."

She tossed it to him, but it bounced off his knuckle and skittered off under the couch. William knelt to fish it out, while Cesar danced around and licked his ears. By the time he found the damn thing, Erika stood over him. A tear ran down her cheek. He jumped up, reached out, and wrapped his arms around her.

"You were right, Will. I should have been more careful. I should have waited until you could run the test." Her hands gripped him hard, and her voice trembled as she spoke. This wasn't right; it didn't work this way. Erika was the one who kept him from falling to pieces. What could he possibly say?

"What happened?"

Erika pulled back. "I looked in her head, Will, and it was there, she's like us, but it's not the same. Something happened. And I can hear people thinking from half a block away, all of them at once."

"That's impossible. How can you pick up the signals without contact?"

Maybe it was something like radio waves; maybe she was casting and receiving an energy signal that connected to the neurons in the brain, a string that stretched between two people like a telephone wire. He squinted at her. For once he wanted to see the glow of energy. It wavered into focus, and he looked for some sign of how her mind might be connecting to others' without contact. Then he heard her voice in his head.

Dakota kissed you and you aren't sure you like her.

William jerked as the soundless words cut across his own thoughts. Impossible. He rubbed the back of his neck, turned away, and turned back. Something in his mind refused to catch, refused to accept what he had heard. Yet not heard. Erika stared at him, her eyes glistening again. He rubbed the top of his head. Then manic laughter burst up out of his chest.

"This is not funny."

"I'm not—laughing—because it's funny. It's because—I don't know—what else to do." He wished he could stop, but it seemed once he had started it would go on forever. He felt light-headed.

Then Erika grabbed the front of his shirt and threw him back into the wall, hard enough to rattle picture frames. He'd hardly felt the flash of pain from the impact when her fist connected with his cheek. He would have gone sprawling to the floor if she didn't have him in her grip again. William stared at her face, which was creased with rage. He didn't know who this was, but it wasn't Erika. His cheek throbbed, his thoughts scattered, and Cesar whined.

"Get it together. You have no idea—right now my head is full of so many voices. I can't even think."

Her fingers twisted the fabric of his shirt. The shadows in the room appeared to shift. No, they *were* moving, creeping out of the corners and into the bright places, which shrank back. The darkness grew, and a senseless fear took hold. William reached up to tear Erika's hands away, but her grip was iron. He was cold, so cold, ice spread over the windowpanes, and his vision began to fade into darkness. There was a roar like ocean waves in his ears. His thoughts felt compressed, trapped, as if his mind was being squeezed. The terror was everywhere. Through it, he heard Erika's voice.

This is what I feel, little brother.

Then it lifted, his vision cleared, and she let go. He leaned back against the wall. What had he just seen? A projection of pure experience, maybe, from her mind to his.

Erika dropped to her knees and wept. Cesar licked her face, and she didn't even try to push the dog away.

William tried to shake off the strange terror he had felt a moment before. He helped her up, and guided her to the couch, then commanded Cesar to stay, hoping his presence would help. He bounded up the stairs to the second floor, into the spare room where he sometimes worked, and found the boxed kit he needed to take blood samples.

William paused there, pressed his hand against his cheek, and winced. No fractures, but it throbbed. What was wrong with her? She'd never hit him in anger before. Sure, there'd been the occasional playful thump, but nothing serious.

He grabbed an extra notebook, a pen, and went back to Erika.

She wasn't sobbing, but tears still tracked down her face. She was now re-plaiting her long hair. When she was done, he held out a tissue. After she had wiped her eyes, he broke open the blood sample collection kit. Erika took the lancet, pricked her finger, and let a drop of blood fall onto a glass slide. William held out two more slides. He wrote a label, and packed it all back into a sealed bag.

He smiled at Erika, but she didn't smile back. "I'll figure out how to help. You know I will. But I need to know what happened."

She shook her head. She looked tired and worn, as if the outburst had depleted her. She had been trying to hear thoughts without making physical contact for years, without success, been trying to send William thoughts for even longer. Now she could do both. He burned to know how, and Erika was silent.

"I know you were trying to find out if someone else has powers like ours. Just tell me who."

"It was there. But it's separated from the rest of the mind. Even if I could concentrate enough to get back to that place . . . " She let her head drop onto the back of the couch. "There's no going back that way. There might not be any going back at all."

Cesar nudged Erika's free hand with his muzzle and she rubbed his head dutifully. Her knuckles were split open. William went to his kitchen where he kept a small first-aid kit.

He sat across from her again, glad to keep his hands busy while he thought. Carefully he cleaned the broken skin, applied an ointment, and then bandaged her hand. He put her blood sample on his desk. Then he filled a glass with water and carried two tablets of a mild painkiller back to her.

"What did you do a minute ago?"

Her eyes flashed open, their green especially bright. "I wanted you to know how I felt, so I pushed it at you. I think I could probably do it more effectively with practice." A small smile lifted her lips. "This could be an interesting development, if I can just get the voices to shut up. A High Guard who knows what people are thinking, who can make other people see things? Sean Ellis won't be in danger from assassins as long as I'm around, that's certain."

Then she frowned, peered at William as if he had spoken. What had he been thinking that could get her attention? This was an inconvenient development, having the contents of his head open to constant scrutiny. Of course, she would see him thinking about that, too.

"Skipper," she said.

No, not that, had he really been thinking about that? But of course he had; he always did when he worried about one of them using their powers too much.

Skip was William's favorite dog as a boy. A long-legged wolfhound with swaths of shaggy gray fur who had slept at the foot of William's bed every night and followed him wherever he went.

Erika sat up, reached out to grip his arm, and pulled him down to sit across from her. He dragged his eyes up, grateful that for the first time that night his sister looked like herself.

"Will. You should have told me. If I'd known, I never would have pushed so hard."

The ribbons of energy that wove all around him could be dangerous, but nothing like that hazy glow surrounding people, animals, anything that lived. That was the force of life. It was a natural extension of the energy manipulations, of *course* he could see it. Chemical reactions and electric impulses ran through people all the time.

Not knowing what would happen, he had tugged at that haze just once. He had wanted to know how it all worked. By the time he had realized Skipper would die, it was too late, the manifestation of the energy in the body too complex to give it back. His mother saw. She always protected him, as Erika did now. She had buried Skipper, and let the rest of the family think the wolfhound had run away.

William bit the inside of his cheek, hard. Erika didn't need this, not right now. She needed him to find out what had happened to her, to be the one who knew what to do next.

"It wasn't your fault. You didn't do it on purpose."

William sucked in a sharp breath and turned away to rearrange the supplies he had pulled out. The way his mother had looked at him when she knew what he could do. He couldn't absolve himself, and he did not want anybody else to, either.

Erika had always been too lenient with him, perhaps to make up for the fact that their father had pushed him to his breaking point more than once. He knew he was dangerous, in a way that neither Erika nor Tristan ever could be.

Of course, now he didn't know what Erika was capable of.

He cleared his throat. "How's your head?"

"Not great. It hurts. And I feel confused. Like everything's all shaken up."

"If we're lucky, then the effect will be temporary. If not, then I'll do everything I can to figure out what's happened, and set it right." He shuffled a stack of notebooks into a tidy pile. "You have to tell me who did this. I need to know everything."

"It doesn't matter. It can't be fixed."

Her shoulders tightened, and her heel bounced up and down on the floor again.

"I don't see the sense in keeping this from me. If there's someone out there who can give other people these powers, that's incredibly dangerous."

"It isn't going to happen again. It only happened this time because I wouldn't stop pushing. Please leave it alone." Cesar abandoned his attempts to get either sibling to pay attention to him, and trotted off to his bed in the corner.

"You aren't protecting this person, Erika. And you're making my job so much more difficult." He reached out his hands to her, but she pushed him away. He didn't know what to do, or how to help.

"Even I couldn't turn back when I should have. If I tell you, you won't let go until this happens to you. I'm protecting them, yes, but I'm protecting you, too."

She stood, and abruptly she wrapped her arms around him again. "I love you, Will. You're a good kid." Then she let go, wheeled away, and was out his front door so fast he didn't have time to respond.

A long time passed before he was able to move from that spot. His mind raced, driving out the feelings he didn't want to deal with at that moment. When at last he moved again, he was quicker than he had been in a long time. He grabbed his notebook, and went back out into the night, leaving his spare key at the top of the doorframe. He would begin his tests that night. He would solve this.

In the corner of his living room, Cesar sighed.

An unfamiliar beep woke William the next morning. He jerked his head up off the table where he had fallen asleep. He stumbled to the middle of the room, where Whir frantically notified him that it was finished.

William gathered up the printed results, page after page of tiny black bars in rows, and took them to his office. Still shaking off the less than restful sleep, he pulled Erika's old results from the locked drawer where he kept the proof of his family's anomalies.

It didn't take him long to find the first difference between the two. Maybe just a smudge, or a printing error. Then he found another.

He circled all the changes between Erika's last genetic profile and the new one, and then placed his pen on his desk with an unsteady hand. Impossible. A mistake. He took another of the samples out of his desk, and went back to the basement.

The second set of results were the same. Erika's genetic sequence was different. But how?

William left Gates to grab some coffee and food, then returned and ran the test a third time.

They were the same. There could be no mistake.

He and Doctor Paige worked on Kardell's monster that afternoon. He couldn't focus, so they didn't make much progress on any of their reports.

William called Erika when he got home that evening, but instead of his sister he reached Sophie. Erika's roommate reported that Erika hadn't returned home the night before.

"That Sentinel she's friends with, Cameron, came to see me this morning. Erika didn't report for a briefing. It's so weird; she's usually so responsible."

William's attempted reassurances sounded hollow. Immediately after, he called Tristan, and his cousin told him that he was already on the job.

That night he slept little. Shortly after midnight he gave up. He and Cesar walked back to Gates, where he ran Erika's sample through Whir a fourth time. He read through his old books of folklore, the only outside evidence of their abnormalities.

The stories had been passed down for hundreds of years before they were set to paper. Most people considered them myths meant to frighten children into proper behavior. No one could have ever moved mountains, and entire cities didn't vanish.

Some of it, however, William didn't question.

One story told of a warrior with extraordinary strength who defended a small band of survivors for years in the midst of the Wars. Though his feats seemed incredible, it was no more than Tristan could do. In fact, William suspected that parts of the story had been toned down to make them more believable. After it, though, was the tale of a woman who could speak to animals, which was pure fantasy.

William had turned the pages of the book until they were soft and frayed, trying to tease fact from fiction. One thing, however, was consistent. In every tale, the people who were capable of something more than human were called The Altered.

He thumbed through to the back of the book, where the tales were the haziest, in spite of being the newest. William had theorized that this was because by the end of the Wars there were few people left to spread and embellish them. Many of the stories here spoke of a new type of Altered, who ended the conflict by stealing powers of the others.

Maybe if the powers could be taken, they could also be given. But the technology needed for that was gone. A person certainly couldn't do such a thing without the help of some serious tech.

William was still reading, considering what was possible and what was not, when Tristan sauntered into the lab. When he saw the bruise on William's cheek, his silver eyes widened.

"Who did that to you?"

"Erika. I don't know what was wrong with her, but I've never seen her that way before. What are you doing here?"

Before Tristan could answer, Whir beeped and the next set of results began to print. William could see now, at a glance, where the bars were shorter, or shifted across the page. "They've definitely changed. But how?"

"When did Erika hit you?"

"The night before last," William said, his mind far away. He couldn't doubt that Erika's genetic code was different now. It might seem impossible, but it had happened. He looked up at Tristan. "What's happened; why are you here?"

"Your dad sent me to find her. She hasn't reported for her job in two days. Any idea where she might be?"

William's mind went blank as he stared at the papers. He should know where Erika would go, but he didn't. At last he shook his head.

"Are you sure? If you don't know, then I've hit a dead end."

William stayed still and quiet until at last Tristan left. All his knowledge, all his books, and still he had no answers.

010

CAM DIDN'T GLANCE at the door, though she wanted to. The procedural review session was about to start, and Erika wasn't there. The Master of the High Guard stood at the front of the room, watching the second hand of his watch make its rounds. When the moment came and went, his nostrils flared. Cam heard him grinding his teeth from halfway across the room. So, lateness was discouraged. Clearly.

He lectured on the honor of the High Guards. His accent grew stronger as he went, with the word 'bloody' making frequent appearances, until it was so thick he was hard to understand. Finally, he looked to Cam, and said, "Go and bloody find her."

She stood, clapped the hilt of her blade to her shoulder, and left. Why jeopardize her chance to look for Erika?

Cam's worldview had already shifted to include the fact that Erika was telepathic. The evidence was too strong to argue against. Erika had also mentioned that her brother and her cousin possessed strange abilities. But what about her? Erika had seen something important in Cam's mind, and she had also been in pain. There were pieces Cameron still didn't understand, and those missing parts quickened her steps. She needed to find her friend before someone else did.

She walked down the hall, out of the building, and across the Military Quarter. She caught no glimpses of Erika's signature auburn braid. Cam quickened her pace to the apartment her friend shared with Sophie. She knocked on the door, and was surprised when Sophie, who she knew to be a late sleeper, answered right away. Her brown eyes widened, and her face paled when she saw Cam.

"I'm looking for Erika," Cam said quickly, before Sophie could assume that she was receiving a casualty notification.

"I didn't see her last night, and she never mentioned that she wouldn't be home. You know how she is, you can set your watch by her, and if she stays out somewhere, she always lets me know." She tugged on her necklace, and the metal disks on it jingled. "If you're out looking for her—"

"There's no reason to worry yet. I'm going to find her."

Sophie's chin crumpled.

"I'll do everything I can," Cam said. "When I find her, I'll let you know."

She escaped before any tears fell, and jogged all the way back to the Military Quarter. When the Master of the High Guard stopped shouting at her for returning without Erika, she explained what she'd learned from Sophie, and that she'd felt the situation would require more than a simple search. He shouted some more, and at last he ordered all of the new High Guards to track down their absent member.

On the third morning of the search, Cam looped around Gates University, debating whether she should question Erika's brother. Sean Ellis's admission the night before, that they would have to call a specialized unit by the end of the day, still rang in her ears. It would be an embarrassment to the High Guards. Surely William Harfield knew something. How could Cam find out what without revealing why Erika had told her their secret?

As she weighed the need to find Erika against the need to keep her potential role quiet, she saw Doctor Harfield turn out onto the sidewalk just ahead of her. He didn't see her, and in fact, he was so deeply preoccupied that she wondered if he saw anything at all.

Stubble darkened his jaw, and his hair was so tousled that Cam's fingers itched to smooth it down. The skin around his eyes was dark. He knew something about Erika, something that kept him up at night.

Cam followed him. As she did, she saw a flash of motion from the rooftops. When she looked up, a man with dark hair looked back at her. Even from this distance, she saw him grin before he vanished. So, Doctor Harfield was already being tailed. Was Erika's brother in trouble, too? Or had someone else decided that he was the key to finding the lost Sentinel?

Without ever looking around him, except to check traffic when he crossed the street, and that so careless that the action was pointless, Doctor Harfield drifted to Three Sides Coffee Shop. Cam turned into a bookstore on the opposite side of the road and pretended to peruse the displays near the window so she could keep her eyes on the scientist. He ordered a coffee and sat at a table far from the door.

The air stirred beside her, and she only kept her eyes on her task with great effort. She hadn't heard anyone approach. He had training of some kind.

"Are you finding anything interesting in the Romance section? I hadn't pegged you for a reader of sultry love stories."

"Who are you?"

His returning smile was engineered to charm. The strong planes of his face lent to the effect, but the expression was too practiced. "Erika's cousin, looking for her, just like you."

"If you're just looking, why do you need all those daggers in your coat pockets?"

He hid his surprise well, but it flashed in his silver eyes. "You're wearing a sword."

"And a uniform. Erika didn't tell me much about her cousin. What's your name?"

"Tristan Rush. Don't laugh. I've heard lots about you. Lucky she has friends so committed to finding her." His grin took on an edge. "Of course, it's not so noble if you want to get to her first so you can hide your part in whatever's happened."

He couldn't possibly know. He was just testing her.

Across the street, Erika appeared from the back of the coffee shop and sat at William's table.

Tristan vanished. She didn't watch him go. Keeping eyes on Erika was more important.

Erika gripped William's hands. She leaned in so that their foreheads almost touched as she spoke. Cam watched, picking up a book now and then, edging ever nearer the door. Finding Erika had been the difficult part. Cam could afford to let her speak with her brother before confronting her.

William shook his head as Erika rose to her feet, confusion in his eyes as she bent to kiss his forehead. Strange. An intensely affectionate gesture, even for Erika.

Cam moved to the door of the bookstore when her friend exited Three Sides. A bell rang as she stepped out onto the sidewalk, and Erika spun at the sound. Their eyes met, and they both paused. Erika's hand went to the blade on her hip, her knuckles white as she gripped the hilt.

A threat, and they both knew it.

Expressions flitted over Erika's face in rapid succession. What was she doing? The door to Three Sides opened, Doctor Harfield spoke, and Erika ran.

That was enough. Cam dashed across the street, avoiding the moving cars by a small margin. When Erika glanced back and saw Cam following, there was fear in every line of her face.

Cam closed some of the distance on the sidewalks, but every time they came to a street crossing, Erika found gaps in the traffic. Cars screeched to a standstill after she had gone by, forcing Cam to weave through the vehicles while angry drivers shouted at her. Meanwhile, the entire city of Advon seemed to be out on the sidewalks, getting something to eat before heading to work. Cam collided with one young man carrying a tray of coffee in each hand, and nearly lost sight of Erika as she disentangled herself from him.

And of course, Erika played dirty. She kicked a shelf of newspapers being sold on one street corner, sending papers flying, and forcing Cam to jump over the stand. In the chaos, Erika turned down a different street, and Cam lost precious seconds regaining sight of her.

Erika seemed in good position to get away until they entered the Arts Block. On the quieter sidewalks and streets, Cam began to catch up. Her hand dropped to the hilt of her weapon.

Erika stopped abruptly and turned back, her sword raised. Cam slowed, changing her stance to intercept. Erika moved her weight forward. The strike was all wrong. Erika's elbows were straight, all the power coming from her shoulders. Cam twisted out of the way.

Erika's blade missed her by a few inches, a comfortable margin. Cam freed her sword and struck in one neat motion. Erika's sloppy swing threw her off balance, and she stumbled back. The edge of Cameron's sword glanced along her ribs.

Erika yelped and dropped her weapon, the steel ringing as it hit the ground. Her face cleared as she pressed her hands against the shallow wound. Cam stepped back to open up some space between them. Her eyes never wavered from Erika's face. She wouldn't miss any sign of what would come next.

"What happened?"

Erika slumped into the wall of the building next to her. "I don't know. I can't stop hearing. I can't turn it off." She held a blood-stained hand in front of her eyes, her brow furrowed. "Please, Cam, just let me go. I have to get away."

"You drew your sword. You struck at me." Attacking a fellow Sentinel meant a dishonorable discharge at best, imprisonment at worst.

Erika closed her eyes and didn't answer. Her eyes moved beneath her closed lids, the corners of her mouth tight. It was the same expression Erika had worn when she'd gone poking in Cam's mind.

Cam stepped forward, her sword rising. Tristan dropped to the ground behind Erika, from where Cam didn't know. They both closed fast.

Pain struck Cam, lancing through her body, everywhere at once. She fell to her knees. Something had hit her, but what?

She gasped and gripped her weapon tightly. The world pulsed, distorted by pain. She pressed her hand to her chest, but felt no reason why her flesh should scream as if on fire. She fought to rise but was overwhelmed, and she fell again.

Gradually the pain faded, the sparks of it fizzling away until she could lift her head. The street was empty except for Tristan, who knelt on the ground across from her, his silver eyes wide. A sheen of sweat gleamed on his forehead.

"Did Erika do that?" Cam said.

They both stumbled to their feet, as if it were a race. "I don't know. Never happened before. Sucked though, didn't it?"

Erika had escaped and would not be caught now on foot. Cam checked for injuries while cursing with all the eloquence she could muster. She wasn't hurt, but the hilt of her sword was scuffed.

Pain was in the mind, and Erika could reach the mind, so it made sense that she could inflict pain. However, she had said that her power depended on physical contact. That clearly was not the case.

If Cam had secret powers, she wouldn't be honest about them, either.

"We found her," Tristan said. "So, what's next?"

"What you do next is up to you." Cam strode away from him, back the way she had come. She wasn't about to give directions to this stranger. She had no way of knowing what he would do with even the smallest hint of her intentions.

Tristan Rush vanished again, so Cam walked back across town alone. If Erika had stopped to say goodbye to William, she had probably stopped at her apartment, too.

There was a knot in Cam's chest, just behind her sternum. It might be fear, not so much of what Erika could do—that would have been an appropriate thing to find frightening—but that she might have had some part in it. The explanation she'd hoped for looked unlikely.

When Cam arrived at Erika's apartment, it swarmed with scarlet uniforms and Advon's investigators. She held her badge out until someone stopped long enough to see the crossed blades stamped below the Sentinel's Eye, and they led her under the tape.

The Master of the High Guard stood in the hall outside Erika's apartment. For once, he wasn't shouting at anyone. He looked up at Cam's approach, his expression grim. "What are you doing here, Kardell?"

"I found High Guard Harfield, sir—"

"Thank God! Is she in custody?"

Cam braced for yelling. "No, sir. She got away."

"You pursued her, she escaped, and instead of reporting to me you came to her apartment?"

"When I saw her, she was talking to her brother. I thought she might have come to see Sophie as well, so—"

"So you decided to launch your own bloody investigation, did you?" he said. "What a nightmare. Do something like this again, Kardell, and you'll be out. At least you can identify the body. You've met Miss Ray, I assume?"

The knot behind Cam's sternum tightened. "Sophie is dead?"

He lifted the tape in front of the door to the apartment. Cam ducked under.

She had to stay impartial, view everything around her as if she were dealing with strangers. Nothing appeared out of the ordinary. Sophie had hung a lot of artwork on the walls, and most of the furnishings were Erika's sturdy family heirlooms. Erika tidied up the few things she had been trained to keep neat and little else, so it was fortunate Sophie had an eye for organization.

The body lay on the floor in the living room. One of the investigators lifted the sheet, and Cam knelt, peered at the familiar face, now cold and pale. Blood, long dried, puddled under her hair.

Erika wouldn't have done this. She didn't even like to hit her opponents hard when she sparred. And yet she'd swung at Cam. Everything had changed; anything seemed possible.

"What is the evidence against High Guard Harfield?" Cam asked.

"She called Miss Ray's parents and told them she'd killed their daughter," the Master of the High Guard said. "The High General instructed me to assemble a team to track her down. I want you on it, if you think you can do what's necessary."

Cam looked at Sophie's pale features. "Yes, sir."

"Good. Go get ready, we leave in four hours."

Cam moved quickly. It was past time she spoke with William Harfield.

011

ERIKA TOLD HIM not to look for her. She told him she was leaving, and he should stop trying to find out what had happened to her. He wouldn't listen, of course. All his life she had been there for him. If she was hurt, he would find a way to make her well.

He kept seeing her as she'd sat across from him at the table in Three Sides, her eyes darting to the people passing outside, to the clattering of a coffee cup, to him, and then back out again. Like she was searching for something and never finding it. Every muscle of her face tense, the skin under her eyes dark, her shoulders hunched with tightened muscles. She had squeezed her fingers around his, so tight that it hurt, but he hadn't complained. She had said goodbye. She had told him to let her go. He still felt the ghost of her grip.

Why had she run? And was that Sentinel Kardell who sprinted after her? William had hesitated, the coffee cup still in his hands, and then he had walked to the corner where they had vanished. They were both already gone. He walked up and down the block, trying to figure out where they'd gone, but saw no sign of them. He didn't know what else to do, so he went back to his office.

A Sentinel waited for him there, a stocky man with a weathered face and bright eyes. William saw the golden pin on the man's uniform, the crossed blades that Erika had worn since joining the High Guard. William invited him into the office, and the Sentinel closed the door behind them.

His name was High Guard Brecht, and he said Erika had murdered her roommate. That had to be a mistake; there had been an accident of some kind. William said as much, several times.

The High Guard asked him a few questions, but William's responses were vague, disjointed. There had been some kind of misunderstanding.

Moments after the High Guard left, Tristan arrived. William was glad to see his cousin. Maybe he knew what to do.

"Hey there, Billy. Has your day been as weird as mine?"

"We have to find Erika."

Tristan sighed. No one sighed like him, with such ferocity. "I was afraid you might say that. Let's go to your place and figure a few things out, first."

Tristan, whose job had made him a paranoid about discussing anything important in public spaces, kept up a string of inane chatter as they made their way back to William's apartment. William did his best to answer appropriately, but his mind was elsewhere.

Sentinel Kardell waited at William's door, and this time she didn't exchange her glare for a smile when she saw him. If anything, she frowned more when she saw Tristan. William's cousin, on the other hand, grinned broadly. Once they were within speaking distance he said, "So, we meet again, Cami. It must be destiny."

That tone was all-too familiar. Why would his cousin would be flirting at such a time, particularly with someone as plain as Cameron? The type of women Tristan normally pursued spent at least ten times longer curling and pinning their hair than Sentinel Kardell did. Maybe

Tristan was losing his mind. Maybe all three of them were doomed to go mad, one by one, killing the people around them as they did.

"He's *really* your cousin?" Kardell asked. William nodded, and she pressed her lips together. Even William recognized that as irritation. "I have questions."

William's disbelief shattered. "Of course you have questions! The whole world wants to know everything there is to know about my sister! But no one really cares. This isn't her fault! And no one cares!" He saw Tristan shifting at the edge of his vision, and William rounded on him. "That's right, get ready to stop me, because you know what happens when I get upset! Too bad you weren't there to stop Erika when she really needed you to!"

He realized what he was yelling about and shut his mouth, unlocked the door, and threw it open. "Go away, both of you." Before either of them could object, he slammed the door shut, and stood in the entryway. He shouldn't have said any of that. He rubbed his hands through his hair while Cesar danced around him, tail whipping the air.

He needed Tristan, because he didn't know how to find Erika on his own. Sentinel Kardell probably wanted to find his sister, too. When the hand rapped at his door, he opened it, resolved to be reasonable.

It was the Sentinel, not his cousin, who stood right in front of him. "I know what Erika can do. Part of it, anyway. But I need to know the rest before I go after her again. Erika wouldn't want to hurt people, but she has, and she might again. So please, help me."

William stood back so she could enter his apartment, with Tristan not far behind. The Sentinel removed her boots in front of the door, much to William's surprise, because Erika always thudded around tracking dirt all over the floors and carpet. "Please sit, and I'll get some water. Do you want water? I think—I don't really have anything else."

"Water is fine, thank you."

Tristan leaned over the back of the couch across from the chair Sentinel Kardell selected, and carried on with his attempts to charm her while William occupied himself in the kitchen. By the time he returned with glasses of water, Tristan had already advanced to a level of innuendo that made William blush, although Kardell behaved as if she heard none of it. The Sentinel quickly drained the proffered glass of water. Running across Advon after Erika was probably exhausting work. He sat the second glass in front of her as well.

"Thank you. So, if Erika is telepathic, and Tristan is part cat, what is it that you do?"

William looked to his cousin, who just shrugged. "Well. Basically, I can visualize raw energy, collect it, and transform it. But how do you know—"

"Just show her, Billy." Tristan said. "Nobody wants a lecture when they can have a show."

William bit back his retort. Erika was only getting farther away with each passing minute. He looked to Kardell. How many years had he kept this secret from his friends, his colleagues, his girlfriends? Erika had trusted this woman, but his sister's judgement was far from infallible. Kardell seemed to understand his hesitancy, and she smiled.

"I'm not afraid."

"That's not really what I'm worried about," he said.

Erika didn't throw away her trust on anyone unworthy. Whatever else had happened, that was still true.

William held out his right hand at chest height. He pressed his middle finger against his thumb, and concentrated, always a bit harder when he had an audience. He shoved down the thought that it would be embarrassing if nothing happened. Instead, he centered his focus on the moment when Erika had struck him. For just a moment, he'd felt the roar of anger.

He let out one long breath, held it, and then snapped his fingers together. When his middle finger struck his palm it made no sound. Instead, a small lick of flame sprang up over his thumb and forefinger. It was a mere flicker, hovering millimeters above his fingertip, fed by the energy of his snapping fingers. He kept it burning with small drifts of ambient energy. He moved it from finger to finger, down to his pinky and back before he let it die out, just to demonstrate that it was not a trick. When it was gone, he looked up, expecting her disbelief.

She stared at his face and not his hands, her eyes a little wide, but she nodded. As if she'd suspected it all along. "So you can make fire."

"I can do a lot more than that. But fire's sort of my specialty."

Tristan grinned. "What does it take, exactly, to get you agitated? Because that really should have done it."

"Erika said she couldn't stop hearing people's thoughts. And when we got close to catching her, I felt pain that wasn't really there," Cameron said.

Tristan nodded when William looked to him for confirmation. "She's never had that power before. She said she was going to try to look into someone's mind and see if they had an ability like ours, and I think something went wrong . . . "

A couple of pieces fell into place. William stared at the Sentinel. Erika never would have told someone what they could do unless she had very good reason. He couldn't believe he had gone this far without understanding.

"You," he said. "It was you. What did you do to her?"

Her face was impassive, unreadable while William and Tristan stared at her. "I don't know. I didn't understand everything that happened."

"We've always known that we were different. And what we're talking about, this is way beyond even the tech anyone has now. Her genetic structure is different. You couldn't have done that by accident."

At last Kardell looked surprised. She appeared to hold her breath for several seconds, and her eyes focused on something far away. "That's not possible."

"That's what I thought, until I ran the test four times. At least let me take a blood sample, and I can be certain you have an ability."

The Sentinel's eyes sharpened again, and she stood. "There isn't time for that now; I'm leaving in just a couple of hours. Is there anything else that I should know about what Erika can do? Anything dangerous?"

"I have no idea what she can do now." William pressed his fingers into his palms, to stop his hands from shaking. "What are you going to do when you find her?"

Sentinel Kardell paused in lacing up her boots. Her eyes met his, dark and still and sure. "I'll bring her in. Thank you for the water."

She shut the door behind her.

William stood there, reminding himself to breathe evenly.

He looked to Tristan. "Kardell is going to kill Erika if she finds her, isn't she?"

Tristan lifted up one shoulder. "Or Erika is going to kill her. Please don't say—"

"We have to find Erika first."

"Will, we have no idea what we're facing here. If Erika killed Sophie—"

"That was an accident. I'm not going to let the Sentinels kill her for that." Not when the whole thing was Sentinel Kardell's fault.

Tristan sighed. "She wasn't lying when she said she didn't know what happened."

"If she changed Erika's genes once, she can do it again. I don't know how, but she has to figure it out. Erika doesn't have any other chance."

Tristan's scowl was so deep that William was sure that he would refuse to help. Instead, he said, "Fine. If we're going to do this, I have to go collect data. You start packing. Take your dog to your girlfriend. And you're going to owe me for this."

012

"GRAY! I WANT another check on all the oil levels. Ford, make sure Grumby packed the ammunition properly."

"Specialist Green, how is the checklist?"

"All the first vehicle checks are complete, and most of the weaponry. Lane, where are you with the med kits?"

Cam stood beside the Master of the High Guard admiring how the Immediate Response Team prepared so quickly. No one appeared rushed, they all just carefully, methodically, went through their checklists. Cam kept out of the way unless Andrew West ordered otherwise.

Her mind danced from Erika sweeping a blade at her, to Sophie's purple-hued lips, to Doctor Harfield with a lick of flame hovering over his finger.

"Sergeant Glover!" Andrew West's bark startled Cam back to attentiveness as Glover, a woman whose name Cam had heard as a Cadet, stopped in front of them. She had a near legendary reputation for being an incredible shot. "You don't carry an edged weapon."

"No, sir. Two pistols."

"Those aren't standard issue."

"I went to Varcove and paid for them myself. I have special permission to carry them. If you want to see the paperwork."

The Master of the High Guard shook his head. "Carry on, Sergeant."

Sergeant Flint had paused midway across the courtyard to watch this exchange. As Glover and West saluted, his eyes shifted over to Cameron. She recognized the long stare of someone picking out the features she shared with her father. She'd been told the resemblance was remarkable, except that he had smiled more.

"Kardell," said Andrew West, "are you certain Sentinel Harfield never demonstrated any instability before now?"

"I never saw anything, sir." He kept asking, no matter how firm her answer.

"What about when she'd had a few drinks? She ever get temperamental then?" he asked.

"No, sir. I never saw her get angry."

"So the steadiest Sentinel in the Armed Forces just decided one day to kill her roommate and run?"

"I may not have known her as well as I thought, sir." Erika had kept secrets, after all, and they were big ones.

Doctor Harfield had blamed her, and Cameron couldn't deny all responsibility. Erika was the one who had gone digging around in her head, but Erika also had been steady, reliable, right up until that point. Something had happened. Those few minutes when Cameron had been in darkness, unable to see Erika, might have been critical.

Cameron hadn't done anything knowingly, though.

A young man, not part of the team, entered the courtyard with an envelope in his hands. He delivered it to West, who scanned the contents before handing them to Cameron. "If you have theories, I'll take them."

The papers were reports on Erika's movements since Cameron had lost her in the Arts District. A stolen car on the outskirts of Advon, and then sightings on the River Road, heading west. For the first time that day, Cameron was sure about something.

She waited for a moment of quiet, and said, "Sir?"

"What do you have, Kardell?"

"I think I know where she's going."

West shouted at a nearby Specialist before saying, "Go on."

"She and I both trained with Master Reese, an expert swordsman.—"

"I know who he is, Kardell. He was already an experienced Sentinel when I was a Lieutenant. You think she went to him in Brook's Cove, then? Why would she do that?"

"Master Reese told us that he would help us whenever we needed it. I doubt she has anywhere else to turn."

The Master of the High Guard considered, and slowly nodded. "If she heads north at the coast, then perhaps you should pay a visit to Reese. I'll keep it in mind."

He dismissed her. As she stepped away, she thought she caught a glimpse of silver eyes in a nearby alcove, but they were gone too fast to be certain. Was Tristan watching her? That would be a whole other set of problems. Someone that quick and quiet was dangerous.

When all the equipment had been double-checked and the members of the team accounted for, Sean Ellis entered the courtyard. He looked at them all with fearsome severity, and when his eyes rested on Cameron his lips tightened. Did he doubt her place on the team? If he didn't want her there, he could easily order her to stay behind.

"As you all know, a member of my High Guard committed a heinous crime. I am personally tasking you with finding her and bringing her back to the capitol. My preference is that she return alive so she can stand trial for the murder of Sophia Ray. However, if that is not possible, then I give you permission to use deadly force." Again, he stared at Cameron. Yes, he doubted her. And proving herself would mean killing her friend. "I do not consider failure an option in this assignment. Bring Erika Harfield back to this city, or do not return at all. Good luck."

The High General strode away, his steps so long that his High Guards scurried to keep up.

When he was gone, the Master of the High Guard said, "You heard him! Let's go catch up while we still can!"

By that evening, Cam had discovered that the hunting party was not much different from a patrol, except she saw less because of her position at the back. They stopped for the night at a large hotel beside the West River Road, a building surrounded on all sides by fields of crops. Rows of small green plants ran off in every direction.

The smell of warming soil reminded Cam of her summers at the farm up north with her paternal grandparents, running through fields with cousins who taught her another language.

The hotel smelled strongly of musty carpets and vaguely of powerful cleansers, and the past evaporated.

While the Master of the High Guard reviewed the new information about Erika's whereabouts with the team leaders, Cam waited in the lobby. She was certain she'd glimpsed William and

Erika's cousin in the courtyard that morning. If Tristan still followed her, she meant to catch him before any of the other Sentinels could.

She sat flipping through a magazine for no more than thirty minutes before the dark-haired man sauntered in through the front door. Even Cam, who knew little about fashion, could recognize that he was well-dressed. The young woman at the reception desk self-consciously tucked away some loose hairs when she spotted Tristan. And then Doctor Harfield followed. Damn. It was worse than she'd thought. Cam dropped the newspaper and moved to intercept them.

Tristan saw her first. If her appearance surprised him, he covered it with a dazzling smile. Doctor Harfield, meanwhile, ducked his head and tried to look smaller.

"Come with me," she said. William moved to follow, and she stopped him with a glare. "Just him." The receptionist frowned at her missed opportunity as the dark-haired man followed Cam to an alcove containing an unused phone. Tristan's smile widened under the force of her scowl. "Take him home. He shouldn't be here."

"He'd just go after Erika by himself if I tried."

Cam looked over at William, who struggled to hold his bags as well as his cousin's. One fell from his grasp, thudded against the floor, and popped open, sending books and clothes across the floor. She cursed softly. "He's going to get hurt. Or he's going to get someone else hurt."

Tristan smirked. "I think he knows a lot more than you do."

Cam ground her teeth together. She didn't want to get Doctor Harfield in serious trouble, but Erika was dangerous. William had no training and no idea of what he faced. "I'm not going to let him get involved in this. Take him home, or I'll arrest you both."

She stalked away to get the paperwork needed to charge Harfield with suspected interference in an ongoing pursuit, in case they hadn't believed her. By the time she returned to the lobby, both men were gone.

The Immediate Response Team was no friendlier toward Cameron the next day. However, the Master of the High Guard believed her theory that Erika had gone to Master Reese for help. Several sightings suggested she had turned north at the coast.

In the morning before they left for Brook's Cove, Andrew West pulled Cameron aside. "The High General insists that the whole team is not to approach Reese's house. He's concerned that it will seem like we're harassing him. However, it's still vital that we know if she visited him. Do you think you can manage on your own?"

Cameron would have much rather faced Erika than pry information from the man responsible for the bulk of her education. However, she knew she was better suited to the task than anyone else on the team. "Yes, sir."

The rest of the morning, Cameron trailed behind the IRT. The sun burned away the morning dew. No hint of the cool night air remained when they reached the coast. The West River Road joined with The Ring, which hugged the shoreline as they rumbled north. Cameron finally caught sight of something besides the tactical vehicle in front of her. When the road twisted with the curves of the cliffs, she saw an expanse of water before her, rolling without ceasing. The Quellan Ocean. She might have heard the crash of waves on rocks, even in the midst of so many engines.

They followed the shore until the road turned sharply, wrapping around the sheer cliff face and inclining up over the top. The shoreline broke with the road, stretching out to form a point of land, while the road crested the lip of a shallow green bowl, into which the ocean spilled from a broad crack in the cliffs. The result was a sheltered bay, too small for large trading ships but big enough for fishing boats. There lay the town of Brook's Cove, an eclectic mix of fishermen and shopkeepers and tourist traps.

Cameron separated from the rest of the IRT when they turned to the town's tiny inn. Instead, she drove past the general store where she, Erika, and the rest of Reese's students had spent precious free time buying snacks. Then Lilly's Frozen Dairy shop, where they'd made nuisances of themselves. The market, where they'd bought fried sweet bread. Had they done anything in Brook's Cove besides eat and meander the streets?

She turned up a gravel road that wound out of town, up the hill, to a house overlooking the ocean cliffs. It was secluded from the village but within walking distance. It was also almost impossible to approach without notice. Reese had probably heard the arrival of the Response Team, and he definitely knew that Cameron had driven up the hill.

She probably should have called before visiting. Hopefully Reese would understand the urgency of the situation.

Cameron brushed the wrinkles from her uniform and tugged the hems into place. She drew her blade and checked to make sure it was clean. As she put it away, she heard the crunch of gravel under tires.

A sleek, black car rolled up the road. It looked too expensive to belong to anyone who lived in Brook's Cove, and it wasn't military. Had Tristan and William ignored her warning?

The car pulled up beside her motorcycle, and the doors swung open. Tristan Rush gave her his usual practiced smile as he climbed out. William Harfield fidgeted and looked everywhere but at her. Clearly they had not given up.

"This is a bold move, driving right up to the house of a man neither of you have ever met. Not to mention tailing a Sentinel who already threatened to arrest you."

William managed to look even more uncomfortable, but Tristan's grin widened. "Seems like you could introduce us. And who, besides you, would deny a man the chance to look for his missing sister?"

Tristan had a point. Master Reese would have more pity for Doctor Harfield than he would for one of his most difficult students. If Cameron asked him to choose between helping the Response Team and keeping Erika hidden, well, Cameron would return to Andrew West with nothing. But if William begged for his help finding lost family, there was a chance.

Even if Reese refused to tell William anything, his presence alone might be enough to draw Erika out. It had worked in Advon, hadn't it?

And if Erika was still in Reese's house, she was much less likely to attack with William there. Erika wouldn't hurt her brother. That settled it.

"Fine. I hope you both have good manners. Master Reese doesn't put up with anything less."

013

SHE ACTED LIKE she was doing them a favor, like they had no right to be looking for Erika. Like her uniform made her more capable.

She led them up a stone stairway. William tripped a couple of times, because each flat stone was a different height and depth. He put aside his thoughts and concentrated on his feet. Only glimpses of the house were visible through cedar trees and rock, all of which were natural in shape but too balanced to be accidental. Sparrows hopped in the currant bushes and scattered as they walked by. William heard the muffled crashing of waves breaking against the cliffs on the other side of the rise.

They rounded a large rock and there perched the whole house. It was one story, low, with long strips of windows tucked under the eaves. The front door was a bright red that contrasted with the otherwise neutral tones of the house.

Cameron knocked. A deep voice called out from around the back of the house. The Sentinel led them to the right, through well-tended gardens. The path opened onto a spacious sunken courtyard sheltered on one side by the house. On the other side it opened to the ocean, a waist-high stone wall separating it from the sheer cliffs.

An old man knelt in the courtyard, plucking weeds from between the paving stones with deft tugs, piling them up to be collected later. His hair was steely gray, but thick. A sword like Cameron's lay on the ground to his left, and he hummed as he worked, just loud enough to float over the thunder of the ocean far below. He looked up at them, a smile creasing the skin around his eyes, but he didn't stand to greet them until he had finished with the row of weeds he was working on. When he did get to his feet, it was with the smoothness of a much younger man. He stood tall and straight in front of them.

The sword master looked at Cameron with a familiar intensity, though the effect was very different with his pale blue eyes. The Sentinel brought the hilt of her sword to her right shoulder in a salute, her head low. He returned the gesture, saying, "The youngest Sentinel ever promoted to the High Guard. I would be proud if I could claim credit, but I can't remember a single time you listened to me."

"I listened all the time. I just tried everything you told me not to do, so I could learn why I shouldn't do it. Master Reese, this is Doctor William Harfield and Tristan Rush, Erika's brother and cousin."

He shook each of their hands. If Cameron's gaze was unsettling, his was like a bucket of ice water dumped over one's head. William wished for a rock big enough to hide under.

"Please come inside, and we can talk. Cameron, if you would dispose of the weeds. Not over the wall. And the compost needs turned." She didn't object, but her lips pressed together. So she couldn't order everyone around.

Cameron gathered the piles of weeds, while Tristan and William followed Master Reese. He took them through the back door, instructed them to remove their shoes, and then led them into the kitchen. "Can I get you some tea?"

They accepted. Within moments Master Reese produced a plate of cookies and placed a kettle on the stove. The cookies were a little plain, but flecked with citrus peels and herbs. Was Master Reese always so prepared for guests?

"What brings you here to Brook's Cove? If you'll excuse the observation, Cameron doesn't have many friends who aren't Sentinels, so I suspect you're here on business."

"I'm looking for Erika," William said. "She's in trouble, and I thought she might come here."

Reese poured the tea. William took the ceramic cup, which nestled into his hand as if made for him. Tea plants only flourished in a small patch of mountains near the northern coast, where the ocean air kept the climate moderate and the elevation was high. William sipped carefully. The flavor was lighter than coffee, and he had to concentrate to pick out the soft, floral taste.

"Along with Sentinel Kardell and the Immediate Response Team?"

"Will was worried about how the Sentinels might treat Erika when they found her." Tristan said. "We tagged along to make sure she doesn't get hurt."

Reese's gray eyebrows went up. "There aren't many who would get between a group of Sentinels and their target."

"We were hoping to find Erika before they did," William said.

The back door opened to admit Cameron, whose eyes lit up at the plate of cookies on the counter. She pulled off her boots, hurriedly washed her hands, and sat next to William. Her sigh when Master Reese put a cup of tea in front of her was long.

"Two cups, then you can have cookies. The tea is good for you."

"It's terrible." She gulped down the hot liquid like it was bitter medicine. William clutched his cup, shocked at her lack of consideration.

Reese tried to look severe, but he smiled too much to pull it off. "Most of my students learn to like it."

She held out her cup for a refill. "I'm sure you know by now that I am not most students. Now, when did Erika stop by, and how did you help her?"

"I seem to remember telling you to work on patience."

Cameron drained the second cup. "I am patient when I need to be. Erika is a danger to herself and others; we don't have the luxury of being patient under the circumstances."

"Your father might still be alive if he had only waited. I hope you learn it sooner than he did."

Reese spoke as if he had said those very same words countless times, and they were growing thin. Cameron's expression remained implacable. This was a well-practiced argument.

"You aren't going to get far by bringing up the mistakes of a man I never met. My mother's been doing that to me all my life and it hasn't stopped me. When did Erika come to you?"

Reese took her empty cup. William watched him consider, decide. "She was here before sunrise this morning, but she wasn't herself. You're right when you say she's dangerous, and I know you don't have a plan for fighting her. I helped her as much as I could. Even if I knew where she was, I wouldn't tell you. Any of you."

William spoke up. "I know I can help her, if I just get the chance."

Reese looked at the three of them, starting with Cameron, who was crunching through one cookie, the next already in her hand. Tristan managed to lounge even on the stool and was doing his best to appear bored. William was last. Reese appeared to genuinely pity him. "I can't tell you where she is. I'm sorry that this happened, especially to Erika. I want to believe that she can be helped, but I'm not going to risk anyone's safety finding out. Someday she might be herself again, but for that she needs time."

"Master Reese—a High Guard murdered her roommate. The High General isn't going to let her disappear." William looked away from Cameron as she spoke, tried to pretend that she wasn't sitting right beside him.

"I'm going to have some select words with Sean for letting you pursue Erika in the first place. Now there's a man who could stand to learn a thing or two about thinking things through."

"He's your High General, now."

"That doesn't stop him from being my student. The same goes for you."

"So I'll be forty and still getting lectures on patience?"

Master Reese laughed, and the subject of Erika closed. Instead, the two discussed the new batch of students arriving at the end of the week, Cameron's disappointment at her assignment to the High Guard, and the ingredients in the newest cookie recipe. Master Reese asked William and Tristan what they did for a living. He seemed interested in William's work on the monster Cameron had slain and promised he would watch for his article.

After little more than an hour Cameron stood. "I have to go report, but it's been good to see you, Master Reese."

"I'm always happy to see an old student at my door. It was nice to meet you, Doctor Harfield, Mister Rush. I hope you will all be careful. I don't think you can fathom how dangerous Erika is."

As the red door shut behind them, the fear and frustration returned. William hadn't even realized that the smell of tea and the soft light inside had soothed them away. He should have pushed for more answers; he shouldn't have accepted the sword master's refusal. Erika deserved better than that.

Cameron, maybe thinking the same things, made a sound of disgust. She set off down the stone steps, and William rushed to keep up, Tristan a shadow behind him. Her feet went easily from one off-set step to the next, while William struggled not to trip.

"What next?"

The Sentinel glanced back, her eyebrows drawn tight. "I hoped Master Reese would help when he met you. Now I have to find Erika, and you need to go home."

"I know her, Sentinel Kardell. I can help."

"Your lab is where you belong, Doctor Harfield. Leave this to me."

William almost objected, but she commanded him, expecting him to obey, leaving no room for his reasons. He was smarter than she was. He had grown up with Erika. It was his responsibility and his right to find his sister. If she was not going to let him help, then it was time for him to go around her.

They had reached Tristan's car and her motorcycle. Before she pulled her helmet on, William tried one last time.

"Sentinel Kardell. Do you have any brothers or sisters?"

Her expression was guarded, but she nodded. "A sister."

"Please, if you find Erika, treat her like you would your sister."

The Sentinel looked away. "My sister didn't murder anyone, Doctor Harfield." She pulled her helmet on, and her face vanished behind the dark, reflective face shield. A moment later she roared down the hill.

Tristan climbed into his car, and William followed. "I don't know what you're thinking ,—" Tristan said.

"I'm not thinking anything. I just want to go home. It's pretty obvious that I don't belong here."

Tristan rolled his eyes but did not say anything else. He probably knew exactly what William thought. He wouldn't give up on Erika, and he couldn't let the Sentinels find her first. Tristan wasn't going to stop him. They drove to Brook's Cove's Inn and checked in, William speaking as little as possible.

He dropped his bags in his room and went back out to look for Erika.

The sun was sinking into the ocean when William cut across the gravel driveway that wound its way up to Master Reese's home. He walked quickly. He could inspect one last beach before darkness fell. The scent of salt water was sharp as he wove his way through heavy shrubs, branches snagging at his shirt. Finally, he broke through the undergrowth.

In front of him the ground dropped steeply; below that curved a tiny spit of sand, and beyond the ocean rumbled, an expanse of gray water banded with white waves. Flocks of small birds skimmed along the surface, and white gulls wheeled over his head, screeching as they fought over scraps of food.

Had he come to admire the scenery? William looked down, to the rock face. His head reeled. This was definitely the steepest and the longest climb of the day. He flexed his sore fingers as he studied it for a good way down. The evening sun shined golden on the rock but revealed nothing helpful.

He turned to put the waves at his back, and slung his legs over the edge, sliding backward on his chest until his toes found purchase on an outcrop. Then he hunted out the next ledge down, blindly because he clung to the cliff with his hands and chest. He tried hard not to think about the great stretch of empty air between him and the sand below. The top of the cliff slipped farther away one painful inch at a time.

One ledge rolled out from under the ball of his foot. His hands slipped. He slid down the rock, scrabbling for something to hold, rock scraping his chest and his legs as he fell.

At last, one of his feet found a crag, and his descent halted. William leaned his cheek against the rock, his eyes closed, fingers wedged so tightly in the crevice he'd could found that they ached and his arms trembled.

He belonged in a lab with humming equipment and equations written out on a chalk board, books spread out on long tables, a coffee mug crusted with a week's work of black rings because he had not washed it between cups . . .

Something grabbed his foot and yanked hard. He yelped as he fell, his arms clawing at the air. When he landed on his back in the sand, the air was knocked from his lungs. He lay there with his mouth gaping and no breath coming. His sister stood over him. Her face was all hard lines. Her clothing was dirty, and her hair whipped free.

"I told you to stay away." Her blade slipped free of its scabbard. The point hovered over William's chest, inches away from the fabric of his shirt and the delicate, very much mortal flesh beneath.

He sucked in air. His head reeled, and his body felt cold, even though he knew that he should feel pain. He followed the curve of the blade up to his sister's hand, her arm, stopping at her shoulder.

He didn't dare look her in the face. He remembered when she struck him, and a small part of him knew that she would not stop there.

They stayed that way for a long time, William listening to the waves roll in and back out, his breath still coming in short gasps, until he couldn't bear it anymore.

"Please, Erika, I just want to help you."

The sword lifted a couple of inches. "Then leave me alone."

He dragged his gaze from her shoulder to her eyes, which gleamed much too bright. The golden glow of the setting sun cast strange shadows across her face.

"Would you be able to leave me, if I was hurt, if you knew you could help?"

She let the blade fall to her side. William scrambled to his feet. He might not be any safer, but at least he felt more in control. Unfortunately, the act of standing brought the seriousness of his injuries to his full attention. Both knees and shins felt like they had been stripped of skin, and his right leg was too sore to put much weight on. His ribs ached, and when he swiped his hands on his pants to rid them of sand, his palms flared with pain.

"You need to give up, Will."

William raised his battered hands. "You've protected me for so long. I have to do what I can for you now."

"You don't understand. It's worse with you. Your brain bounces all over the place, and it's too much. I was starting to feel normal again, until you got in range—you just never shut up. I can't be near you, Will."

He took a step back, flexed his fingers. "I can work this out in my lab, and then you won't have to hear any of it. Just come home with us."

Erika's eyes lit up. "Kardell is with you."

William watched her face change as she saw the truth in his mind. She screamed, and he stepped back. Her eyes burned, and William felt a pressure in his mind.

"No one is here to hurt you!"

"She did this to me!"

"She's trying to help."

"She wants to take me back to Advon, where I'll be tried for murder and executed." William swallowed. The point of her blade rose.

"What am I supposed to do, Erika? Pretend you're dead, when you aren't? I can't do that." He lowered his voice and reached out to her. "Just come with me. Let me help you."

She let him get so close. She was going to let him help her. His hand was only inches from her arm when she raised her blade again. It cut through the air, and then bit into his torso.

William stared down at the steel, at the patch of red spreading out around it. Blood made hot tracks down his belly. When he looked up at Erika her eyes were wide, her face pale. She withdrew the sword quickly and stared at the blood on the end as if she didn't understand what it was.

William grunted. The pain radiated through his abdomen. He clutched at the wound with both hands, surprised at how swiftly the blood flowed, surprised at how the pain grew with each breath, and shocked at the rush of anger coursing through him.

Erika reached out, touched his shoulder. He threw out a hand to push her away. He felt the great pull and tug of energy from the constant rush of water in the ocean, difficult to see because it was everywhere. In his agony and fury, he grasped it easily.

Instead of fire, the energy coalesced into electricity. He watched it leap from his hand to her shoulder, a shock that knocked her off her feet. William had not meant to do it, had not even known he could.

He collapsed to the sand and lay looking into his sister's eyes. The waves rolled in and out, a continuous pounding. William felt the whole world rock back and forth. Erika mouthed, *I'm sorry.* William shut his eyes. He couldn't forgive this.

When he opened them again, she was gone, and he was alone, his blood slipping through his fingers onto the warm sand. Above him, the gulls cut silent circles.

014

"THERE'S ACTIVITY ON the cliffs at 11 o'clock from our current position, facing due south. A man just climbed down; looks like he has a buddy waiting for him up top."

Cameron stood beside the Master of the High Guard as the search teams made their reports on the radio. She noted this new piece of information and put a pin in the map. She listened carefully as West said, "Keep your eyes on them. Full description?"

Sergeant Rhodes described William Harfield and Tristan Rush. Cameron double-checked their location on the map before saying, "Sir, I believe that they are on Master Reese's property."

West checked the map. "Of course they would be. And what do you think the High General will say if the whole team storms in?"

The radio crackled. "Sgt. Rhodes reporting. The second guy dropped down the cliff. Looked like he was in a hurry."

The Master of the High Guard looked at Cameron. "Go check it out. If Harfield is there, don't engage. Call for backup."

They exchanged salutes, and Cameron escaped her note-taking duties. Tristan didn't seem the type who would hurry unless there was trouble. What could Doctor Harfield have gotten into?

Erika would never harm her brother. It was the reason Cameron had told William to go home, knowing that he would do the opposite. Only he was guaranteed safety. As long as he hadn't fallen off one of the cliffs.

Cameron's bike engine roared to life, attracting stares from some locals on the street. Brook's Cove wasn't accustomed to the flurry of activity that had descended on it over the past few hours. Cameron should probably have attempted a friendly nod to make amends for disrupting the peace, but she was in a hurry.

As she neared the edge of the village, just before starting up the hill to Reese's house, Cameron spotted something strange. A young woman jogged along the sidewalk. Her long, pale hair stuck to the perspiration on her face, and she clutched at her side. A large bag beat against her back. Cameron had never known Melanie Stillwater to do anything in a hurry, so she pulled up beside her and lifted off her helmet.

"Hey Mel. What are you doing in this part of town?"

Melanie jumped, her hazel eyes first going wide, and then narrowing to slits. So, she still hadn't forgiven Cameron. Clearly.

"I'm on my way to Reese's place. I didn't know you were in town; it's good to see you." The smile she adopted was as much a lie as her words.

"I can give you a ride up."

Melanie bit her lip, looked up at the climb still in front of her. At last, she accepted the helmet Cameron held out. Cameron smiled as Melanie climbed onto the bike behind her. Whatever was happening, Melanie was a part of it, and now Cameron would know about it.

Melanie gripped Cameron's waist as they rumbled up the hill. Cameron heard her swear on the particularly violent bumps. When they stopped, however, Melanie grinned. She shook out her hair, then tossed the helmet back to Cameron. "Here I thought for sure you'd push me off halfway up the hill."

"I don't hold grudges."

Melanie laughed, then bounded up the path to Reese's front door.

"So, any reason you were in such a hurry to get up here?" Cameron asked as she followed.

Melanie tried to put the gentle waves of her pale gold hair into order. "There's *action*," she said.

Mel did not knock on the red front door. She turned the knob and pushed it open without invitation. Impolite as always.

Cameron followed, but stopped just inside the door, staring. William Harfield lay on a couch, his face white, blood bright on his hands and his shirt. Tristan stood over him, appearing calm except for the creases at the corners of his mouth. The shoulder of his jacket was stained red, too.

Melanie went to William's side at once, slinging her bag to the ground. Her fingers swiftly arranged medical equipment on the nearest table. She ran through a series of diagnostic questions in a clipped voice while pulling her hair into a chaotic tangle on top of her head.

"This is the doctor?" William asked. "She can't be more than twenty-five!"

"Twenty-two, in fact. And I'm not exactly a doctor. Reese just loves to exaggerate."

William's protest became a grunt as she prodded the area around the wound.

Cameron stepped back by the wall and watched while Melanie cut away the fabric around the wound. It had been made by a blade, just like the one at Cameron's hip.

Surely, Erika couldn't have done this.

Master Reese entered the room, carrying blankets and his own emergency supplies. His pale blue eyes lingered on Cameron's face. She maintained her neutral expression in spite of his stare.

She wasn't comfortable with what she had done. Her attempt to draw Erika out of hiding had resulted in harm to Doctor Harfield. Cameron didn't need Master Reese to tell her that she had made a mistake.

"Melanie, you got here quickly." Though Reese spoke to Melanie, his eyes were on Cameron, and now she looked up to him. William begged that someone with a medical license see him.

"One of the Sergeants reported that he saw two men near your house. I came across Melanie on my way over, and I gave her a ride."

Melanie had started an IV. Cameron had never seen her be serious before, but she certainly was now. "Do you know your blood type, Doctor Harfield? No problem, I have some universal on hand. Feeling light-headed? You've lost a good bit of blood." She looked over her shoulder at Cameron and Master Reese. "If the two of you wouldn't mind taking your conversation elsewhere, I have work to do."

"I need some answers from Doctor Harfield first," Cameron said.

"Maybe this doesn't seem like a serious injury to you, but I do need to work. The sooner you get out of here, the better."

"I'll be quick." Cameron didn't wait for Melanie to assent. She left her place by the wall and knelt on the floor at William's side. When she took his hand, his fingers curled tight around hers. She was close enough to see his pupils contracted with pain, the green of his eyes bright. "Did Erika stab you?"

"Yes," he said. The corner of his mouth twitched, as if he had suppressed a smile. Strange.

"Do you know where she's going?" His eyes glazed over and Cameron increased the pressure on his hand. "She hurt you and she knows she's being chased. Where would you go?"

"Home. I would go home."

"There you go," Melanie said. "Now leave, I need quiet."

Cameron paused. There was more, but the man was in pain, maybe even in danger. She could make do with what she had. She squeezed his hand one more time, then let his fingers slide from hers.

She followed Master Reese and Tristan to the kitchen. As soon as the door closed behind them, Cameron turned on Reese.

"You *knew* Erika was down there."

"I'd hoped by withholding the information that this might have been prevented. Of course, you wanted him to draw out Erika."

Cameron held her breath for a few beats. It was true. Reese's expression was cool and distant, more than Cameron had ever seen before. She wasn't going to get any more help from him. When she turned to Tristan, he took a step back from her.

"What does home mean to William and Erika?"

Tristan shrugged. "Up north just before The Ring turns east, there's the old Harfield Estate. We lived there as kids, before the money ran out. It was seized and I don't know what happened to it after that. But to them, it's home."

Cameron nodded and breathed again. "Master Reese, I hope that you will stay here with William. Tristan—I'm sure you'll do whatever you're told."

Master Reese didn't flinch at what had bordered on an order, only nodded as if this was acceptable. Tristan shrugged as if he didn't care what happened.

Before Cameron reached the door, Master Reese spoke. "Don't push her, Cameron."

"The High General ordered us to bring her back. That's what I'm going to do. Everything else is up to her."

Cameron left Master Reese's house, anger coiled just behind her sternum. Master Reese must bear some part of the blame. He had known Cameron wouldn't stop and must have suspected William wouldn't, either. He could have forced Erika to keep running, or brought an end to it all by telling Cameron where she hid. It should never have come to this.

At least Cameron was sure now that this was no misunderstanding. She would find Erika, and she would stop her. It had all become very simple.

Cameron had counted on love to restrain Erika. A miscalculation. She wouldn't make the error again.

When she arrived at the inn she found the IRT already mobilizing. The Master of the High Guard shouted at her to move quickly. Risking damage to her eardrums, as he was in full roar, she ran up and told him of Erika's attack on her brother. Her story was absorbed with little change in expression besides a slight deepening in the lines on his face, and then he burst out, "I've never seen anyone lose it like this. Do you have any idea what's going on, Kardell?"

"No, sir." Any ties that Erika's behavior might have to her were tenuous at best, impossible to explain, and revealing them would not tell them anything about Erika's capabilities. "If she would hurt her brother, then she might do almost anything."

"Be ready to leave within the next five minutes. She fled north, probably after she attacked Doctor Harfield. We're going to get this over with, hopefully before the sun comes up."

"I'm glad to hear it, sir. I'm ready." Cameron had not unpacked when they arrived, so she went to her bike as engines came to life around her. The air rumbled, and uniformed figures dashed across the parking lot.

For the first time, Sergeant Glover approached Cameron.

"Sergeant Flint says you're good with that sword."

"Best scores in my class, Sergeant."

"You keep your eyes open. West is good, but he's been behind a desk too long. Watch us, and keep your head down when I shoot."

Sergeant Glover went back to work. She did not glance Cameron's way again.

When everything was ready, the party moved out. Sergeant Flint and Specialists Holmes and Fleet quickly pulled away from the rest of the group on quieter, speedier bikes. The scouts vanished rapidly into the night.

The darkness drew around them as they rode with the ocean pounding away to the left and cliffs jutting into the sky on the right. Cameron tuned her senses into every scrap of input, even though she was near the back, and by the time she caught sight of the road in front of her the rest of the team had already wiped away any evidence. Mile after mile, the scouts checked in to report that they saw nothing out of the ordinary.

Twice they stopped for a break, and twice they returned to the road. The treacherous ocean cliffs smoothed into rolling sand dunes, which muffled the sound of the ocean and allowed the road to run in a straighter line. Cameron knew from her patrol that the towns here were farther apart and smaller. She had very little to look at besides the hulking vehicles in front of her. To either side the mounds of sand were mere silhouettes.

"Full halt; dismount your vehicles and circle up." The Master of the High Guard's voice crackled over the radio in Cameron's helmet.

The bikes and the larger vehicles skidded to a halt. Doors slammed, booted feet hit the pavement, weapons were readied. Then a deep silence fell.

Cameron, at a nod from the Master of the High Guard, went to the front of the group, awake to every sound and motion. A figure stood in the headlights, a man holding something round in each hand. Cameron squinted. The slope of the shoulders, the set of the feet told her it was Sergeant Espen Flint.

A thick fluid dripped from both of the round objects. Cameron saw hair, the line of a nose—Flint held the heads of his fellow scouts.

015

SERGEANT GLOVER FACED south, the way they had arrived, and Sergeant Rhodes watched the north where Flint stood in the road. Cameron looked to the Master of the High Guard at the center of the formation. His eyes were bright, and she was not sure if it was with excitement or fear.

"Flint!" Rhodes said. "Talk to me!"

Cameron gripped the hilt of her blade. She peered into the shadows, looking for some sign of motion in the sweep and roll of the dunes. Could this be Erika?

Flint's hands relaxed, and the heads thudded to the road. He reached to his holster and very slowly pulled out his gun. Rhodes switched off the safety on his own weapon.

Some of the younger soldiers turned to watch the events unfolding down the road. Even the more senior members could not help glancing over as Sergeant Flint stood, his pistol hanging at his side.

"Stay sharp," the Master of the High Guard said. "Keep your eyes on your section." Cameron's skin was too tight, and her heart beat hard against her ribs. Flint's hands shook, dark with blood. Slowly he raised the pistol, not toward the team, but up to his temple.

"Flint! Put that gun down!"

Rhodes's shouts had no effect on Flint. Cameron touched the Sergeant's shoulder, and he stopped yelling. Flint's last few breaths were fast and heavy, and then his finger tightened on the trigger. The gun went off, and the man's body thudded against the pavement. Blood pooled rapidly around his head in a dark, wet halo.

Sergeant Rhodes's curse overlapped with the rising hiss of wind. From the dunes to the west, a cloud of sand swirled in a sudden gale. The flying grit enveloped them, and any orders from West were lost in the roar.

Cameron raised her arm to shield her eyes, trying to protect her face without completely obscuring her vision. The sand felt strangely soft. She had expected it to scour her skin. The puffs and clouds of sand began to clear after a moment, leaving them all coughing.

Staff Sergeant Lane shouted, "She's over here!"

Cameron wheeled. Erika was through the front of the line facing the ocean dunes. Andrew West swung at her, but she slipped under the blow and drove a dagger into the space under his sternum, angling up to his heart. Cameron raised her pistol but couldn't get a clear shot.

Erika leaped onto the armored vehicle, knocked aside the lookout's rifle, and then spun him around to face away from her. She gripped either side of his head in her hands. His body shuddered, his face went slack, and he fired the heavy weapon down on the rest of them. There were several grunts as soldiers hit the ground and took cover, a cry when someone didn't move fast enough.

Cameron dove down in front of the car, hoping the bumper would be better cover than a motorcycle. All around her metal pinged as bullets flew. She was now the ranking officer. Their line was broken, and they were taking fire from their own team members.

"Open fire, even if the shot isn't clear!" Cameron stood and took two shots, ducked. The bumper at her back vibrated as something struck the vehicle. When she glanced up to the roof, Specialist Green lay very still on top. Erika was gone, as was the long-range rifle.

"Report!" Cameron shouted, hoping her voice was steady, hoping someone would answer. She stepped back from the bumper, knowing Erika would keep moving. She wasn't going to run and disappear, not without making her point first.

A hand closed on Cameron's elbow, then yanked her back behind the armored vehicle. Several more shots rang out from the dunes to the east, the bullets shattering the pavement at Cameron's feet. Sergeant Glover pushed Cameron flat against the side of the vehicle. Glover raised one hand slightly, and made signals that Cameron didn't recognize. "You didn't tell us she was an excellent marksman."

"I didn't know," Cameron said.

Sergeant Rhodes crouched behind one of the larger bikes, signaling back to Sergeant Glover. Cameron tried to ignore the Master of the High Guard's body slumped against the vehicle next to her, the form of Staff Sergeant Emily Shoal on the pavement in front of her. Two more members of the team rushed from their cover to join Cameron and Sergeant Glover.

Another shot rang out, and Sergeant Rhodes stumbled to their sides as well. "Damn, she got my leg."

Ford quickly dressed the wound while Rhodes leaned against the side of the vehicle. When this was done, Sergeant Glover gestured them all nearer.

"Ford and Grumby will come with me to flush her out. Rhodes and Kardell can lay down cover fire." Sergeant Rhodes nodded. Neither of them even glanced at Cameron for confirmation.

Ford and Grumboldt followed Glover out into the open. When Erika fired at them, Rhodes and Cameron took a few select shots with their pistols. Erika didn't bother to fire back in their direction, and Cameron ground her teeth together. The three figures slipped toward the dunes to the east. Erika didn't fire again, but she didn't make an appearance, either.

"Did you notice that when she shot at you, she aimed at your feet? She didn't want to hit you." Sergeant Rhodes pulled off a couple more shots. Cameron couldn't see Erika and she was sure he hadn't, either. "She's saving you for last. Glad I'm not you."

Sand lifted up from the dunes and swirled around them again, much harder than before. Sergeant Rhodes cursed some more. While Cameron's eyes stung, the sensation was ghostly, only half there. She didn't feel any grit catch in her eyes or nose, even when she lowered her arm.

"It's not real," Cameron shouted over the roar of sand. "It's in your head!" Sergeant Rhodes let out a bark of laughter, and coughed.

She could drive away the illusion, if she just tried hard enough. If Erika could create it from nothing, then Cameron, knowing that it was false, could dismiss it. *Not real. It's not real.* The sensation of sand on her face faded a little, but not enough that she could see through it. Like the pain she had felt in Advon, knowing that it was an illusion didn't help her stop it.

More muffled shots went off to the east. It was impossible for Cameron or Rhodes to fire, because they couldn't see more than a few feet in front of them. The lights of the bikes were dim, amber-colored orbs. Cameron peered through the haze, trying to see beyond it to what was really there. The shots tapered off, then went silent.

The sand vanished as rapidly as it had blown up, leaving the pavement clean. Cameron looked over at Sergeant Rhodes. He looked back, their fate written in every line of his face, the set of his shoulders.

The smell of the ocean mingled with the reek of burning rubber and the sulfur of gunpowder. Cameron reached with shaking hands through the window into the armored vehicle. At least she could get the long distance radio, send out a warning.

She didn't hear the warning footsteps, just a gasp from Sergeant Rhodes, and the sound of heels scuffling for traction on the road. Cameron spun.

Erika held the sergeant in front of her as a shield, a dagger at the man's throat. Her green eyes glowed in the lights of the parked motorcycles. Her grip on Sergeant Rhodes was tight enough to make her tendons stand out.

"You should never have sent my own brother after me. If not for that, I would have let you wander around looking for me until you got tired and went back to Advon."

Cameron's hands steadied. "I thought he was the best chance at capturing you peacefully. I didn't mean to put him in danger." Erika's knife pressed harder against the sergeant's skin. A helmet lay on the ground by Cameron's right foot, and she waited for the opening. She might have to sacrifice Rhodes to stop this.

Erika smiled. "You really think you have a chance, don't you? That a sword is the only solution you need, even after everything I've done. It's time for you to stop."

Erika pressed and pulled the knife, let Sergeant Rhodes fall. Cameron slung the helmet at Erika. It missed and shattered on the road. Pieces broke off and spun through the air. Cameron kept moving, sweeping her blade down. Erika didn't bother to draw her sword. Maybe she'd had enough of murder—

Cameron's sword passed right through Erika as if she wasn't there at all, striking the motorcycle behind her. Metal clanged on metal, sending a shock up her arms and shoulders.

Just another image. Erika could control all she saw. Cameron stood with her battered sword raised in front of her and waited. There wasn't anything else to do.

The all-encompassing pain struck her just as it had in Advon, the quality of it sharper. Erika was getting better, Cameron thought as she went to her knees. *It's not real.* Her body curled around the agony. The problem was, it *felt* real.

A booted foot connected with her side and she heard a rib crack, felt the difference between the false and the genuine pain, just before the former lifted. Before she could regain her feet, Erika shoved her flat and planted a knee on her sternum. She unsheathed her sword and held it to Cameron's neck. With her free hand, Erika reached out and pressed her palm to Cameron's temple.

"Show me what you remember," she said. Cameron's head itched as Erika rifled through her thoughts. Memories from the gym flashed across Cameron's vision, over and over again until it all blurred together. At last, Erika sighed. "You didn't mean to do it. You still don't even *know* you did it."

Erika leaned closer, her face tight, her eyes bright with tears. She set the cool blade against the skin of Cameron's face, and then she applied pressure, opening a cut from the corner of her left eye down to her jaw. Cameron remained very still as blood welled along the curved line. "You still did it." Then Erika leaned back, her eyes cast up to the sky, the blade resting against Cameron's collarbone.

Blood tracked down Cameron's cheek and jaw, prickling as it ran into her hair and under her earlobe. Erika smiled. "That is going to be one kick-ass scar."

"Probably won't get me many dates."

Erika threw her head back and laughed, a bright and brittle sound. "Here's the deal. You owe me, so I'm going to let you go this time. I think I've made my point about what happens when you come after me, and I need you to take care of my brother. He's terrible at coping. Help him. Think of it as my dying wish."

Cameron held her breath, then Erika tapped the flat of her sword against Cameron's skin. "I'll take care of William."

Erika slammed the hilt of her blade into the side of Cameron's head. The world went bright, and an engine roared. Cameron drove herself back up on her feet, the unbalanced sword still in her hand, and she stumbled forward. She reached Erika just in time to be pelted with shards of gravel.

As Erika vanished, Cameron leaned against the massive armored vehicle. Her ribs ached, and her face burned.

She caught her breath and then she went to the bodies all around, checking for signs of life. She found a single pulse. It was Henry Gray, the youngest of the group, a Private of Sergeant Glover's. Cameron hoisted him up—something she'd been working at since she was fifteen, never thinking she'd actually have to do it—and carried him south out of the carnage. She checked his injuries and then folded her jacket underneath his head.

Just then, Tristan pulled up in his sleek car. Horror marked his features as he stepped out, but at least it wasn't a contrived expression. He paused, one hand gripping the door and the other on the hood of the car, while his eyes went over the accident scene behind her. She understood his hesitation. He was the man who created chaos, not the one who cleaned it up.

"Do you have a first-aid kit?"

He nodded and went to the trunk of the car, returning to the young man's side with the box. As he worked, she went back to her bike, found the emergency flares, and then picked up her helmet. She tuned the receiver in it to an emergency channel and sent out a warning that a government vehicle had been stolen, the person using it was extremely dangerous, and should not be approached under any circumstances. She put out a call for assistance, even as she lit the flares and placed two in each direction of the carnage.

She returned to where Tristan had finished administering what first aid he could. He didn't seem to have any words, so he went to work cleaning the cut on her face with disinfectant and gauze. The pressure of his hands was light and clinical, and she was relieved to see that he was capable of being serious. Finally, he decided what he would comment on first.

"Erika did all this?"

"Yes."

He scrunched his face in a way that was not at all attractive, but again, it wasn't a practiced, contrived expression. He looked out across the road, then quickly away, and his gaze landed on the battered blade still in her hand.

"Your sword."

"Yeah, it's trashed."

The screams of emergency sirens drifted up over the sound of the ocean, and Cameron felt some of the knots in her chest tighten. She was going to be asked questions for which she had no answers. At least not sane answers.

"So, are you still going after her?" Tristan asked very quietly.

That, at least, was easy. Erika had become an enemy, and Cameron would destroy her.

016

ERIKA SAT ASTRIDE that piece of metal and fire and sound, but she didn't feel it beneath her, just as she didn't see the road ahead of her. She felt the cold air whipping around her, though, tearing at her skin and hair, felt it worming down through her flesh into her bones. She was oddly cold on the inside, too.

All her connections and her relationships were severed. She was adrift, lost, alone, and in the midst of it all was a freedom she had never experienced before. No longer would she be pushed by her father's aspirations, or thrall to her concern for William. Nothing existed for her now except her own flesh and her roaring mind.

When she got too close to a town, she *heard* them, and then she altered direction to escape. Even when they were asleep, they made noise. She began to imagine that she heard the hum of voices all around, like a swarm of bees between her ears. Maybe she *could* hear it. Or maybe that was just the motorcycle engine.

She pulled over to the side of the road, the wheels skidding on gravel, and shut off the vehicle. In the stillness her senses settled. Her thoughts swirled like detritus in a pool at the bank of a river, rather than crashing around like pebbles in the rapids.

She dismounted and walked into the trees. She was going home. She was running from—something.

A quail whirred out of the brush near her feet, the sound of it a soft rush. She rested her hand against a tree, her thoughts broken by the gentle noise. It was real, not just something she had heard someone else think. When she pushed away, the skin of her hand left the bark reluctantly. She looked down. Her fingers were dark, tacky, and smelled of iron. Blood.

Oh yes, that was why she ran.

How many people had she killed? She had lost count in the darkness and the rush of power. Never had she felt such complete control. Yet she had only intended to scare Cameron into giving up. Clearly, she had done much more than that. How many? She remembered the push of a rifle into her shoulder and the trigger tight beneath her finger. She remembered the heft of a dagger in her hand, the hard crunch of bone and connective tissue.

That was bad, but worse was the memory of breaking open their thoughts and planting the destructive suggestions that had led to Espen Flint killing his own team. The false sandstorm had been a stroke of brilliance, simple and believable, though Cameron had begun to doubt at the end. The rifle training she had stolen from Oland Green still rested in her brain. She shouldn't have done that.

She found water, a tiny rivulet wending down to join the ocean, and she washed her hands clean. Her anger rose again as she scrubbed, but she wrestled it down.

There had been no flicker of fear in Cameron's mind. Erika didn't understand how this was possible. It was as if Erika had only set her friend's determination, made it as hard as iron. They would face one another again, in spite of all Erika had done to prevent that. Ghosts of Cameron's thoughts still flew through her mind, cutting like the blade that was so sure in the younger woman's hand. She blamed Erika for all of this. Images of Sophie's pale face and William's fingers wrapped around hers—no, that was Cameron's memory, Cameron's hand.

She had hurt Will, as no one ever had before. At least she had kept enough self-control not to kill him, but that was small consolation.

Erika stood and walked on through the woods, trying to forget, trying not to feel, and failing at both. She had made her own nightmare and dragged everyone she loved down into it.

She walked for many miles, giving towns a wide berth, afraid to go near people, afraid of what she might do. The stars in the night sky gave way to the brilliance of the sun, which arced overhead in a lazy path. So many thoughts flashed across the surface of her mind as she went.

She thought of arriving home, cold and hungry, and encountering Sophie's rush of thoughts, and pushing her away, too hard. She remembered Master Reese's calming, steady voice in the face of her confusion, and his eyes had gleamed when she sent him her thoughts. She remembered the rumble of the waves and the rush of rage, and the numbing spark that ran through her when she reached out to help William up. She tried not to think about the blood on the point of her sword. She remembered the satisfaction of slicing through the skin of Cameron's face, the care she had taken to make the cut artful, the knowledge that this was madness. If only Cameron had winced. She remembered the falling of bodies, the life in them fled or fleeing, the blood pouring.

The small pieces of other minds echoed through hers, gradually fading. In the midst of it all, she at least managed to hold one thought. *Home.* She would not forget that.

She walked over loamy forest floors; she passed through many miles of giant evergreens that scattered tiny, compact pinecones; and finally, her feet felt the thick moss, great ferns brushed her shoulders, a gray mist hung soft and ethereal in the air. These were the forests of home, cast in shades of emerald, gray, and brown. It was soft and still and dark. Her heart had never really left this place, nor William's.

She had hoped it would envelop her, soothe her. As she passed through trees that she recognized like friends, as memories spun around her, as her movement ruffled drifts of fog, she knew she was not who she'd been, and she could not go back. The tempestuous child, the combative student, the strong and steady Sentinel, all of those things were gone.

She was not free. She was dead. Her life was gone. She had enough sense and reason to see that. She had driven a blade through her brother's belly, killed Sophie, and spilled so much blood on The Ring. That was not who she was.

Her feet followed the paths she had run alongside William, the places they had lived like little wild things. These woods had been their retreat from their life inside the house, which had rarely held much warmth or comfort. She broke at last out of the forest and there it was, all the pillars and windows, a grand clean-lined structure in the dense green forest. A drizzle, barely distinguishable from the mist, fell upon her head and the roof of the estate where she had been born and where she had grown up. She felt as if her feet no longer quite touched the earth. It stood empty. This building was indelibly stamped as the Harfields' home and it would be theirs for as long as it stood.

In less than five years, the banks would sell it off to reclamation companies, who would strip out anything of value. Whatever remained would be plowed into the earth. That was the end that awaited their family. A blankness, where there had risen pillars and glass.

As Erika pushed her way through grass and ferns where the lawn had once been smooth, she considered that coming to the end might not be such an awful thing. For so long they had prolonged the death throes, borrowing money, selling off smaller properties, bargaining for just a little more time, when instead they might have made something new.

She went to the rear entrance, stumbling a little on the stairs. She couldn't remember her last mealW. Massive locks at the bottom and top of the door held it closed. The wood and metal were strong. Erika kicked until the screws holding the lock in the frame wrenched free, throwing out shards of wood.

The halls and rooms were dusty, but not terribly so. The pieces of furniture that were too big to move lay under heavy white sheets.

Erika didn't know where to go. She didn't want to wander the halls or remember anymore. She wanted to move on. She'd made a mistake, as many Harfields had before her, but maybe she had the answer to what came next. Rather than scrabble for a foothold, she would abandon all she'd been, leave behind the death and destruction along with her ties and accomplishments. She didn't know what that meant, when her thoughts twisted and turned without direction, but she did know that she was ready to be rid of this monument to ambition.

She reached out, placed a palm against a wall paneled with pale wood. The grain was smooth, the surface cool and dry. She pulled the lighter from her pocket, a gift from her grandfather, just like the one William fiddled with when he didn't have a pen. She flipped it open, rolled the striker, and saw the tiny fire dance. Then she held it up to the wall.

The smooth surface blackened, and the fire grew, climbing and leaping like a living thing. Erika smiled a little. Life for the fire meant death for the wood.

She went from room to room, lighting more fires as she went. The hungry flames rushed along, belching out black smoke and casting a glow that shifted in color and brilliance as the heat increased. It danced. It lived, brief and fierce.

When she was satisfied that the flames would consume it all, Erika kicked out the front doors and escaped into the cool air, while her monster roared and raged and destroyed everything before it. She went back into the forest, now alight with strange shadows as Harfield Manor crackled and burned. Embers drifted through the trees, and she heard a window burst behind her.

She could vanish, become a ghost. She would stay away from people. If she disappeared completely enough, maybe Cameron wouldn't find her.

Ash and mist mingled in the air as a glow in the eastern sky strengthened. Erika followed the tug and pull of her own feet, found it easier to go forward without direction than she had hoped. She soon left the smell of smoke behind her, and she wandered.

As she went, she took what she needed on the outskirts of civilization, picking up hardier boots, a hunting bow, a small pack, and a tarp for shelter from rain. Summers in Northwest Cotarion were pleasant, and she was able to steal food from unattended gardens. The forests were expansive and dense, easy to hide in.

It was a strange thing to go day after day hearing nothing at all but her footsteps, the swish of wind in the trees, and the chattering of birds. She had rarely ever gone more than a few hours without talking to another person.

Eventually, she came to the most northwestern point in Cotarion, a rocky spear of land that jutted out into the steely gray ocean. The wind blew fiercely, little plovers ran up and down the rocky shore plumbing for shellfish, and smooth pebbles rattled in the crashing waves. Offshore, a pod of black and white whales crashed through the water, their fins throwing up white spray. Erika turned back inland, and kept going.

Soon after, she found the door. She had been letting her feet go where they wished, so she couldn't be certain where she was. The patch of forest where the door hid was so dense that she almost didn't see it. She stood and stared at its outline for a long time, afraid to go near after avoiding civilization for so long. Yet moss obscured the metal, and a heavy covering of vegetation all around suggested that no one had been this way in many years.

She reached out and struck her knuckles against the surface, just once. The metal was cold, and the sound it made was heavy. From a great distance, a memory rose up, of Cameron and a doorway she found in the mountains, a beast's lair, and a strange room with two doors that would not open. Erika hadn't paid much attention to any of these things at the time. None of it had seemed nearly as important or mysterious as Cameron believed, but here was a metal door matching that description, set into a sheer rock face.

Erika went up and inspected the door carefully. She climbed the rocks beside it and prowled along the ridge above, looking for any clues to what might lie underneath. Then she dropped back down.

It was made like nothing Erika had ever seen before. The metal was smooth, without any sign of joins, the texture and color strange. There was no rust and no pitting.

So. This was why Cameron was so obsessed with that door she'd found in Palisade.

Erika brushed away the moss on the door, then pulled down the vines and ferns around it. As she yanked and tore at the vegetation on the right side of the frame, she heard a distinct electronic tone. She saw a red light flashing through the greenery. She reached out to it, her fingers brushing aside leaves. She found a smooth dark surface beneath; when she touched it, another tone sounded, this one brighter and clearer than the last.

The door opened. Erika leapt back. The space behind the door was formless shadow. She abhorred the idea of going into the darkness beyond after so much time out in the open air.

Her feet, used to having their way, went forward. The door shut behind her.

When she emerged later that evening, she tried to hold the jumble of what she had found together in her mind, but she could feel it all slipping out. For the first time in a long time, she went into a town, to the mail office. The clerk on staff lent her paper and pen, and then agreed to send the letter she wrote to Advon. He offered to buy her something to eat when she set down the pen, but she dashed out without answer.

017

WHEN WILLIAM WOKE, all was darkness and confusion. He heard strange sounds, the hushed crashing of waves, the whisper of wind around walls that were not his own, and an empty space where the clacking of his grandfather clock should be. He saw unfamiliar shadows across the ceiling, he felt the weight of a strange blanket, and he smelled wood, lemons, tea, and salt. Hunger gnawed at his belly. Then he heard the soft creak of a floorboard, and a moment later, a hushed voice.

"Of course I didn't predict this. No one could." There was a long pause, and no matter how carefully William listened, he couldn't hear a second speaker. Master Reese must be on the phone. "It will look better for you if you extend her a reprieve. She isn't ready for the High Guard, but it's too late for that now. Show her forgiveness and she might remain loyal. She's an instrument, well-made, and in time she might be more, but for now that's all you can expect. Cut her free, and someone else might pick her up and use her against you."

William couldn't help eavesdropping. He closed his eyes again. "You can do what you like. However, the consequences will be much greater than they have ever been before. I advise you not to punish someone just because you're angry." There was another pause, a quiet exhalation, and then the click of a phone receiver connecting with its base.

The distant roar of waves lulled William back to sleep a moment later.

When William woke again, morning light filled the room. His stomach rumbled. Fortunately, a plate heaped with eggs and ham and fruit sat on the coffee table beside the couch. He ate it all, then looked around.

A full set of clean clothing lay neatly folded next to the plate. William had never seen creases so perfect. He looked down at what he wore. Someone had changed his clothes, because everything he wore was free of blood, if a little rumpled.

He frowned and dropped a hand to his abdomen. There, under the shirt, was a scar. The ghost of an intense pain hovered there. It couldn't be healed already; Erika had just stabbed him the day before. Unless he'd been unconscious for weeks.

William stood. Spots danced in front of his eyes, but he ignored them. Either he dreamed, or the world had turned upside-down.

He forced his feet to move, though they were heavy, through a hallway. The house was quiet and empty. Any other time it might have been peaceful, but William needed a person who could give him answers.

He found the kitchen where he'd sat—the day before, it must have been. Out in the courtyard he saw Reese and a young woman with silvery hair. He'd seen her before, hadn't he? The memory was ghostly.

William went out, though he didn't have on any shoes. Both of them looked up as the door opened. The woman rushed over, and steered him to a bench. Reese knelt so he could be at William's eye level.

"You're safe, Doctor Harfield. Nothing will hurt you while you're here."

Did he look like he needed the reassurance?

"How long was I unconscious?"

Reese smiled. "Just for one night."

William's hand dropped to the scar on his abdomen. "How is that possible?"

It was the young woman who answered. "I gave your body some extra focus. Healing can be kind of slow, but a little encouragement can move it along and get your energy to the right places. That's why you're so tired."

Someone else with powers. Erika had been right, they weren't the only ones; the proof of it was written on his own body. The young woman smiled at him, her cheeks dimpling. Perhaps he and his abilities were equally important to her. It was always good not to be alone.

William extended his hand to her. "Doctor William Harfield."

She looked at his hand as if uncertain, and then shook it. "Melanie Stillwater. Are all you Advonites so formal?"

William's cheeks burned. "No, it's really just me, probably."

She laughed. "Good, I don't think I could stand city life if everyone went around shaking hands all the time. I'll be back to check in again later today." She shook William's hand again, with false sincerity. "Ever so pleased to meet you, Doctor Harfield, I do so look forward to continuing our acquaintance. Have ever such a nice day."

William attempted to smile. Under almost any other circumstance he would have been amused, even if the joke was at his expense, but just then he had too many worries running through his head to laugh.

She was gone in a swish of skirts and a flutter of silver hair—the ends, William noticed, bright with blue dye. He turned his attention to Reese.

"Where is Tristan?"

"I sent him after Cameron as soon as you were out of danger. I hoped that he would be able to help, and he looked like he needed something to do."

"Did any of them find Erika?" The question was fraught with danger, and William feared the answer.

"The Response Team caught up to her last night. Doctor Harfield, I'm very sorry to tell you that Erika killed them. She left only Cameron and Private Henry Gray alive. Tristan arrived too late to do anything more than slow down the investigators who wanted to blame the whole mess on Cameron—"

"How do we know Cameron didn't do all of it and just point the finger at my sister?" William finally looked up and met Reese's gaze.

"What do you think the odds of that are, after your conversation with Erika yesterday?"

William stared back into the bushes. He couldn't escape the memory of Erika's face, lined with fury. His scar was no accident.

Cameron had held his hand, her expression fierce. But her dark eyes had been steady and sure. She would not have slaughtered her fellow Sentinels, either.

"Erika is not a murderer." Even Tristan had never gone so far.

"You're right. Erika is gone."

William watched a sparrow foraging in the shrubs. Harfields did not break, that's what Erika would say to him. Harfields fought through and found a solution. Harfields did not put their heads in their hands and give in to despair.

"If I might make a suggestion, I have whole stacks of books inside gathering dust. Some of them will probably interest you, and I think a distraction would do you good. What do you think?"

William nodded, and Reese led him inside, showing great patience with William's slow pace. The sword master even provided him with a notebook and pen. Then William dove into the books, and didn't leave them until Reese brought him dinner.

William sat on a bench in Master Reese's courtyard, alternately watching the ocean waves and the students sparring. After two days of rest, he felt almost back to his old self. His anxiety to get back to Advon so he could continue his research rose every hour. He had skimmed through all of the books Master Reese had lent, and he wanted to compare the information to notes in his office.

Master Reese raised a hand and stopped the practice. Rather than launch into instructions as he so often did, he stood silent at the end of the line of pupils. Then William saw Sentinel Kardell approaching from the opposite side of the courtyard.

A long, scabbed cut ran in a wicked red line from the outer corner of her left eye, to her jaw, almost touching her chin. It looked like the track a tear might have made, retraced with the edge of a knife. Erika had made that cut. William held his breath as Cameron stopped in front of Master Reese.

His surprise grew when she dropped to her knees in front of her instructor, laid her bent sword at his feet, and rested her forehead on the ground. Her words were muffled, but William heard her say, "I failed, Master Reese. I'm sorry."

Getting the apology out was clearly a struggle. Even when it had been delivered, Reese did not tell her to stand. All was silent except for the crashing waves and a finch chattering in the gardens. Surely it was not necessary to make her kneel on the ground like that.

"Rise, High Guard Kardell," Master Reese said, and she got to her feet, wincing slightly as she did. Otherwise, her face was still, her eyes dark and unreadable as she met Reese's gaze. "Their names and how they died."

William's skin went cold and he looked around for an escape route. He didn't want to know what his sister had done, but there was no way to leave now without interrupting.

Kardell sucked in a deep breath and kept her eyes locked on the master's. "Specialists Natalia Fleet and Evan Holmes were beheaded. Sergeant Espen Flint took his own life. Erika stabbed Specialist Emily Lane, and then the Master of the High Guard, Andrew West. Private Henry Gray was wounded by friendly fire, Private Mary Schumacher killed, and Erika broke Specialist Oland Green's neck before stabbing Staff Sergeant Michael Hayes. Specialist Christian Ford, Private Sam Grumboldt, and Sergeant Charlotte Glover pursued Erika and were shot. Erika cut Sergeant Stratten Rhodes' throat. They were all experienced warriors, among the best in their fields. And because of me, they died."

Master Reese nodded. "What was your mistake?"

"I was impatient. I tried to draw her out by letting her brother go after her. You warned me not to pursue her, but I recommended to the Master of the High Guard that we chase her, anyway." She looked away then. Reese dismissed the students. They left rapidly, turning to one another and whispering before they were even out of sight.

"Come inside," Reese said when they were gone, his voice quiet. "I'll make you some tea." He picked up the sword and handed it back to her.

Cameron didn't follow Reese inside at once. Instead, she approached William, and he stood to meet her. He wished he knew what thoughts passed behind those dark eyes. On the other hand, considering what had happened to Erika, he probably didn't really want to know.

"I pushed you. I wanted you to look for Erika when Master Reese wouldn't tell me where she was. If I hadn't let you go off on your own, you wouldn't have been hurt. I'm sorry."

William frowned. He knew she could read people, but he didn't believe she could have predicted his actions so precisely. He was the one who had run after Erika with no idea of what the result would be.

"Please don't worry about it. I'm sorry she hurt you and all those other Sentinels . . . " He stopped and swallowed. "I can't believe she did it."

The Sentinel looked at him for longer than he liked, and then said, "You're recovering very well, but you should still probably sit. It's not good to push yourself too much."

"Oh, that." Knowing he could not explain entirely, he pulled up the edge of his shirt to show her the scar. Her eyes widened noticeably as she looked at the remnant of the wound. Did she understand its importance? To William, it was confirmation the abilities were not just a fluke of his family, as well as a reminder of Erika's rage.

"Melanie did this?" she breathed at last. He nodded and dropped his shirt as she turned to Master Reese, who still waited at the door. "How much do you know?" she asked him.

"Come inside, and I'll tell you."

Cameron followed Reese, and William went behind her. They sat in the kitchen just as they had a few days before, distinctly worse for wear now. Master Reese placed a kettle on the stove, then stood in front of Cameron as the water warmed, his eyes moving across her face, lingering on the cut. William was glad he didn't have to endure those cold blue eyes. Reese sighed.

"The most exceptional Sentinels in Cotarion come to me. Many years ago, one of them confessed to powers even more amazing than the rest. After that, I collected all the information I could find, and I learned to recognize when someone was something more. I try to help as much as I can. This is the first time I've seen something like this happen."

The water simmered in the kettle, and Master Reese poured the steaming liquid over the tea leaves to steep, a pronounced sadness in his features as he watched the shriveled green shapes blossom in the pot. "I hope you can learn more than I have." His gaze turned to William for a moment.

Cameron spoke. "You say that you've learned to recognize people like Erika. How?"

"I trust my instincts. I learned in my training to observe, just as I taught you, and when a student is more cautious than normal, I watch even more carefully. Erika always took a long time shaking someone's hand the first time she met them, and sometimes she knew things she shouldn't. When she was young, sometimes she forgot what had been spoken aloud and what had not." He paused, and then said, "But that's not exactly why you were asking, is it?"

William was glad Reese turned away to tend the tea, because he knew what his face must be showing. Cameron was asking if there might be a way to tell if she, too, had one of these powers, but he guessed she must not want her instructor to know that. She kept her expression blank and said, "It's good to know."

Master Reese dispensed the green tea into cups, and Cameron drank what was placed in front of her with only the occasional grimace. Was she tired, or trying to make amends for being too brash?

"Sean said he's going to send you after Erika again as soon as your ribs are healed."

Cameron nodded. "He can't afford to let her go, not now. She's caused too much highly visible damage. Leaving it unresolved looks bad."

The older man nodded with great solemnity. "Well, you can at least stay here and rest tonight; I've made room for you. If you'd like, I can have Melanie take a look at your injuries."

Cameron shook her head. "I'd rather let it heal on its own, thanks." William did not blame her for refusing to let someone use an ability on her, after the events of the past few days. Reese didn't push the issue.

Reese replaced the cups of tea with lunch, a salad of grains and chopped vegetables unlike anything William had eaten before. It was crunchy, bitter, and tart with lemon juice.

"I noticed that pine down at the bottom of the hill is finally filling back in," Cameron said between mouthfuls.

"It was ragged for a long time, but the work you and Erika put into it is paying off."

"After three days on a ladder, I was disappointed when it wasn't the prettiest tree in your garden."

"It was no less than you deserved," Reese said, and then explained to William. "Cameron thought she should add challenge to her training regime by sparring in a tree. She convinced Erika that it was a good idea, too, and up the largest tree they climbed."

"That branch was perfect. I'm sorry it broke. It was going very well before that."

"There aren't many branches that will hold over two hundred pounds of highly active people. So, Erika fell on a rock and broke her leg, while Cameron hit every branch on the way down."

William chewed thoughtfully. "I've always assumed that Erika's schemes were her own ideas."

"Most of them were," Cameron said. "She didn't participate much in my plots after that."

"Two weeks later I found Kardell on my roof," Master Reese said. "Erika learned to be careful, and you just kept on climbing things with weapons in your hand. I never could teach you anything."

Cameron stood, her exhaustion increasingly apparent in the stoop of her shoulders. "You taught me how to wash dishes and pull weeds." When she tried to take William's plate, he stood and reached for the ones she already carried.

"I can clean these. You look like you need rest." He winced and cleared his throat. "I'm sorry, that didn't come out—I meant, you look tired, and . . . um. I really am trying to be nice, I swear."

She smiled again, as if she found his fumbling amusing. "I understand what you're saying." She put her plate on top of his. Was that gratitude he saw? Then she turned to Master Reese and said, "You might want to supervise him. Based on what I saw in his office, I'm not sure he knows what he's doing." William didn't know if he should be mad or not. Fortunately, she walked for the door to the living room, and he was spared any more teasing.

He was stacking the dishes to be washed when he realized there was a question he needed to ask of Cameron. He found her stretched out on the couch in the common room, and he was sure she was asleep, until her eyes flashed open at his approach.

He said, "I'm sorry; I just need to ask. Where is Tristan?"

"Hell if I know. I thought he was right behind me." She closed her eyes again, and within moments appeared soundly asleep.

William took up his perch on the wall that encircled the courtyard. He read through his notes and watched Master Reese's students practice. Some of the older Cadets helped instruct the newest in basic techniques. Cameron followed Reese as he circled the group, fine-tuning the placement of feet and elbows. Her lips remained a flat line and she spoke very little. Reese's students watched her whenever they had a chance, as did William. There must be clues there in her face, ones he hadn't learned yet.

Finally, he went back to his notes, writing to the rhythm of the training blades clacking. When he looked up again, he was surprised to see Cameron had joined the practice.

Even with broken ribs and a scab running down her face, she could move. She sparred with one of the older students, instructing him between blows. Her strikes were smooth from beginning to end, her feet so light that they seemed to float over the ground. The young man across from her struggled to keep up.

"Sentinel Kardell, I told you not to push yourself," Reese said.

"I'm not, sir."

"I don't think you understood."

"I wasn't able to describe the Farrow Offense. I thought it best to demonstrate. I didn't want there to be any confusion."

Reese smiled. "Well, if you're determined, you can help me show them a few more of the trickier techniques."

William's notes lay on his knees, completely forgotten. The students formed into a line, and Cameron took up position across from Master Reese. She stood tall, her shoulders loose, poised like a bird as it prepared to fly. As Reese brought a practice blade into the ready position, Cameron kept hers down at her side.

"Please note that Sentinel Kardell is taking a risk that I do not encourage."

Cameron's lip twitched. "You said you wanted them to see how I fight."

The sword master reset his position and moved in for an attack. Only when he struck did Cameron raise her weapon. She slid his blow away and stepped lightly to the side.

William lost track of what was happening almost immediately. Both combatants sprang from attack to defense. Cameron's feet moved across the ground with precision and care, and always she watched her opponent's face, her eyes alight with purpose. She moved in ways that must be painful, and yet her face remained smooth, her attacks relentless.

She was very good; even someone as clueless as William could see that. But Erika had beaten her.

Master Reese stayed even with Cameron for several minutes, and then he made a strike at her face, which would have landed right on the scabbed cut. Cameron caught the blow. Something new rose in her eyes. It should have been anger. Instead all her weariness and frustration drained away, replaced by a cold focus.

She moved faster. She jabbed and cut, forcing Master Reese to twist to defend himself in ways that were uncomfortable and made balancing difficult. Then she turned, opened her weakened side for just a moment. When the master moved to attack, she dove in, hooked his knee with her leg, pushed against his shoulder, and brought him down to the ground. He managed a few more blocks before she disarmed him, and then she brought the point of her training blade down to his chest.

The young students stood in silence. Cameron remained in place for a moment before sweeping her blade away and helping her opponent to his feet. They exchanged salutes. Reese turned to the trainees, and said he wanted an essay from each of them on what they had learned within two hours. As they scattered, he turned to Kardell.

"I hope you aren't hurt."

"I'm fine, though if that blow had landed there'd be some blood to clean up." Her voice was light, her vengeance already won.

"Better to see if you hesitate now than when it really matters. You're getting closer to finding your style. It is gratifying to see something entirely new in the making." He turned to look across the courtyard. A shadow William hadn't noticed moved, and resolved into Tristan. "I'm guessing you're here at last to take Doctor Harfield home."

Tristan shrugged and avoided the powerful gaze. "Yeah, if you think I got the job done."

"You did." Reese turned to William. "It has been wonderful to have you, Doctor Harfield. I hope we meet again soon. Make sure you keep getting enough rest for the next few days, but not too much. And feel free to take those books with you."

William protested that he couldn't accept, but Cameron interrupted.

"Just take them, Harfield, he's read them all, anyway."

Tristan packed the boxes in the trunk of his car. Master Reese shook hands with the cousins at his front door and watched Cameron as she, too, made her escape.

"Are you sure I can't convince you to stay a little while longer? Sean can't expect you back so soon."

"He does. Also, I'm afraid that if I stay any longer you'll make me part of your lessons for the rest of the summer."

Master Reese laughed. "I can't help that you make such an interesting study." His eyes moved across the three of them.

William felt the space where Erika should be. She was the reason they had travelled here, the reason two of them bore new scars, and this was a moment when she would have said something that would bring all that had happened to an end. Instead, there was nothing.

Kardell looked to William. "I'll call you and arrange a meeting." Then she exchanged one last salute with Master Reese, carefully pulled on her helmet, and left in a roar of engine. William gave Reese a final awkward wave, and they departed not far behind her.

"Where have you been?" William asked.

Tristan grinned. "That's an interesting story. You know that pretty girl who fixed you up?"

"Yes."

"Well, she wants to go to Advon."

"Tris', you didn't offer to take her, did you?"

"Maybe a little," Tristan said, his smile fading. "Do you think that was a stupid thing to do?"

"Yes, I do."

Tristan was quiet until they came to the bottom of the hill. "Do you think it would be stupid to let her live with me until she finds a job?"

"Yes!"

"Oh." Tristan paused again. "Billy. I've done a stupid thing."

018

CAMERON STOPPED HER bike in front of a small house in the suburbs on the south side of Advon. It was made of brick, and flowers lined the stone path to the front door. It was all so unfamiliar to her. She didn't visit enough, and they never said so outright, but it was always there under the surface. And this visit wasn't just about catching up.

Cameron knocked gently on the front door before letting herself in. As soon as the door shut behind her, she let her hair down and desperately tried to arrange it so her scab was less visible. Then she stripped off her boots and jacket and shoved them in the closet with her helmet. She was debating whether to leave her ruined blade in the entryway when Owena floated in.

Owena's slender hand flew to her mouth. "Cam! Mom is going to lose her mind! Your *face*!"

Cameron sighed, and her ribs creaked. "Do you think you could say that any louder?"

"But, your face!"

Seren Kardell's voice drifted from farther inside the house. "Cam, what is your sister shouting about?"

So, it was going to be a thing. Cameron went into the living room, met her mother just leaving the dining room, and found Armel was also there, reading on the couch and taking up far too much space. He tried to appear disinterested, but he leaned forward and stared. He and Cameron's mother both wore the same expression of shock.

Seren reached out, brushed aside Cameron's hair with her long and delicate fingers. Cameron wanted to fade into the corner, but her mother pulled her into a painful embrace instead. Cameron glared at Armel, who raised his book to hide his face.

Finally, Owena cleared her throat and said, "Mom, I think you're hurting her."

Seren let go and dried her eyes. "Well, it was going to happen eventually, I guess. I can't believe Erika would do this to you, though."

"She isn't herself."

Cameron's mother struggled for a moment, probably fighting down a lecture. "Dinner is almost done, so you should wash up." She kissed Cameron lightly on the forehead and returned to the kitchen.

Armel once again raised the book up in front of his face as Cameron's gaze locked on him. She went over and plucked the novel from his hands, gently closed it and set it aside, then sat on the coffee table across from him. He folded his hands in his lap, trying to look contrite, but he grinned too much.

"You should have told me."

"Told you what?"

"Armel!"

Owena sat on the couch next to him and took one of his hands. She stared back at Cameron with her eyebrows raised.

"We decided we shouldn't say anything until—"

"Until I showed up at my parents' house one evening and you were there? She's barely eighteen."

Owena spoke again. "I'll be nineteen in two months, actually."

Cameron cast around for another argument, but she couldn't land on any that made much sense. "I just wish you'd told me." Then she left to wash up.

They couldn't be good for each other. Neither of them had any idea what they wanted in life; they had no course for their futures. Owena was still a girl, and Armel had only given up responsibility for running an entire country a couple of weeks before. This couldn't possibly last for long. Then, when it ended, Cameron would be asked to take sides, to carry messages of regret and anger from one to the other, and both would be annoyed with her because of course she would refuse.

The idea that they might not break up was almost as awful. If they stayed together, married, had children, how much would her relationship have to change with Armel? She didn't know how to predict that, and she didn't want to find out.

But things changed. It was unreasonable to expect not to.

The timing was bad. She had been thrown into a job she didn't want, her confidence was shaken, she had lost Erika, and she had no idea how to stop her.

Someone should have mentioned it before Armel was being invited over for family dinners. Of course, if Cameron ever attended those family dinners, she probably would have noticed sooner.

She dried her hands and put it out of her mind. She had more important things to worry about, and this was none of her business.

"Dinner's ready!" her father called.

Cameron went back through the living room on her way to the dining room. Armel thumped her on the shoulder as she passed, not entirely certain, but she smiled at him with the good side of her face.

The table held an impressive spread, complete with a roast chicken, a rice dish, and some vegetables that Cameron was guaranteed to like. It was a rare thing that both her parents took time off on the same evening, even rarer that they would spend that time cooking, and Cameron felt the tug of gratitude.

Her dad was careful when he wrapped his arms around her shoulders. Seren must have prepared him well for the cut, because he didn't stare. "It's good to have you home, Cam."

She kissed his cheek. "Thanks, Dad. This looks great; you didn't have to go to all this trouble."

He gave a deep-throated laugh. "I can hardly take credit, since I was demoted to assistant and did very little besides chop and make whatever sauces your mother directed." He lowered his voice. "Don't tell her that I didn't add the nutmeg to the glaze on the chicken. No matter how much I said you didn't like it, she insisted it was part of the recipe."

"How dare you violate the sanctity of the recipe?"

Seren entered with the last couple of dishes. "I heard that. Please, everybody sit down. What would you like to drink, Armel? I have a nice white, or some ale, or water of course."

Armel hesitated, looked at Cameron, then at Owena, and finally muttered that the white wine sounded nice. Both sisters rolled their eyes, and Owena whispered to him as they sat down that she didn't care if he had ale instead of wine. Their dad carved and served the chicken, while Seren distributed drinks, and she put both a glass of wine and a bottle of ale in front of Armel, who took another minute of deliberation before opening the ale, grinning at Owena.

"I've been reading up on the history of the High Guard," Bryce Kardell said. "It's a very exciting topic."

"You probably know more about it than I do," Cameron said. "History was never my best topic. Armel knows just about everything on the subject, though."

"Not as much as my dad. He's been collecting and cataloging documents since he was fifteen. But history was definitely one of my best subjects."

"Your tutoring was probably the only reason I passed."

"Fair exchange, since you got me through weapons classes. Which books have you read on the Guard, sir?"

"I started with Marven's but he meandered a lot. Graves' *The Unseen Watch* was much easier to follow . . . "

Cameron listened as they discussed the formation of the High Guard in excruciating detail. Her mother contributed the occasional rumor she had picked up during her time in the Sentinels. Cameron had rarely before heard Seren admit to her time in uniform.

"Does your face hurt much?" Owena asked during a lull in their father's discussion with Armel.

"When I smile. Mostly it just itches."

Armel grinned. "You smile? When did that start?"

Cameron's family stared at him, surprised that anyone would dare make fun of her. She threw a roll at his head, and it struck him even though he ducked. "Shut up, you're giving away all my secrets."

"I could tell them what the other Sentinels call you."

"Some of my nicknames aren't suitable for my family's ears." She raised her eyebrows at him, but he was unrepentant. Her parents didn't need to know what the other Sentinels thought of her.

"Now I'm curious," Seren said. "Go on, Armel."

Armel's smile was broad as he swallowed, and savored for a moment Cameron's concern over what would come next. "They call her 'Queen of Laws'. When they're feeling polite."

Cameron relaxed. That was only what they said when they thought her strict adherence to procedure would help them. When it made their lives more difficult, the names got a lot more colorful.

Owena laughed, declared this ridiculous, especially when her middle name made such an easy target. As Seren defended the choice as a perfectly good family name, Cameron sought a way to change the subject. If Armel knew she bore the moniker 'Eustella,' she would hear about it every day for the rest of her life.

When the meal was done, Owena and Armel offered to clean up the dishes. They retreated to the kitchen, where they completed the task with much clattering, splashing, and the occasional burst of laughter. It was time to ask the favor. Cameron went back to the front hall to retrieve her box.

Her mother's expression when she saw the ruined steel was more aggravated than devastated. A battered sword paled in comparison with a scar on her daughter's face. Cameron's concerns tipped the other way. The cut would heal, but the blade would not.

"How did this happen?"

"I missed Erika and hit a motorcycle. I hoped you might have another sword that I could use." If not, she would be forced to carry one of the standard-issue blades, and their balance was notoriously poor.

For a moment, Cameron thought her mother would refuse, but then Bryce squeezed her hand. They exchanged a long look, which Cameron had difficulty interpreting. How many years of conversations and worries did their silent communication encompass? Cameron waited. At last, her mother stood.

"I still have something that should work for you. Come with me."

Seren led Cameron to the second floor and into her bedroom. Cameron stood near the window. She didn't want to receive something that was given half-heartedly, only because her father's hope and confidence won out over her mother's experience and fears. She stared at a line of trinkets on the windowsill. Heirlooms and souvenirs from her parents' occasional travels. Cameron picked one up, a deep blue stone egg streaked with a paler, opaque mineral.

Her mother finally emerged from her search under the bed. Cameron replaced the stone egg as Seren laid a wooden box on the bed. Her elegant hands ran across the surface and popped the locks. The lid opened without a creak, and Cameron leaned over to see what was inside.

The sword had a stronger curve to it than the one she had been using, though the difference was slight. The steel was bright, as if it had been polished recently. The hilt ornament depicted a hawk in flight peeking out through golden-brown silk wrappings. The guard was almost solid, unlike some of the more fanciful openwork designs Cameron had seen, but the metal had been worked to depict a mountain range. The temper lines were long and low, and seemed to mirror the shape of the mountains on the guard. Overall, the weapon was elegant but simple, made for hard use, but still formed with care.

"It was a wedding gift to your father. It's good steel. Better than good, really. I think it will suit your style well." She reached down, lifted it out with practiced care that had remained over the years, and presented the hilt. Gently, Cameron tested the balance and weight in her hands. It really was good steel. Few Sentinels had blades so fine, excepting the High Guard. She smiled involuntarily at the feel of it in her hands, the scab tugged, and she forced away the expression.

Her mother sighed. "I know how good you are, but this time you were lucky. Still, if you aren't going to stop, you might as well have good equipment."

Cameron laid the sword back in the box, alongside the scabbard. "Thank you. I do my best to take care of myself."

Seren couldn't seem to help looking at the cut. She reached out and brushed Cameron's jaw just at the end of the scab, the motion quick, almost involuntary. "You were lucky."

Cameron didn't know what to say. There was nothing she could do to ease her mother's mind, no way to guarantee she would be safe besides leaving the Sentinels. Even if she could do that, she wouldn't. She had invested too much of her life training.

"I understood, once," her mother said at last. "I was just as devoted as your father. Maybe if he'd died protecting the people of Cotarion, I would have understood, but in training . . . " She shook her head and closed her mouth for a moment. "It was senseless. And here you are following the same path, and I can't seem to stop you, no matter what I do. I just don't understand how you can be so much like a man you never even met." She lowered the lid of the box, then pushed it in front of Cameron. "You've seen what can happen, and you know the dangers you face. Please try not to get yourself killed."

Cameron nodded. "I'll do my best." She reached out and wrapped an arm around her mother's slender shoulders.

Seren smiled, then. "I still can't believe they put you in the High Guard. I have to admit—I'm proud of you."

Yet another feeling Cameron couldn't share. She'd seen Master Reese's concern over Sean Ellis's motives for selecting her, and she still wondered why. She worried now and then that the position may not be as temporary as she had been told. There were so many questions that she would like to ask, but she couldn't afford to appear disloyal. She would have to observe, rely on what happened around her to determine why she had been given this job.

"I hope that I can do well at it. So far, I've felt a little unprepared."

Seren nodded. "I think it's good to have some doubts. It gives you a chance to question what you've learned and find your own way." She lowered her voice. "What do you think of Armel dating Owena? He's always seemed to have a good head on his shoulders, and I have to give him credit for stepping down when he could have ruled the entire country. Their ages aren't that far apart, but she seems so young for him."

Cameron shrugged. "Armel will treat Owena well."

"Is it strange for you?"

"A little," Cameron said. "He's been my friend for a long time."

Her mother sighed again and shook her head. "All right, let's go back down and make sure your dad isn't interfering too much."

Cameron followed her mother back downstairs and found Armel setting out a board game with the help of her dad, while Owena studied the rulebook. The three were wedged into the couch on one side of the coffee table.

Armel eyed the box Cameron put down next to her chair. He would pester her into telling him every story, later. But for the time, he handed her a game piece and made her promise not to stretch the rules to their limits.

019

"THE ARTS DISTRICT is always safe, but the night scene there is boring. The Wharf District has the most interesting bars, but you don't want to go there alone. And stay off Hale Street entirely. There are some good places between the Military Quarter and Gates, but mostly it's trash—"

"The market on Second Street is the best place to get food if you ever feel like, you know, eating," William said.

Tristan rolled his eyes, but Melanie turned in the passenger seat and winked at him. William had been forced into the back so that Melanie and Tristan could flirt all the way from Brook's Cove to Advon. Now as the tall buildings of the city rose around them, Tristan pointed out the most important landmarks. Melanie stared up at the towers, her eyes wide with wonder.

William had stopped trying to figure out either of their motivations several hundred miles back. Tristan had brought a young woman he'd known perhaps a day to the capital, and Melanie had moved to a strange city with an equally strange man. Neither seemed concerned about the wisdom of this.

Erika would have berated Tristan for acting so impulsively, and Tristan would have listened. William didn't have the courage to try.

At least Melanie helped carry one of the boxes from Tristan's car into William's apartment, though after that she wandered off to use the bathroom and didn't return for some time.

"So, here's the thing," William said as he unpacked the boxes. "This book, *An Extended History of Ancient Civilizations*, it's really old, and it makes reference to a lot of other texts, most of which I have, but it keeps talking about this one that I've never seen before, and it sounds important. So, I was wondering if maybe you could find it."

Tristan rolled his eyes. "*Why* do people keep asking me to do these things? At what point did I give the impression that I work for free?"

"I can't exactly afford to pay you." Hopefully uncovering secrets would be more interesting to Tristan than making money. He'd relied on Erika as much as anyone, and he should want to do what he could to help her.

"What's the damn thing called?"

William turned away to hide a smile and wrote the title. "It's *The Altered Compendium*. Written by Anonymous, which is incredibly unhelpful, and it has no date. It sounds like it was rare even at the time this book was written, so there may not be any copies left, and if there are, they'll be difficult to find."

Tristan took the scrap of paper William handed to him, trying to look annoyed, but William saw the spark in his silvery eyes. Tristan loved finding things.

"If I should manage to locate this mysterious tome, what would you like me to do?"

"I just need to know what it says."

Tristan smirked. "What I mean is, do you want me to make a copy, or do you want me to steal it?"

Oh. So this would mean operating in legal gray areas. William hadn't considered that. "I would prefer that you not steal it, if you don't have to. However, I mean if the quality of the paper is very bad—I'm just saying—I have to be able to read it."

Melanie finally reappeared and stood next to Tristan with her arm hooked through his. "I'd love to see more of the city. If my interview goes well tomorrow, I won't have much time for exploring."

"Of course. Be good, Billy. I'll see you around."

William watched them pull away. For a few minutes after they were gone, he unloaded books, sorting them into piles based on how useful he thought they would be. The grandfather clock seemed inordinately loud, the pauses between its ticks unusually quiet.

William remembered Cesar, and along with him, Dakota. He needed to pick up the dog, but his stomach knotted at the idea of having to explain what had happened. Better now than later. He called her, confirmed that she was home, and then set out to cross the city.

She was outside when he arrived at her place, with Cesar straining at the end of his leash, sniffing every light post in his reach. When at last the dog spotted William, he made a mad dash, and Dakota had to run to keep up.

William finally escaped Cesar's effusive greeting. He tried to meet Dakota's eye, and failed. "Thanks for watching Cesar, especially when it was so sudden."

"No problem. I'm sorry you couldn't help your sister."

He looked up. He hadn't said anything about what happened, not to anyone.

"It was in the newspapers. Well, her name wasn't, but I assumed—"

He couldn't scrape together any response. The whole world knew. He hadn't said a thing, and still everyone knew. At least he wouldn't have to bring it up at work, but it would always hang over him, his family, like a cloud. There goes the brother of that crazy Sentinel, didn't you hear, she killed a bunch of other Sentinels . . .

"Don't worry; I know you've been through a lot the past few days. Just call me when you feel like it. And when you're up to another concert, I have a few on my calendar."

"Thanks, I will." She hesitated, then reached out and hugged him. It didn't last long, but he was grateful. They exchanged smiles, hers almost as reticent as his.

He went back to his apartment, which was much more comfortable with Cesar's presence. He straightened the frames on the wall in the entryway, still askew from the day Erika had struck him. The shock of that moment when her fist hit his face now seemed so distant and small.

He sat on the couch and organized his notes, pulling more information from the books. Always his mind went back to Erika, the way a magnet wheeled to north.

Her face a mask of rage and her eyes blazing as she thrust her sword. He couldn't even remember what had upset her now; he couldn't remember if afterwards her face had held remorse. He did remember the way she reached out to him, and the upwelling of fear and anger that drew together into the lance of electric light.

He held his hand out in front of him, snapped his fingers, and produced a short flicker of flame. Then he breathed deeply, remembered the beach, the salty smell of the air, and the sound of waves throwing themselves onto the sand, one after the other. He grasped onto that swirl of emotion and snapped his fingers a second time.

The air sparked, and he heard a pop of static. It stung his skin. Not much, but enough.

What else could he do that he hadn't tried? He needed to do more than just investigate the energy transformations that he already knew, he needed to find new ways. He could break it down, make the processes more efficient, and find a way to stop Erika. Maybe even a way to save her.

He put down his pen. Was that what he wanted to do? What purpose would it serve, to go after her again? Did he still think that he could help her? He recognized the little shred of hope, that he might make her back into the sister he knew. No matter how much he told himself she was gone, a part of him refused to believe that she was beyond help.

"She stabbed you, fool. What could possibly be left, after that?"

But still, he hoped.

William spent the next few days in his office or the labs, updating a new draft of his article, pulling together lesson plans for the coming school year, and in general avoiding a deep analysis of the books Master Reese had lent. He was waiting for the *Altered Compendium*, hoping that it would bring him something more than hints and vague summaries. So far, all the information he had read was merely source material for what he already knew. Reading allusions to knowledge lost, to history unrecorded, chafed.

At least he had plenty of time to work without interruption, because most of his fellow professors preferred to do field work during the summer. He probably would have done the same, if he had been able to organize an excursion, but he was glad he had the equipment mostly to himself. He also took the opportunity to practice his energy transfers, trying to make them as efficient as possible. It didn't take long to remember his old skills. Within a couple of days, he could keep a flame from a single finger-snap burning for nearly ten seconds.

He was pushing this time even longer, a stopwatch in one hand and his other raised in front of his face when Kardell showed up, throwing open the door to his office without knocking. He jerked in surprise, burned his finger. He felt the guilt rise on his face. Kardell must have meant to catch him off guard, because she gave him a knowing look as he shook his hand.

"I thought what you could do was a secret." She leaned over his desk and peered at his finger. The intensity with which she regarded the mild burn reminded him of how she had held his hand as he lay on Reese's couch, and he felt now, as he had felt then, a sense of calm. Her certainty was a powerful force.

Then she looked right at him. "You'll recover. If you're going to play with fire, you should probably lock the door."

"Why are you here?" he asked.

She sat across from him and couldn't entirely suppress a wince. She leaned a new sword against his desk. "It's past time we find out whether or not I have one of these abilities. Erika was convinced that I do, and I'm curious."

"The collection kits are in a lab upstairs."

He stood, and she fell into step slightly behind him. "How have you been the past few days?" she asked.

"Oh—all right. I was tired at first, but I've been working a lot. How about you? That cut looks like it hurts." He regretted saying that at once. Perhaps she would prefer people ignored it. She almost certainly didn't want reminded of what Erika had done.

"It looks worse than it is. The ribs have actually been a lot more trouble."

"I'm sure that's especially true if you've still been sparring." She didn't smile as he unlocked the lab door, but her eyes gleamed.

"A brand new High Guard can't stop just because of some broken bones."

He hadn't thought that any Sentinel might match his sister's determination. Maybe she didn't know that a bad fall would mean a pierced lung, even more time recuperating. If she did know, then it was a stupid risk.

William pulled a small sample kit from a box in one of the tall storage cabinets. "Why do you do it? What could be so important that you put yourself through all that?"

The Sentinel took the package he handed her, and without bothering to read the instructions, she opened the sealed bag. "It's my job." She pricked her finger, squeezed out a drop of blood, and a second later she was handing back the blood sample. "I want to be good at it. There isn't much point in doing something if I'm not going to do it well."

Her eyebrows were raised, and he knew his thoughts must have been showing, so he busied himself labeling the sample as an excuse to keep his expression hidden. When he finished and looked up, he was a little surprised to see her still sitting there. Did she have to look at him like that?

"What are you going to do if the test shows that I do have one of these powers?"

"It's going to bring up a whole new set of questions, but at least we might have an idea of what happened to Erika."

Her eyes softened. "She isn't coming back, Harfield."

"Then what is your plan? If she's really gone and there's nothing we can do about it, why come in for these tests?"

"I have to start somewhere."

She tied her sword to her belt. William gathered his resolve. "Maybe we could just leave her alone. Let her disappear."

"I don't know if she *can* just disappear. And after all the people she's killed, I won't just let her go."

That was a dangerously unrelenting attitude. She'd already been hurt because of it, and other people, too. By her own account, William among them.

"Promise me that you'll at least try to help her," he said. "I'll give you these results and I'll tell you everything I find out, as long as you try."

Kardell stared at him, and he could almost feel the force of her disapproval. "You're asking me to help someone who killed almost an entire Response Team, who stabbed you, who killed her roommate. That isn't reasonable."

"I'm asking you to do what you can for someone who spared your life when she could have killed you."

If he'd seen anything gentle in her eyes a moment ago, it was gone. "I'll do whatever my orders allow, and with the safety of the people of Advon my priority. Which is what I always intended to do."

"That's not enough."

She started for the door. "I'm not going to make promises that I can't keep. I hope to hear from you on those results." She paused with her hand on the doorknob and looked back at him. "We have to work together, Doctor Harfield. I believe that if we don't, more people are going to die."

She closed the door behind her, leaving William with a thousand replies on the tip of his tongue and no chance to say any of them. What kind of friend was she, to refuse helping Erika? It didn't hurt anything to try.

He balled up the bits of plastic wrappings from the sample kit and threw them at the garbage can, but they bounced off the edge and scattered.

Most irritating of all, he knew he would give her the results. He didn't know how to proceed, and she always did.

William dreamed of Harfield Manor.

The trees and flowerbeds still stood neat and orderly, but he had little interest in them. He went through the landscaping quickly to the back of the property where the wilderness began. It was a misty forest, where the earth was always cool, damp, and sweet smelling. The path, no matter how often it was used, always seemed to be on the verge of being swallowed back into the forest. Just a few steps in, and the house and the gardens were gone, and William was in another world entirely.

When he said "home", this place was where his mind went, not to the halls and rooms of the house. He walked along the loamy pathway, noting the deer crossings and the bird roosts, marked by empty seed casings. His mother and grandfather had taught him how to hunt and fish in the early years, so besides his lab, the forest was the only place William felt competent, even though Erika had always been better.

He crossed several creeks, which flowed with water so clear that looking down into the creek bed was like looking through glass. He paused at a place where water spilled over an embankment and swirled into a little pool. He found a comfortable rock to sit and watch the splashing water, and waited there until Erika arrived.

She sat next to him, and without speaking shared her lunch; sandwiches on dark bread and red-fleshed blood oranges. She watched in fascination as he sent ripples out across the surface of the water, even though they were small and did not travel very far. Water was slippery, and the energy he sent through it never wanted to stay in one place. She tried to speak to him telepathically, but the attempt was fruitless. He was annoyed when she ruffled his hair and called him *little brother*.

In the distance, they heard a dreadful screeching, a howl that raised the hairs on William's arms. Erika gripped his hand, fear written across her face.

William woke, the dream lifting away from him at once. In his mind remained a connection, a filamentous thread stretching between two far-flung points, delicate and fragile but important. It must be so, there was something to it, the two things were not random, they were bound together. The odds were astronomical, but he didn't care. He put on random clothes and jogged to his office. He pulled out copies of two genetic profiles and circled.

When he was done, he sat heavily in his chair, rubbed a hand across his eyes as if he could clear away a film and see something different. Nevertheless, there it lay before him. The genetic sequences that he, Erika, and Tristan had in common were also there in the code of Kardell's monster.

020

CAMERON WOKE EARLY the first morning of the Summer Solstice Festival. She leapt into the shower and out of it as quickly as possible. Then she ate a cold breakfast, dressed in the pressed uniform hanging in the closet, and went to the door where her boots waited. When she pulled on the soft-soled shoes, her toes encountered a wad at the end. She quickly extracted her foot, upended both boots, then laughed as red confetti cascaded out onto the floor.

"Weak, Armel. Weak."

She picked every piece of confetti out of her boots. As she plucked the stray bits of it off her uniform, she discovered the scraps of paper were the exact same shade of red as the fabric. She gave up and went to her closet for a new uniform, glad to find that Armel had not been clever enough to sabotage her extras.

She found the instigator of the prank out on the sidewalk, attempting to appear nonchalant.

"I know you can come up with better than that," she said as he fell into step beside her. He struggled to keep up, especially since she was trying to regain the time she had lost changing. Armel broke into a sweat immediately.

"It's only the first day; I'm saving up my good ideas for later in the week. Besides, I didn't want to go too far and really inconvenience you. You've been so cranky ever since your patrol, and especially after Erika. I figured you just needed some cheering up."

"I appreciate the effort, but I really am fine. Now, you better move faster if you want to talk to me; my shift starts before the High General's breakfast."

"Breakfast with my cousin, better you than me."

"How is the search for an apartment coming?" She knew Armel hadn't made much progress adjusting to his new lifestyle. His grace period within the walls of the High General's residence would end soon. If he didn't find a place to live, he would be forced into one of the dormitories in the Military Quarter.

"All the places I've looked at are too small, or too far away. I can't find a single one with parking." They paused at the gate into the Military Quarter, handed their identification to the guards, and went through.

"That's pretty normal for the budget we get. You might have to make a compromise on something. Especially the parking."

He sighed. "You know, being a normal person is a lot more difficult than I thought it would be."

She smiled at him, and then paused. She wanted to broach this subject before they got too much closer to their destination, but not so close that he did not have time to answer. "The High General wants me to take one other Sentinel along when I go back out after Erika next week. He gave me a list to pick from, and you were on it. I have to give him my answer today, and I'd like you to come with me."

He frowned. "It's not like you to wait until the last minute on stuff like this."

She had known that given enough time, Armel would talk himself out of going. Or her sister would convince him to stay. She couldn't risk letting him have time to do that. He wasn't the best fighter, but there was no one she'd rather have with her if she had to face Erika again.

"It's okay if you don't want to go; Gordon Palmroy is on the list too, and he would work."

"Like hell are you taking Gordon on some adventure instead of me. I mean, he's a nice guy and all, but he doesn't belong out there in the field. You got me; I'm in." They arrived at the side entrance of the High General's Residence, and Armel said, "Happy Solstice Week. Enjoy breakfast."

"Happy Solstice Week. You better have something better planned for tomorrow."

He waved as the door shut behind her, and she went down the hall to the Master of the High Guard's office. Thea Clemens had replaced Andrew West in the position with some reluctance, which was considered the proper way to approach the job.

Her uniform was impeccable, and she kept her gray-streaked hair twisted at the back of her head. In her second week, she had changed the training schedule. The High Guards practiced in smaller groups but with a higher frequency, so that their sparring had greater variety and more time opened up for the mentoring of new recruits. Of the five pinned on the same day as Cameron, only she and one other remained.

"You're the left hand guard today, Kardell. For your first day on personal guard, remember that you are the last line of defense. All the usual rules about speaking to no one but the High General remain. Don't let him distract you, he's been very chatty. We bumped up the threat potential a point yesterday due to the heightened tensions in the north, and he has a meeting in the afternoon with some of the officers who have expressed dissenting opinions over his handling of the situation, so be particularly wary. He wants to personally get a feeling for how tense things are within the Sentinels." Furrows appeared between her eyebrows. She didn't approve. "The High General also needs your decision on who you plan to take with you in your pursuit of former High Guard Harfield."

"I've decided on Armel, ma'am."

Her frown deepened. She didn't approve of that, either. "That is all. Go relieve Morran."

Cameron saluted and left the office, then climbed up to the top floor, counting all one hundred and fifteen stairs along the way. Eric Morran stood to the right of Sean Ellis's bedroom door, partnered with High Guard Lin on the left.

The change in guards occurred without ceremony, just a salute and an alteration in position. High Guard Morran left with the slightly stiff gait of someone who had been standing in one place all night, the price of pulling duty while Sean Ellis slept.

Cameron's feet fit within the impressions left in the carpet by his boots, with over an inch to spare in many places. She had never thought of herself as a small person, but she was easily the shortest of the High Guards, who tended to rise to heights of six feet or more. She guessed that a longer reach was a significant asset, and only her speed made up for those inches she lacked.

After a few moments, she settled into the waiting stance used by the High Guards, with squared shoulders, well-rooted legs, and a gaze that never rested. Fifteen minutes after Cameron's duty began, the High General exited his room. He wore his dress uniform, with all its glinting awards, and his posture said he knew he looked magnificent.

He paid little attention to either of his guards. He grabbed an orange from a bowl on the coffee table, then strolled around the room while he peeled away the skin, staring at the art and books as if the space was still unfamiliar. He dropped the peel into a garbage can in the corner and jerked his head to indicate he was leaving. He then pulled open the door, eliciting a sigh from Lin. She and Cameron quickly moved to keep up with Sean Ellis's long strides. He chewed a segment of orange, swallowed, then looked over his shoulder at Cameron.

"Are you enjoying that reprieve, Kardell?"

Cameron stepped forward to open a door for him. How would Erika tell her to answer? "Yes, sir, I am grateful."

"It was one hell of a disaster. Fortunately for you, Master Reese is convinced that your potential far outweighs any mistakes you might have made that day. That scar will scare off any potential assassins, at least."

"Yes, sir, I hope so."

One eyebrow arched. "Was that a joke, Kardell?"

She kept her face expressionless, a skill she had refined to perfection while the cut was healing. "No, sir, I was merely agreeing with you." She stepped forward to open the door to the formal breakfast room.

The roomful of Seat Members rose to its feet as Sean Ellis entered, then sat along with him. The two High Guards became shadows near the wall behind his chair. Cameron watched and listened, not for the words spoken as much as the tone.

Seat Member Harfield was at the table, not far from the High General. He and Doctor Harfield were nearly identical, which made the cunning gleam in his bright green eyes startling. His gaze flicked from one person to another as they spoke, and the false smile he gave in response to the conversation around him was well practiced. If he had lost any sleep over his daughter's unfortunate actions, it didn't show.

They talked and talked, with a strange mixture of polite restraint and competitive jockeying. Every politician wanted the High General's attention, yet none of them dared let it show. Once Cameron understood how the maneuvering worked, she was able to pick out who did well and who failed utterly. More importantly, she could tell who was the most desperate, and therefore the most dangerous.

Seat Member Harfield seemed to have less respect than most, but more skill. If he'd tutored Erika, it was no wonder she'd been so good at knowing just what to say.

The High General had hardly eaten more than five mouthfuls when an aide gave the signal. "Ladies and gentlemen, I must move on. Good luck in your sessions this afternoon."

They scrambled to the second floor for the next meeting, and the High General focused his chatter on Lin while they walked. Her responses were terse and so uninteresting that eventually he gave up. They arrived at the conference room before he had an opportunity to pester Cameron again.

The room was full of advisors. An engineer gave a long presentation about relying more heavily on hydroelectric dams for power, although Cameron thought he underestimated the lack of infrastructure for building them.

When Sean Ellis suggested that they raise the wages and increase recruitment for wind turbine engineers, an economist argued that the money was not available. A general scoffed that if access to power was not stabilized, then they would have to prepare for the expense of war, which would be much greater. A fight broke out which soon enveloped the entire table, and it went on for some time before Sean Ellis stood. This was enough to quiet them all.

"Keep your heads, people. Cotarion has survived greater challenges. There are solutions here, but we won't get anywhere saying they're impossible; unless of course it has been attempted and failed, in which case, I give you permission to call each other fools. The next person who mentions war in this room besides myself will be fired on the spot. Now, please continue, if you can be civil about it."

They carried on for the rest of the morning with presentations that Cameron didn't have the knowledge to follow, while aides came and went with messages for the High General in a steady stream.

Eventually, Sean Ellis left for lunch with representatives from manufacturers of ceramic-ware around Cotarion. Cameron's feet hurt, her stomach rumbled, and she missed the challenge of perimeter duty, particularly as she stood listening to arguments for lifting the restrictions on importing foreign clays.

After lunch, High Guard Brecht replaced High Guard Lin, and Sean Ellis shook off the swarm of aides so he could walk to Braydon Hall in peace. Two of the peripheral High Guards joined them as they crossed the Military Quarter. The air was heavy, and black-bottomed clouds rumbled over the city. The low hills beyond Advon, visible between brick buildings, were obscured slightly by the rain already falling in the distance.

The peripheral guards peeled away once they entered the building. Sean Ellis griped at High Guard Brecht that none of the other guards made him walk so slowly when they were in front of him. It seemed Sean Ellis's way of relaxing between meetings. He shuffled a green apple back and forth between his hands as they went.

When Brecht opened the door into the Map Room, all the officers were already present and waiting. They greeted the High General with silence and glares. Cameron stayed close as Sean Ellis went to the side of the table furthest from the entry, with the banks of windows at his back.

Brecht closed the door. Sean Ellis's first bite of the apple was louder than the click of the latch. He chewed while the officers watched him. At last, he swallowed. "As we discussed a few days ago, the situation in the north has grown more tenuous over the past few weeks. Sentinels on The Ring have noticed the dissent spreading from the isolated villages into towns along the main road. It's dangerous to fly the flag of Cotarion in the mountains, so even those cities that remain loyal have drawn down the colors for fear of what their neighbors will do. Last week, secessionists attacked one of my Sentinels on patrol. This situation is coming to a head, and I don't know what side any of you will fall on."

The room was silent. Cameron scanned the faces around the table. She saw anger, courage, and shades of fear, but she didn't see any sign that these men and women were prepared to pledge their undying loyalty. She remained as still as possible.

Sean Ellis's teeth cracked through the skin and flesh of the apple again. He chewed, swallowed, and then smiled. "Well, I suppose at least you aren't liars. However, if it comes to war—which I hope it does not, but if war cannot be helped—I will not have people at my back who are disloyal. I understand that most of you grew up in the north and that you sympathize with their struggles, but I don't want to lose your skills merely because the quality of life in some areas has fallen. I am working to restore power and protection to all people in Cotarion, and I hope that you will work with me to amend the wrongs committed by my uncle."

The man across the table took a sharp breath. "Yes, Major O'Shea? Is there a problem?"

All the eyes in the room should have turned to the man being questioned, but instead everyone kept a steady gaze on the wall opposite them.

The Major squared his shoulders and clasped his hands behind his back. "Sir, my family lost their farm to a governor run rampant, and this is after two years without power other than what they've managed to provide on their own. No Sentinels were ever sent to protect them in spite of their pleas. This is not law; this is not the order promised by our nation."

"With too few men and too little power, what would you have me do, Major?" The pause stretched too long, and Sean Ellis brought his fist down on the edge of the table hard enough to rattle the glass and send the markers skittering a few centimeters away from their original positions. "Major, I have asked a question and I await your answer. Do not forget who I am."

The Major's eyes burned, and Cameron's hand didn't waver from the hilt of her father's sword. She hoped that she wouldn't be called on to protect the High General; she did not want to strike a man wearing the red uniform.

"You are not *my* High General! You stole this job from a worthy man, who was willing to compromise, who was willing to try! You are nothing but a warmonger, and I won't follow you."

Sean Ellis dropped the apple, leapt onto the edge of the table, drew a gun from the belt at his waist, and balanced there with every eye on him. His finger was firm on the trigger. The officers to either side of the Major leaned away. Cameron glanced over at High Guard Brecht. Her partner remained where he was, attentive, his jaw tense.

"Major O'Shea, I find you guilty of treason. If you have last words, I recommend you get them over with now."

"You know what is happening. Cotarion is falling to pieces; it cannot last, but you will hold onto it until there's nothing left, until every last bit of power is drained, until every person rises up against you, and then you'll hide behind the red uniforms who still fight and die—"

The High General's finger moved, the trigger clicked, the hammer fell, the gun went off. Everyone at the table flinched. Major O'Shea dropped with a strangled cry of pain. Not a fatal wound.

Cameron's pulse raced; her scar itched with the memory of a blade.

Sean Ellis walked across the table. Cameron, moving to fulfill her duties, leapt up beside him. Potential enemies surrounded him.

The High General stopped at the edge, poised on his toes over O'Shea, who lay on the ground with a hand to his shoulder, breathing raggedly. Cameron did not often take the trouble to record things in her memory, but she etched the defiance on that man's pale face into her mind.

Sean Ellis dropped to the floor, Cameron at his side. He planted one foot to either side of O'Shea, then drew a dagger from his boot, dropped to one knee, and plunged the short blade into the Major's chest. He at least had the decency to put it straight through the man's heart.

Cameron glanced around the room and saw nothing now but shock. They were all fools, to choose this path without seeing this result. Had Armel VI really allowed this disloyalty to fester, or was this a response to the change in leadership?

Sean Ellis stood and spoke in a cool voice, "You will all commit your loyalty to the service of Cotarion, and to me. Otherwise, you will leave Advon before sunrise tomorrow, and never return. My uncle Armel might have tolerated your treason, but I will not. If you rebel, I will crush you. Cotarion will remain whole. Now, go."

They fled as fast as they could without breaking into a run. When they were gone, the High General held out an open palm to Cameron. She stared in confusion before he snapped, "Your cleaning cloth, before I drip any more blood on the rug. Thank you." He paused while he wiped down his dagger. "That went much worse than I hoped."

"O'Shea has talked of the mountain regions seceding for a long time, sir," Brecht said, and Cameron was impressed with how evenly he spoke considering the powerful smell of blood in the room. Did summary executions happen regularly? Her skin felt strange, too cold in some places, too hot in others.

"Well, I doubt I'll see any of them again, but at least that's done. Now, let's go find someone to clean up. I have another meeting here in a few days, and I'm probably going to catch hell for staining this carpet."

Cameron strode along in the High General's wake for the last few hours of her shift, pushing aside all the stray thoughts that threatened her concentration. At last, her replacement arrived, and she turned to go, but Sean Ellis stopped her. He told the other two guards to leave the office. He gestured at the chair across from him, and she sat as he began signing his way through a stack of papers on the desk.

"You've had an eventful first day on personal guard. I don't often have to deal with treasonous behavior. I understand that your recent experiences might have made it unpleasant for you, so I appreciate your level-headedness under the circumstances."

She was not sure what kind of a response was required, so she nodded and said, "Sir," allowing him to interpret it as he liked.

"I doubted you after Erika Harfield's escape, but I'm beginning to think that you genuinely couldn't help what happened. If you can finish the job, I will be convinced."

"I will do my best, sir."

He glanced up from the papers. "It's a relief, after a day listening to false promises, to hear someone who avows no more than their best. That said, I do expect you to put an end to this mess. While you're at it, I need you to report back to me on just how far this secession talk has gone."

"Yes, sir."

"You may go now. Send my guards back in."

She stood and saluted, but he held up his hand to stop her once more. "By the way, it's in regulation 26–2.3."

"I don't understand, sir."

He looked up, his eyes bright. "That's the article which states that the High General may execute anyone under his command without trial, when said person commits an act of treason or speaks direct words of treason. I just thought you might like to know."

"I see, sir."

He went back to signing papers. "Now go, before you end up pulling a double shift."

She did leave, and went straight to practice. She should have had trouble concentrating, but her focus was as good as ever. She spent most of the session using just one hand, something she hadn't done in a while, so she lost a few matches, but the challenge kept her mind occupied.

She walked home alone. Armel's day had ended hours before. She went up the rickety stairs to her apartment and exchanged a brief greeting with a neighbor she passed.

She found the book of regulations on her shelf, and she opened it to the place Sean Ellis had mentioned. She read it through a few times, seeking a place where he might have gone too far and broken the code, but it wasn't there. Such severe punishment might have fallen out of favor, but it was legal.

O'Shea's expression hovered in her mind. She had seen fear, but also certainty. Of what, she didn't know. She wanted to wipe it away, to fulfill her duties without doubt or question, but she couldn't dismiss it. Killing a man for his dissent, without a trial, said a great deal to her about how Sean Ellis used power. She didn't like it.

Of course, would she have acted any differently under the circumstances? Faced with turmoil within and without, the High General had taken a short and certain path to getting rid of the dissent within the Sentinels so he could focus on Cotarion. No one would speak against him again after hearing what happened to O'Shea.

She shut the book, changed out of her uniform, and ate a quick dinner. She didn't know everything. She hadn't predicted that Erika would harm William. She hadn't seen the relationship beginning between Armel and Owena. Maybe the High General knew things that she did not.

Cameron let it go.

021

WILLIAM STARED AT the sheet of genetic markers. It looked the same as it always did. No matter how many times he ran the beast's blood, the same circles were always there. Like some horrible join-the-dots puzzle that only spelled 'monster'.

Time to move on, to test Melanie and Kardell, to learn something new . . .

His phone rang, and he absently picked up the receiver. "Hello?"

"Your etiquette has not improved."

"Sorry Dad, I'm a little distracted."

"I got you a seat at the High General's Solstice Feast. I hope you will remember how to behave between now and then."

William dropped the papers on his desk. "That's three days from now. I made plans weeks ago."

"You'll have to cancel."

So much for good manners. "Can you at least get a seat for my girlfriend?"

"No. I'll be sending some clothes to you tomorrow evening. Arrive early. Try not to say anything foolish during the meal."

William hung up the phone, dread in his stomach. Dakota would be disappointed, and he wished he could say he'd put up more of a fight. Worst of all was the little twinge of relief that he wouldn't have to spend an entire evening with her, trying to come up with the right things to say.

He slouched down the hall to her office and peeked around the open door to where she sat refining one of her lectures. Her headphones were on, and she tapped out complicated rhythms on her desk with her pen. As he approached, she looked up at him and pulled the headphones down around her neck.

William swallowed. "I have bad news. My father wants me to go to the High General's Solstice Feast."

She was disappointed, even he could see that, but she rallied rapidly. "That's too bad, but I understand after what happened to Erika that he would want you to be there." Her expression seemed brittle, her smile forced. "In that case, though, I'll just go ahead and give you this."

Dakota opened a drawer in her desk and pulled out a wrapped gift, just the size and heft of a book. William unwrapped it, wishing that he had just stayed in his office, or that he had something to give her.

Myths from Bleak Days was emblazoned on the cover in gold. It was a finely bound copy, and he smiled at her as well as he could.

"I noticed that you read your copy a lot, and it was looking a little worn out—"

"Thank you, Dakota. It's really nice."

She poked him gently. "I think you're pretty much the only adult I know who reads fairy tales. It's a bit dorky, even for a scientist."

"You never know what you might learn from this book," he said. Especially when it turned out the monsters were real.

She kissed him, and smiled again. He promised he would see her later and went back down the hall to his own office. He put the book on his desk, and resisted the urge to pull out the test results again. He wondered what Erika would have told him to do.

The clothes for the Solstice Feast were delivered by an assistant. William tried to puzzle out what his father had in mind as he studied the pale yellow button-up shirt with a mandarin collar, rust-orange summer jacket, and gray pants. Even shoes and socks had been included. He considered rejecting the ensemble and dressing himself, but a survey of his closet turned up nothing that would be appropriate for such a formal event. In fact, he would have been hard pressed to dress himself for a casual morning wedding. He had no choice but to wear what had been provided.

He spent the morning with Dakota, attempting to make up for canceling their evening plans. They strolled around Advon, admiring the banners and buntings fluttering over the streets, and visiting stalls in some of the squares. She bought a paper bag full of fried sweet-dough studded with spicy pepper and coated in sugar, which was pleasantly crisp on the exterior and soft and fluffy on the inside.

They sat for some time on the edge of a fountain, drinking iced coffee and carrying on a surprisingly pleasant conversation. William had expected annoyance, but instead she was more engaging than she had been in a long time. He endeavored to be at ease and was partially successful, even though a large part of his mind was still on that monster and the code it shared with him. It was just a small scattering of markers. He probably had many more in common with that ant crawling across the concrete. However, when he thought about what had happened to Erika, he felt chilled.

He still procrastinated over running Mel's sample, even more so Kardell's. He wasn't sure he wanted to know anything more. Of course, he would have to get around to it eventually.

Dakota cleared her throat next to him, gently, and he realized he had fallen into silence.

"I'm sorry," he said, even as she waved away the apology.

"Don't worry about it. But you probably will want to get home; you'll need to leave soon." She stood, extended her hand to him, and he laced his fingers with hers. They wove around bare-footed kids slinging homemade paper water-bombs on the sidewalks.

William felt bad to have been so unenthusiastic about his plans with Dakota. He'd never had a date to the Solstice Feast before, so he had usually avoided it entirely. Of all the holidays, it was perhaps the most awkward for anyone without a date.

He decided to try harder. He might have fun if he did.

They kissed at her front door, and she smiled at him, her eyes bright. He squeezed her hand before they separated and walked home under the streamer-bedecked trees.

His anxiety resurfaced as he dressed. Erika would have known what to expect from the evening, would have understood what their father was trying to achieve, but William only knew that he could look forward to further maneuvering and manipulation. He suspected, now that Harfield Manor was nothing more than ashes, that his father's constant talk of getting it back had been a ruse to get William's cooperation. If that had been a primary goal, there should be little point in him going to this party tonight.

He looked at himself in the mirror, narrowed his eyes, and muttered, "You have control over your own life, you know. Just because he tells you to do something doesn't mean you have to comply." However, he didn't quite believe it when he was wearing clothes picked by someone else, going to a party where he didn't belong.

An hour later, he arrived at a makeshift parking lot in the forests southeast of Advon and parked next to a shallow creek. He stepped out of his car and found the air much cooler than it had been in the city. A thrush called nearby, and a squirrel barked overhead. Sunlight slanted down through the forest canopy, speckling shadows with golden light as the afternoon moved into evening. The air smelled of loam and leaves.

What a strange location for a feast. Of course, it was probably more appropriate to the Summer Solstice than the middle of Main Street. The origins of the holiday were rather wild, after all.

A wooden bridge arced over the creek, connecting the parking lot to a path flanked by lanterns, delicate glass orbs that hung from tree branches and glowed with candlelight. He paused on the bridge and spotted the flash of a trout. As he lingered there, a couple came up, and the man peered over his shoulder.

"See, Owena, I told you I should have brought my poles." William looked up at a squarely built, dark-haired young man. The younger Armel. Standing next to him was a tall, willowy woman. Something in the curve of her hands and the height of her posture suggested she danced. William did not belong within a hundred yards of such a perfect pair.

They both smiled. Armel said, "You're William Harfield, right? Erika said that you like to fish."

"It's been a while since I had a chance, but yes."

"Then you should go with me sometime; almost nobody wants to fish with me anymore. Owena, this is Doctor William Harfield, Erika's brother; William, this is Owena Kardell, my girlfriend. I think you know her older sister, Cameron."

William shook hands with the young woman and his brain stumbled a little as it tried to put her together with Sentinel Kardell. The extremity of their differences was perhaps emphasized by the fact that Owena wore a fluttery dress, but he had never seen Cameron display even a hint of the bubbly, warm friendliness currently exuded by her sister.

"We're half sisters," Owena said, as if reading William's thoughts.

"It's very nice to meet you."

Armel's memory for names must be impressive, considering the infrequency of their meetings. William was in the company of someone much more socially adept than he was and decided that he would stay nearby if he could. Armel gestured that they should move on down the path, and William was glad to be included in the sweep of his hand.

"So, where do you normally go angling?"

"Mostly in the northwest, when I was still a student. I haven't done much of it since then." William sensed that Armel was an enthusiast and knew the conversation could easily drift into the technical aspects of the hobby.

"When I get back from whatever Cameron's mission is, you will come fishing with me." Owena nudged Armel with an elbow, and he amended, "After I've spent some time catching up with my girlfriend. So, have you ever been to one of these parties before?" William shook his head, and Armel grinned. "Excellent! Owena hasn't, either; you're both in for a treat, as long as you can keep away from anyone who tries to talk business."

As Armel outlined his personal technique for keeping away from said attempts to 'talk business', the path opened out onto a clearing set for the feast. A tent-like structure had been formed by lashing together saplings as a frame for strips of fiery orange silk. One long table stood at the far end of this tent, set for twelve. Smaller round tables sat in front of it, draped in yellow linen and decorated with lanterns and flowers.

In the center of the clearing, where the cover of tree branches gave way to open sky, an enormous pile of logs stood for the bonfire. Tucked back into the trees, William saw clusters of lanterns over smaller groupings of chairs. It was an interesting array; a meshing of the formality that came with a High General's feast and the more casual atmosphere of the Summer Solstice.

With fifteen minutes until the feast began, William, Armel, and Owena wandered among the tables, looking for their name cards. Armel went for the round tables closest to the head table, and found his place right away, with Owena's name next to his. William eventually spotted his tag, at a table near the center of the tent.

Armel glanced around at the people starting to arrive, lifted one of the tags from his table, and with a mischievous grin, he rushed over and swapped it out with William's.

"Isn't there a lot of political, you know, importance to where people sit at these things?" William asked.

"Sure, but I don't really give a shit." He ignored a look from Owena at his use of language. "By rights, I should be up at the long table. But I'm not, so I'm going to sit with whomever I want." He dropped the tag on the table to the left of his seat, grabbed a bottle of wine from a nearby bucket of ice, and filled their three glasses.

"Tonight, William-brother-of-Erika, you are going to party with me, and there is no party like an Armel party. Now, for our first game, Cameron is on perimeter patrol until the start of the festivities. Last person to spot her has to do something embarrassing, which I'll come up with in the meantime."

"So you can give yourself something easy if you lose?" Owena said. "No way."

"What do you suggest, dearest?"

While they debated, William looked around, sipped the wine, which hinted at pears, and smiled. This evening had potential.

Then he spotted Cameron striding toward them, looking almost as severe as he'd last seen her. Owena and Armel were still debating the rules when they saw her. Even Sentinel Kardell's closest friend looked cowed by her expression.

When she was near enough to be heard while speaking quietly, she said, "The High General noticed that you've repositioned some of his guests. He doesn't like that very much."

Armel forced a smile, but it was edged with annoyance. "I'll gladly move closer to the back with Doctor Harfield if that would make him feel better."

Cameron shook her head, her expression softening just a little, but not much. "He said he won't make any one move, but he doesn't want to see it happen again. You know how these things are. Just try to remember this isn't your father's party anymore." She nodded at William. "Doctor Harfield. You look very nice, Owena. I'll see you all later."

She swept away, weaving through guests trying to find their places, and vanished into the dark forest. They were all very quiet until Armel sighed, "Well, that game is over, with no clear loser. Suggestions?"

"I will never understand her." The words burst out of William before he remembered who he was standing with. His face reddened.

Then Owena said, with a wry smile on her lips, "Neither will I."

"She's not that complicated," Armel said. "She tells the truth. It takes some getting used to, but it's better than the people who lie to you because they're telling you what you want to hear. She has never let me down, not once. So, I'm going to listen to her, try not to make too many more waves, and get back to our games."

The certainty with which Armel spoke would have been enough to sway someone who had never met Cameron. William had, and found her personality abrasive, her attitude unyielding, and when considering her single-minded pursuit of his sister, he could not bring himself to like her.

Yet Armel's words reminded him of when he had lain in an unfamiliar place, in pain, afraid, and she had held his hand. He had felt protected. Every moment since then, she had confused him more, but maybe there was something to Armel's words.

"So, for our next game, I challenge you each to find five people who are already intoxicated, must be verified by the other two players, no overlaps, first one to five wins. This shouldn't take long; I've already got two."

022

CAMERON HEARD SEAT Member Harfield's discussion over dinner. William wouldn't be nearly so cheerful if he knew the plans being laid for his future. She could ignore the promise she'd made to Erika. It had, after all, been drawn out of her at sword-point. And the professor, as a grown adult, ought to be able to fend for himself.

If they forced the choice on him, at this party, in a public way, that wasn't fair. Seat Member Harfield had set up the situation to make sure William had the least possible leverage. William deserved to know what was coming.

Cameron's shift ended with dinner, and she went in search of William. She found him near Armel and Owena, laughing, his face pink. He sobered quickly when he saw her approaching. The way his smile fell was a little insulting.

Armel exchanged a few jests with Cameron to cover for the sudden fall in joviality. She frowned at the number of people jostling around. What she had to say was sensitive. Then the band started up a new song. It would be awkward, but alternatives were sparse.

"Doctor Harfield," she said, "would you like to go dance?"

He frowned, and stared into the woods over her shoulder. His mind seemed very far away as he answered, "Yes."

She grabbed his arm and pulled him to the dance floor, hoping she was doing the right thing.

They did not begin smoothly. William seemed afraid to take her hand, terrified to touch her waist, and unsure about her sword. Cameron allowed them both a few moments to fall into step before she began.

"Your father wants you on the High General's Council."

William's attention snapped to the present. He laughed, all nerves. "That's insane. There's no way he actually thinks I could do a job like that."

"I'm sure he'll make the argument that you'll have resources working for the High General that you wouldn't have otherwise. Freedoms that you will never have working at Gates."

They made a complicated series of passes between the other couples. Cameron watched William's face as he considered. If his father thought to make that argument, he would be tempted to accept the job offer. As they came back together, moving a little more comfortably than before, Cameron said, "If it comes up, I suggest you think hard about what you really want. Don't let them manipulate you as easily as I did in Brook's Cove."

William smiled, though the joke was at his expense. "I've never said no to my father before. Not without Erika."

Cameron tightened her grip on his hand just before they launched into a series of complicated turns that gave them little time to speak. They moved easily through the other couples now. William had lost any signs of self-consciousness as he thought about the choice he faced. He wasn't afraid of her as long as his mind was occupied.

"You don't have to do anything you don't want to, Harfield," Cameron said when she finally had a chance. William raised his eyebrows and glanced at her sword, at the pin on her scarlet jacket.

"I think we all have to do things we'd rather not, sometimes."

Cameron held back her response. She wished she could say what she knew about Sean Ellis, make William understand the danger he might be in if he took the job. Seat Member Harfield might be masterful at hiding his emotions, but his son lacked that skill, and his temper around someone like the High General—nothing good could come of it.

If only she could say that without risking her career.

They completed the last turn, and while the other dancers broke apart to applaud the good work of the band, Cameron leaned into William, bringing her lips up to his ear. William, surprised, automatically began to pull away, but she clamped a hand around his arm to keep him in place.

"If you take the job, be careful. He's dangerous."

She withdrew slightly, but kept a grip on his arm. He met her gaze, seemed to be trying to read the extent of her meaning. If he knew her better, maybe he would trust her, but under the circumstances she couldn't do any more.

William nodded, and she released him. Then she smiled. Before he could say anything, she slipped away into the crowd around the dance floor.

One quick circuit, then maybe she would go back to visit with Armel and Owena.

Cameron moved back through the people, looking on them with fresh eyes. She kept a hand on her sword to prevent it from snagging on the gauzy fabrics floating about. Cameron had never seen so many beads in all her life. A great many of them had worked free of the fabric and glinted in the dirt.

Underneath the noise of overlapping conversations, the music, and the fire, Cameron heard the unceasing sounds of the forest, the swish of leaves in a gentle breeze, the humming of cicadas, the chirruping of tree frogs near the creek. The ground was cleared of plants, rocks and sticks, but there was still earth and moss below her feet. Only the ground under the dining tables and the dance floor had been swept flat.

She moved through the people, listened to them speak. Now and then, she drew a stare. Eyes held on her scar, which was still bright pink, except at the very ends where it had begun to pale.

A man stood at the edge of the dance floor. He paid little attention to the dancers, even though the current song was rowdy, and most of the crowd laughed and clapped in time with the music. His dress was indistinguishable from the other men except for a burr caught on his sleeve. Cameron sidled a little closer. At some point he had been deeper in the woods, because no bushes of that type stood near the clearing.

It was not enough to sound an alert, but she kept his location in mind and looked back to him regularly.

A few minutes later, he raised his hand to smooth his hair, throwing his elbow up high as he did. He stepped away from the dance floor. At the same time a couple on Cameron's opposite side, near the edge of the woods, also disengaged from their embrace and moved towards the bonfire. Meanwhile, near the path that led from the parking area, another man turned from his conversation with the young woman tending the bar there. He stumbled into the underbrush with an exaggerated drunken sway.

Cameron moved as well, looking for her fellow High Guards. Vincent was far to her right, halfway between the band and the bar. He had been on duty since before dawn and was mostly staring at the glowing red embers rising up into the sky from the fire. Cameron dared not break away for long enough to go get his attention. High Guard Lin was by the bonfire, looking sharp, and Cameron caught her eye.

Cameron brushed the middle finger of her right hand over her left eyebrow to signal that she had noted a potential threat, possibly serious but unconfirmed. Lin tugged at the cuff of her sleeve. *Where.*

Cameron flicked her eyes at the man who had signaled, then the couple, then where the too-drunk man had staggered off.

Lin followed her gaze to each one. She brushed the shoulder of her jacket as if ridding it of dirt, the signal encompassing a range of meanings from *Carry on* to *Hold steady.*

Cameron gathered from the context that she was to keep sight of her marks. Then Lin turned and moved around the bonfire, out of Cameron's sight.

The couple split up between the dance floor and the bonfire. The young man, who had a heavily hooked nose, crossed in front of Cameron, going toward the bar where the too-drunk man had begun. He passed just behind where Armel stood with her sister.

Her friend was not her responsibility tonight. She had to defend the High General.

The hook-nosed man didn't glance at Armel, which was suspicious, because his voice and his laugh pierced through all other conversation. The man stopped at the bar and ordered a drink, then stood there with one finger tapping the side of his glass.

The woman stayed on the other side of the bonfire and paused just on the edge of one cluster of guests, melding in with the group. Unlike most of the other women at the party, she didn't wear much jewelry. The dress was right, but the tailoring should have been better. The group she joined didn't welcome her, either, and she made no effort to join their chatter.

The man who had signaled walked more slowly around the dance floor. Cameron kept just short of level with him. He made a wide turn around the bonfire. To follow him, Cameron would have to put the hook-nosed man at her back, and he was well placed if Armel was his target.

Carry on, Lin had indicated, so she stayed with the man still moving.

The young woman passed out of Cameron's sight behind the bonfire as the man who'd made the signal rounded it, and Sean Ellis came into sight, surrounded by Seat Members. The Master of the High Guard stood over his right shoulder and High Guard Anais over the left.

Behind them all was High Guard Lin, her eyes sharp. To the left was William with his father, talking quietly well away from the main body of supplicants.

Then the man Cameron had followed across the party was joined by a Seat Member, an older man from one of the southern regions. High Guard Lin's lips thinned with annoyance and she glared, certain that Cameron had made a mistake. Yet the young woman appeared now from the other side of the bonfire and slipped closer to Sean Ellis, behind the Harfields.

Cameron stood just outside a closing net.

Someone screamed over Cameron's right shoulder, beyond the tables—where the too-drunk man had gone, perhaps? Every head turned, and even High Guards Lin and Anais glanced for just a moment. Cameron's left hand closed on the hilt of her father's blade.

The man who had made the signal reached under his jacket. When his hand came out, he held an impossibly small firearm.

Cameron moved. She was halfway through her sweeping draw when she heard a gun crack over her left shoulder, where she knew Armel stood. She didn't flinch, didn't let her mind consider what might be happening there. She couldn't change it. But she could deal with what was in front of her.

Her first sweep took off the hand that held the gun. A swift second blow removed the man's head. The balance of her father's sword was right in her hand. The Seat Member had started to turn as the man beside him fell. Cameron slammed her hilt into his temple, dropping him to the ground.

She had never fully turned away from Sean Ellis, so she saw Master of the High Guard Clemens push the High General down. The young woman pushed through the crowd and raised another small firearm. Her first shot dropped High Guard Anais, and shouts filled the air.

From back in the forest came a soft sound, like an exhalation. A dark object arced through the air overhead, sending down a cascade of leaves as it ripped through tree branches. It landed in the bonfire with a dull thud.

Cameron moved into the gap left by High Guard Anais, could see the woman's finger tightening on the trigger again as she took aim at Sean Ellis, who was being pushed away by the Master of the High Guard.

The bonfire erupted, sending flames high into the sky as white-hot logs burst out and streaked through the crowd. The assassin flinched as an ember struck the side of her face, causing her second shot to waver and strike the ground. Heat washed across them all, and light flared as Cameron's sword swept out again and brought the woman down.

Two more High Guards moved in to shield Sean Ellis and remove him from danger. High Guard Lin dashed for the forest from which the canister of accelerant had flown, but she stumbled and fell, bleeding from one thigh. Although she hadn't heard a shot, Cameron was certain a gun had wounded Lin. The weapon must have excellent accuracy for the wielder to hide in the brilliantly lit forest and still make the target. Cameron ran for the forest in Lin's place.

She felt a presence at her side and recognized William Harfield before she lashed out at him. His hand brushed the edge of her jacket.

"You were on fire," he shouted in her ear. "Also, I can see where the gun went off."

She glanced down at the blackened edge of her uniform, looked up at his face, saw the shock in his eyes, but also something familiar. It was the same steadiness she had always counted on from Erika. She took his hand and pulled him along behind her. It was better than running blind.

As she went into the trees, William jerked and Cameron ducked down, pulling him with her. She heard a high-pitched whistle and saw leaves fall along the path of a bullet fired at them. It went just over their heads. She had missed the sound and flash of the gun firing, but he had seen it.

William pointed with a surprisingly steady hand, a little farther to the left than Cameron had been headed. He said quietly, "Thirty meters, maybe a little less." With that guidance, Cameron saw the figure, a small and slender shadow, stumbling through the undergrowth, hands working on a rifle. Cameron dropped William's hand and dashed forward, in a race now with this assassin's quick fingers.

She closed in just as the enemy clacked a bullet into the chamber. The only thing that saved Cameron was the length of the barrel. She dropped to her knees, hooked the rifle with the curve of her sword, and slid the weapon high. Metal scraped on metal, and the gun went off right next to Cameron's ear.

The hooded woman was fast enough to draw a smaller pistol, but Cameron leapt back onto her feet and took the last step to get in range. Then her opponent let out a tight-lipped curse in a language Cameron recognized but had never heard in Cotarion. The woman was from Varcove.

Cameron twisted her strike and slapped the woman's wrist with the flat of her blade, and then kicked her down to the ground. With the point of the sword at the sniper's face, Cameron said, "Who are you?" The Varcovian words were rough on her tongue, but good enough to be understood.

Footsteps behind her. It had to be Harfield; he scraped his left heel when he walked. She needed to have a conversation with him about approaching her from behind.

The woman's eyes went wide. From this close, it was easy to see that they were the same color as Cameron's. The assassin could easily have passed for her aunt. She was certainly from Varcove like Cameron's father.

The woman's lips parted instinctively to respond to her native language, but then she clamped her mouth shut. Cameron saw her hand flash down to her boot. Cameron would have stopped her before she grasped the throwing knife, but a gun went off next to her, the bullet catching the woman in the chest.

Cameron spun around, bringing her weapon halfway up. William stood by her. He held the woman's dropped pistol in his hands. The brilliance of the bonfire was behind him, and his face was in shadow, but she could still see the white of his eyes.

She wiped her blade with a cloth from her pocket and returned it to the scabbard, while he knelt and put the pistol down on the ground with shaking hands.

"Damn it Harfield, you should not have done that. I had it." She confirmed the woman was dead, and then picked up her fallen weapons.

"I didn't know. I saw the knife, and I thought . . . " He ran a hand through his hair as he looked down at the dead woman.

"My sword was in her face. I couldn't have been safer." Hot fury rose up, surprisingly strong, riding on the waves of adrenaline still coursing through her. She fought it down. Anger wouldn't help.

"How did you know where the shots were coming from?" She ensured that both of the firearms were safe to carry and that the rifle was unloaded. Neither of them was like any weapon she had ever trained on. They operated smoothly in her hands.

William finally brought his gaze up to Cameron. "I could see the burst of energy when the gun went off."

"That's handy. Come on, we need to get back and check in."

"Are we just going to leave her here?"

Concern for the body of an assassin he'd shot? William Harfield was a strange man. "I'll send someone back for the body. Now, let's go."

William didn't need help to navigate the forest; even in the strange, slanting shadows, he kept his feet clear of grasping roots and rocks. He walked so close that his feet caught her heels a few times. He apologized profusely, but she didn't tell him to walk farther away. Once again, she had dragged him into trouble he wasn't trained to deal with. It had seemed necessary at the time, but she was certain Erika's request had included, unspoken, *For the love of God, don't put him in a position where he feels it necessary to shoot somebody.*

They stepped back into the light and chaos. The assassins had done well creating distractions from their primary attacks. Most people were still either on the ground, or milling around in confusion.

High Guard Lin stood where the bullet had stopped her, shouting orders while leaning on one guest for support as a medic bandaged her leg. It was the most Cameron had ever heard her fellow High Guard speak.

There were not nearly enough medics to go around. Many guests had moved to the tables and were helping the injured there.

Cameron did not see Armel or Owena. She spotted a cluster of scarlet uniforms beyond the tent, mostly high-ranking Sentinels who stood speaking with their heads close together. Blood splashed the ground all around where Sean Ellis had been standing.

High Guard Lin flashed a grimacing smile at Cameron. "You got the bastard who shot me?"

"With Doctor Harfield's help. The body is in the woods, and I retrieved her weapons. Where am I needed?"

"The boss wants to see you. Or he wants you close enough to kill anything that gets within three feet of him." She glanced over Cameron's shoulder at William. "You should probably leave your boyfriend here, though."

William finally stepped back from her with a burst of nervous laughter. She turned to him. She had to be quick. "Thank you. I probably would have been shot without your help." She pressed her lips together. She did not know any words that might help him. Before tonight, she had never killed a person, either. "I'll meet with you again as soon as I can."

She turned and left him.

She went upstream to the rally point, where the slanting roof and windows of a log house looked out on the surrounding forest. It was part of the High General's property along with the grounds downstream where the feast had been; it was familiar to Cameron because it had always been Armel's favorite place to go fishing on long weekends. She passed through heavy front gates, where her identification was checked, even though she was expected. High Guard Morran stopped her again at the front door. He looked ruffled as he let her pass.

Inside, every light was on, and no feet but her own tread on the hardwood floors. She went through the expansive entryway, where the dark of night pressed up against the windows, and down a narrow hall to the interior rooms. She found Sean Ellis in one of the safe rooms, along with the Master of the High Guard, High Guards Vincent and Wells, and Armel.

The High General looked surprisingly placid. He stood when she entered, and she barely finished her salute before he reached out to take her right hand. She thought he meant to shake it, but instead he spread her palm flat against his hand, keeping his eyes on her face. Then he smiled, a cold upturning of his lips.

"A little bit of a tremor, but slight. I think you are in the proper career path, High Guard Kardell. Wells, go get a towel or something so she can clean up a bit. And a fresh uniform, while you're at it. I want her at my right hand for the remainder of the night while a few of you get some rest." He sat down again and watched as his commands were followed.

Clemens spoke. "Sir, Kardell needs rest just as much as any of us, perhaps more. She killed two assassins, chased a third . . . "

"If you are trying to dissuade me by pointing out how Kardell almost single-handedly saved my life tonight, then I would suggest a different tactic."

"High Guard Anais died protecting you."

"Very noble of him and a sacrifice I appreciate. But she saw the threat before anyone else did, and neutralized it while the rest of you were still trying to find your weapons."

This was not entirely true; Cameron had just moved a little faster, been a little more prepared.

"At least let her shower," Clemens said. "She shouldn't have to spend the rest of the night caked in blood."

Sean Ellis shrugged. "I can concede on that point. You heard her, Kardell, but I want you back here in fifteen minutes."

Cameron, knowing the size of the house, trotted down the halls to the High Guards' Quarters. She passed the unfortunate Wells who was returning with the towels and new uniform. She explained the change in orders without breaking her stride.

When she removed her jacket, she was surprised to see just how much of the edge had burned. William could not have put it out with that single, gentle brush of his hand. He must have used his powers to do it. She wouldn't have believed it if she hadn't seen the flame he made. What else could he do?

The blood was fresh and washed away easily. Cameron dried her hair as well as she could, and then brushed it back even though it was still damp. A clean uniform replaced the old. She didn't exactly feel fresh as she tied her sword back on, but she could last the night.

Only the stony-faced Master of the High Guard was still in the safe room with Sean Ellis and Armel when Cameron returned. Former High General Armel was not there, and she understood the distress on her friend's face. She assumed that if anything had happened to Owena, Armel would probably look more upset.

She took up position at the High General's shoulder, but he waved a hand to indicate that she should stand at the side of the room, across from the door. " I want your eyes on the entrance. Besides, I have questions, and I don't like talking to someone who's standing behind me." Cameron moved as told, and when she was in position, Sean Ellis continued, "Tell me what you saw."

She reviewed the events of the past forty-five minutes as concisely as possible, every movement still fresh in her mind. Sean Ellis absorbed the narrative without interrupting. As she concluded, he sat back and folded his hands behind his head.

"So, the sniper was from Varcove?"

"I believe so, sir."

"And yet you think one of the assassins was walking up to me with Seat Member Hill. Are you certain that this was not merely incidental?"

"I can't be sure, but they were close together, closer than strangers usually like to walk."

Sean Ellis raised his eyebrows. "You weren't certain, but you hit Seat Member Hill on the side of the head, anyway."

"I thought, at that point, that it was best to be safe."

Armel leaned forward in his chair and growled, "I don't care about Hill. I want to know what happened to my dad." He looked at his cousin, then to Clemens, who looked away at once, and at last to Cameron. "Come on, Cam, did you see him?"

The Master of the High Guard gave her a warning look that was not difficult to interpret. Cameron wished she had not, because that told her why the former High General was not there.

"I didn't see him," she said, and knew that her voice was too quiet, too gentle, and that Armel had known her long enough to understand. The High Guard had been spread too thin to offer protection to anyone besides Sean Ellis, and the elder Armel would have been an easy target. She remembered that first scream. It had been more than just a distraction.

Armel sat back again, his face white. Sean Ellis put a hand on his cousin's knee. "I'll find out who did this," he said.

For a moment, Armel's expression cleared, and Cameron saw a cold fury there. "I know who did this," he said, his voice quiet but clear. "It was you."

023

WILLIAM REMEMBERED THE warm glow he had felt after a few glasses of wine, how easy it was to get along with Armel and Owena. The music had sounded good. He had danced with Cameron Kardell, and he hadn't minded. In fact, for two whole minutes of the dance he had felt lighter. She looked entirely different when she smiled.

He remembered the chaos all around as guns had fired. He had seen Cameron flying over the earth, her face awash in brilliant light and flecked with blood. He had not been able to look away, so he had watched her raise her sword, saw it glint and gleam, saw every part of her body move as she cut.

He remembered Master Reese's words. *She's an instrument.* What he had meant, William understood, was *weapon.*

He remembered she had turned away, and he had seen the licks of flame eating rapidly at her coat, and something had moved him forward. He had reached out and pulled the energy out of the fire, extinguishing it. Then he had seen the flash in the woods, and knew it was a light invisible to everyone else. Her hand had closed around his. She had drawn him into the forest and he had followed.

He remembered picking up the fallen pistol, and that he had turned the safety on. His ears had roared with the sounds of shouting and fire burning. Cameron had said something he did not understand. The metal was cold in his hands.

He did not remember switching the safety off. He had seen Tristan practice with throwing knives, once, knew how fast they flew, how they stuck and quivered in the targets. The thud they made as they sank deep into the block of wood. When he saw the woman reach for the knife in her boot, he had fired.

He remembered that, but he still did not believe it.

Then he remembered Cameron had shouted at him, and he didn't understand why she was angry. He had only been trying to help her.

He slept the entire day after the Solstice and was upset that he woke as the sun set. The last thing he wanted was to spend the night alone with his thoughts.

He took Cesar on a walk. His feet carried him to Dakota's house and up to the front door. She was home, and as she stood in front of him, he felt numb. His mind went blank, which was not so bad.

"I was worried," she said and reached to the table by her door. She showed him that day's newspaper. The front page, horrifyingly enough, was splashed with the words "Assassination at High General's Feast." He stood in the doorway and read the whole thing. It was a surprisingly long article, considering the reporter seemed to know very little besides the fact that former High General Armel was dead.

"I met Armel, the younger one, last night," William said at last. "He was really nice to me."

"You weren't close to any of it, I hope."

William's skin went cold, and he couldn't speak. Finally, Dakota said, "You know, I learn more about what's happening in your life from the papers than you."

"I'm sorry," he said. "Dakota, I just—I can't." What could he possibly say about Erika, about what he could do, about what he had done? He didn't want her to know he had killed someone. He wanted to pretend it hadn't happened.

She stood on her toes and kissed his cheek. "I'll see you around, Doctor Harfield." Then she closed the door.

He walked for a little while longer, feeling relieved and bereft all at once. Maybe he should have tried harder. He should have found something to say.

He went to his office, then, and found the blood sample he had taken from Kardell, and he went down to Whir with it. It was time to be certain.

He had fed in the sample and was listening to all the hums and buzzes as the machine worked, when Tristan appeared at his side. His cousin was like a ghost. Cameron was the opposite of a ghost, more than merely alive. Once he had thought it easy to compare them. They were both strong, fast, and skilled with edged things, but they were not the same at all.

"You've had another couple of interesting days, haven't you?" Tristan lounged against the wall. He always looked like he belonged, no matter where he was.

"I think Dakota just broke up with me," William said.

Tristan laughed. "Yes, she did."

"I think I killed someone last night."

This time he didn't laugh. "Want to talk about it?"

"I don't even want to think about it." He folded his arms over his chest. "I was protecting Cameron, I think. It was stupid."

"Yeah, I'd say that's pretty dumb, but you've done stuff for much dumber reasons than that." Then he laughed again.

"It's not funny," William snapped.

"If you saw it from my side, you would laugh, too. "

"If you're going to be cryptic, then please shut up."

Tristan leaned over the machines. "Are you finally running Kardell's profile thingy?"

"Yes."

"Good. Working is good. I think you're going to be okay." He returned to stand in front of William and clapped him on one shoulder. "Just remember, your intentions were pure. You came to the aid of your fellow man. Woman. It was stupid, but it was noble, and that's more than I can say about half the stuff that I've done." His silver eyes lit up with pride. "I found that book you asked about. You can come over to my place, have a drink or two while you're waiting on this to get done. Melanie is pulling a shift tonight, so I don't have anything better to do."

"You know, you aren't as bad as you make people think you are."

Tristan scowled, but it was half-hearted. "I am pretty awful, but I'm trying."

William went to the lab the next morning and picked up the results from Whir. He found a copy of his own code in his lab, and went to one of the larger rooms down the hall to work.

He rolled two chalkboards across from each other at the far end of the room, in front of the banks of windows. He attached the papers to them with magnets, Cameron's on one, his on the other. Sets of red circles had already marked his papers; he started up in the top left corner of his board, located each circle on the first page, and then turned to the coordinating sheet on Cameron's results. He knew the markers he was looking for and their positions on the paper by heart, but he wanted to be careful. He started circling.

He went back and forth from one board to the other, over and over, for more than an hour. Finally, he put a cap on the pen and spun both of the boards so that they were lined up next to each other. He stared for a long time, running his hands through his hair, then uncapping and re-capping the pen. He walked in front of the boards, staring at them from every angle, until the little red circles seemed to float in front of his eyes even when he looked away.

He ran back to his office, picked up Erika and Tristan's old results as well, and pinned them up on two new boards. He pulled a chair up in front of the massive wall of results and sat there staring at them for a long time, his chin propped up in his hands.

That was how Cameron found him. She opened and closed the door quietly and smiled slightly when he glanced over at her. The skin under her eyes was dark, her pace slower than usual. Had she had slept at all since the feast? She picked up a chair as she crossed the room, sat it next to his, and sank into it. Her eyes moved across the boards for a few minutes.

"You ran the test?" she asked.

He nodded. She looked over all the circles a few minutes longer. "They're the same, aren't they?"

"You have the markers I theorized are connected to an ability, yes."

She didn't appear shocked by this, but then he had seen no surprise the evening before, either. If she were going to show surprise, that would have been the time. "Then it was me. I did something to Erika; I changed her. But I don't even know how it happened!" She dropped her forehead into her hands, and groaned.

"It doesn't seem possible," William said.

He raised his hands and let a flicker of electricity jump from one to the other. It was getting easier, although it didn't come as naturally as the flames. If he could do that, why couldn't Cameron alter genetic code?

He paced in front of the boards again. "If Erika triggered your ability, then there must be something in your mind preventing you from using it. A block of some sort. That's well outside of my knowledge base, so let's focus on the mechanics."

He spun one of the blackboards around to the blank side. Papers broke free of their magnets and cascaded to the floor. He ignored the mess and wrote. "Everything requires energy. My theory is that because the focus of my ability is to alter energy, I can see it and control it. Erika needed to draw energy, too. I could see it happening, but she wasn't aware of it. The process happened on a subconscious level for her. I'm absolutely certain that to make the changes in code like we're talking about, you would require ambient energy, probably a lot." He turned back to see if Cameron followed, but she still had her head down. When he paused, she looked up.

"Harfield, I haven't often been in over my head, but just now I'm getting there. If you wouldn't mind keeping it simple, I would appreciate that."

He put down the chalk, dusted off his hands, and went back to his chair. "I'm sorry. I get carried away, and this information—

Cameron, Erika has been hoping to find someone else like us for years now. It changes everything." He paused. "What is it that's bothering you, besides, well, this?"

"Let's see. Besides finding out that I have some kind of magical powers which I unknowingly used to destroy your sister, yesterday— no, the day before that—I prevented an assassination attempt, my best friend's father was murdered, and Armel now believes things that are going to get him killed. In three days, I still have to go out and somehow find whatever is left of Erika, and stop her. I don't know where she could be, or what she can do."

She stopped and rubbed her temples. "I didn't come here to tell you about my problems. I came to see how you're doing."

He shrugged. "I'm trying not to think about it, to be honest with you."

She turned back to him and studied him hard, though her eyes were bleary from lack of sleep. "Tristan told me you and your girlfriend broke up yesterday. Why?"

"I don't know how to talk about any of this. I don't know how to feel about any of it. I don't think I *can* feel anything about it right now. I should be angry with you. I should be horrified at what happened at the feast." He tried to put to words exactly what it was. "It's all on hold. Everything is hanging above my head, just waiting to fall on me whenever we figure out how to save Erika, or she's really gone. Until then, I don't think I can deal with anything else."

The Sentinel looked at him now the same way she had looked when she was speaking about the position on the High General's Council. It was not as intense as her usual stare, but still attentive.

"Maybe that's okay, for now."

The silence hung there for a moment, and they both looked back at the boards, with all the red circles. "What about you?" William finally asked.

"I know that I acted as I should have. If I hadn't, Sean Ellis would be dead, and Cotarion would be in chaos, without a clear leader at a time when some areas are talking about secession. But I've seen a lot of people die recently."

Her eyes cleared a little and she sat straighter. "The funeral is tomorrow. I need to go rest." She got to her feet and extended her right hand to him. When he took it, she shook his firmly. "I won't see you again before I leave Advon, but I'd like you to keep thinking about all of this. I might call you for help at some point."

"I'll do my best. Be careful out there. And just, try to help her, if you can." He walked with Cameron to the door and felt that he should say something else. Nothing that came to mind seemed right, so he said nothing at all.

The good thing, William thought as he stood outside of the High General's office, was that recent events made a meeting with Sean Ellis seem small. This was nothing compared with facing down a furious Erika, or running into the trees looking for an assassin with a long-range rifle.

For some reason his palms were still sweating.

He tried to smile at the High Guards standing outside the door, but they stood as stiff as statues. He turned away from them to study the painting on the wall, a depiction of Armel I defeating the bandits who had once plagued the Bluestone River Valley. It was one of the seminal events in Cotarion's formation.

Armel I couldn't have been wearing such a brilliantly red cape, the bandits certainly didn't look so ghoulish, and the clouds had never parted to cast light only on the man who would be the first High General of Cotarion. However, what were paintings for if they depicted things precisely as they were? William studied the face of that first Armel, trying to find features similar to the progeny he had met, but Armel VII was entirely different.

He heard a door open behind him, and he turned to see Sean Ellis standing there. He was taller than William had realized, and appeared particularly imposing dressed in black.

"High General Ellis, thank you for inviting me here." The words came out faster than he had intended, but at least they were the right ones.

The High General stepped closer and nodded at the painting. "Are you learning anything interesting?"

"Either people once dressed very impractically, or painters wish that they did. And neither you nor your cousin appears to have much in common with your great-great-great-great grandfather."

"Very true, although if you've read all the stories associated with the first Armel, it's fairly obvious he's more invention than fact. Now, as for familial resemblance, it would seem that you Harfields are all copies. But you are not your father, or your sister for that matter. Are you?"

"No, High General. Sir." He felt that this was probably not going well, but Sean Ellis revealed nothing.

"Come on into the office; I'd like you to look at a problem for me."

William followed, keeping his mouth shut now, because he didn't trust himself. He was already regretting what he had said thus far.

Cameron's words kept running through his head. *He's dangerous.* Sean Ellis sat behind an enormous polished desk, and William took the chair across from him.

"I am surrounded by clever people, Doctor Harfield. People so clever that they can talk circles around themselves, or carry both sides of an argument at once. Now, as useful as all this can be, I'm beginning to see that I need something else to complement all that dodging about. I need a mind that cuts." Sean Ellis opened up a folder and spread a few papers out in front of William. "I'm told that you are very intelligent. If you can tell me how to solve this, then we might be getting somewhere."

This, William was comfortable with. He liked when things were on paper and he had time to think. He looked at the charts, graphs, and maps. His frown deepened as he did.

"May I ask a question?" The High General nodded and picked up a handful of almonds from a bowl on the table. "This is a layout of Cotarion's current power system, isn't it?" Sean Ellis nodded again, crunching nuts between his teeth, his eyes narrow. "And you are trying to find a way to get the current output to match the current need, correct?" Another nod. William stared for another minute. "How long does it take to manufacture and install a wind turbine?"

"A year to manufacture, six months for installation, more depending on the location."

William pulled a pen from his pocket and began to calculate. After a few minutes, he looked up and said, "With this budget, and that kind of output, at best you are looking at ten years. But nothing here accounts for the fact that Cotarion's population continues to grow at a rate of 1.1% per year."

The High General nodded, looking annoyed. "Yes, I already know that. What I need is a solution. The outer regions need power, and the sooner the better."

William wrote in the margins of one of the pages, scribbling faster as he went. After a few minutes, he forgot entirely where he was and started muttering at himself under his breath. Finally, he threw his pen down, leaned back in the chair, and once again saw Sean Ellis watching him. He cleared his throat and said, "This is going to sound a little radical . . . "

"I'm inclined to think that radical is what the situation requires."

"Instead of waiting for the grid to overload, I recommend a system of power rationing. You see, at the moment, priority is placed on the power coming into Advon, and so there is a great deal of waste here within the city; all the other larger cities, as well. Meanwhile, there are regions in the mountains that run on very little, places far from the Ring that see almost nothing at all. During the summer and winter months, when people require power the most, the amount available in the smaller towns dips the lowest. If you allot power to each area and restrict how much the larger cities use, then I think that you can get a fairer distribution of what's here until the turbines are constructed."

Sean Ellis did not pluck up another handful of almonds. "What kind of power reduction would we be looking at here in Advon, for this to work?"

"About fifty percent. Sir."

The High General laughed. William hoped that he was about to be thrown out of the office and told to never come back. "Do you realize that I would have to deal with an uprising here within the city if I did something like that? Doctor Harfield, you are as insane as your sister."

The statement struck William with all the force of a blow. He knew that his fury must show on his face, but he pulled another piece of paper in front of him and wrote some more. Then he slid the string of calculations across the table.

"These are only estimates. By which I mean, I have estimated on the low side. But these are the possible savings if all the major businesses in the city waited until half an hour after sunrise to open. Now, I'm not an economist, so I don't know the exact effects that will have, but I know the situation you are already facing, and that's what I think is possible with just one change. In some cases, this is already being implemented, but for it to be effective, you must go further. Um, High General, sir."

Sean Ellis's eyes dashed over the paper and he considered a long time before he rose to his feet. "Well, you have the job, Doctor Harfield. Your first meeting is going to take place as soon as I can get that economist and a few other experts in here."

William stood as well and tried to get a grip on every ounce of courage he possessed. "I have one requirement, sir, before I accept the position. I've spoken with the University, and I would like to continue my work there, at least part of the time."

The High General raised his angular eyebrows. "What would be the purpose of that?"

"I grew up with a full-time politician, sir. And I would like to maintain at least some connection with reality."

This earned him a genuinely amused smile. "And if I don't acquiesce to this request?"

"Then I decline your offer. With all possible respect, sir." William held his breath.

Sean Ellis laughed. "Yes, you will do very well. I will meet your conditions. Welcome to the High General's Council, Doctor Harfield."

024

CAMERON STOOD IN her parents' entry, staring first at her bootlaces, then when that became intolerable, the ceiling. Armel and Owena stood to the side, saying goodbye, or trying to convince each other that the separation wouldn't last long. Or something.

Armel had been doing so well, too. He had been admirably composed during the funeral proceedings.

When at last he collected himself enough to open the front door and go out for his bike, Owena clasped Cameron's hand, tears in her eyes.

"I wish you wouldn't take him with you."

"You've heard what he's been saying. I'll get him back safely, but not until he's stopped talking about conspiracies."

Owena wore a rare frown. "He trusts you."

"He should. You should, too." Owena's eyes lingered on the scar and Cameron sighed. "I'll return him home safely, even if it kills me. I swear."

Her sister shook her head, but the tension went out of her face. She reached out and threw her arms around Cameron. "I'd prefer it if you came home, too."

"I'll do my very best."

Her thoughts said, *Maybe you can't have both*. Owena didn't think that way. Not even after the Feast, where she had seen Armel escape assassination. If anything, that had been a reassurance. How many times had a gun gone off without killing anybody? In Owena's eyes, the odds of survival were high.

In Cameron's eyes, a few inches farther from the sniper, and she'd be dead.

Owena went out to Armel on his motorcycle. Cameron had requested plain bikes, rather than those stamped with the High General's Seal. Sean Ellis had even allowed her to swap out the awkward standard-issue revolver for one of the sleek pistols carried by the assassins. She liked it much better. She and Armel were both dressed in plain clothes, and she hoped they would pass through the difficult areas with little notice.

Armel lifted the visor of his helmet and spoke with Owena for a few more minutes, their faces close. Then they exchanged another lingering kiss. Cameron waited until Owena stepped back to start up her engine, and Armel's came to life a moment later.

The trip up to Harfield Manor took longer than it should have because Sentinels were advised to spend the nights at military outposts as much as possible, which broke the drive up into oddly sized chunks. Cameron didn't dare speak to Armel much while they were in the midst of other Sentinels, afraid of what he might say and who might hear. Other Sentinels approached regularly when they stopped, and all their expressions of condolences, which would have worn at Cameron's patience, seemed to give Armel comfort.

On the road, Armel hunched over his bike, his shoulders round. He glowered at the world with his entire body.

In four days, they arrived at the entrance to Harfield Manor. Armel whistled low, lifting up his visor to stare at the ornate filigree of the iron gates. Ferns grew to shoulder height all along the stone wall that fronted the property. Beyond the wall, ancient trees stood tall and dense, their branches dripping moss.

The morning air was cool, and a soft gray mist curled in the dips of the land. The air was fresh, earthy, with hints of cedar.

The local PSO had been investigating the fire, and their lock barred the way. Cameron dismounted with the key in her hand. She dragged the gate open, the metal groaning as it swung aside. Armel revved the engine of his bike and swept past her, tearing down the gravel lane. Cameron went back to her vehicle, drove through the gate, and locked it.

The gravel drive ended in a loop where the front entrance of the manor had once been, but the building was mostly gone. Only stone, concrete, and metal remained, their surfaces blackened by the flames. It was a sprawling skeleton surrounded by a verdant sea of wild grasses, landscaping gone feral, and the ever-present ferns.

Armel stood at the top of the stone steps, looking at the ashes beyond the threshold. Cameron cut her engine and went up to stand by him, biting back a warning not to run ahead of her. The air was still, the sun shining down on the sooty remains of the house and lifting away the mists out in the emerald forest. She could just hear the splashing of a hidden stream.

"Do you really think Erika would do this?"

"Erika as she was, no. But as she is now, she is capable of anything."

Armel's frown deepened. "What happened to her?"

Cameron finished moving her blade from her back to her waist, with her mind on all those red circles in Harfield's lab. The truth was she didn't know what it meant. "It's a long story, and one that I think William Harfield is more qualified to tell."

"Cam, don't try to feed me bullshit. I know better."

"You wouldn't believe me."

He rolled his eyes. "I already know it has to be a strange story. Erika couldn't beat you in single combat, let alone a whole team. You've been keeping too much stuff to yourself, and I really need my friend right now. So tell me."

The loneliness in the lines on his face unraveled all her reluctance. If she couldn't trust him to keep the secret, she couldn't trust anyone.

"Let's start searching, and I'll try to explain."

Cameron explained as well as she possibly could while they investigated the area immediately around the remnants of the manor. Armel's flood of questions was difficult to grapple with. She did her best to provide answers as they scoured the scrubby vegetation and the flame-blackened walls, but she didn't know much. At least it provided a good distraction from his anger.

"Are you sure Doctor Harfield didn't pull some kind of trick on you? Like an illusion or something?"

She knelt in the grass in front of some stone stairs and looked over a set of locks tossed on the ground, splinters of door still caught in the bolts. "Yes, I'm certain. The fire was real."

He was quiet for a long time, but as they finished looking around the house and started to move into the woods beyond the gardens, he said with ponderous slowness, "So, you're saying she made everyone think there was a sandstorm? And made you see her when she wasn't really there?"

The shade of the forest was cool, and great tree trunks rose up dark all around them, but sunlight cut through the canopy here and there, dappling all the verdure below. It was impossible to move through without brushing the shoulder-height fronds. "I think so."

"You know, Dad collected a ton of old texts and stories and stuff, and he knew a lot about correlating information from one text to another to figure out what was accurate and what wasn't. Something about two sources written at the same time by people with no connection to each other, I forget what that's called. But some strange stuff like what you're talking about comes up as potentially true when you do that." He stopped talking, then abruptly halted and sank down onto a log.

Cameron went and sat next to him. She put her arm around his shoulders. His head hung heavy, but he seemed to have spent all his tears with Owena.

"Sean knew the attack was coming," he said.

"You don't know that."

His eyes burned. "Of course I do. You're a fool if you don't believe it." He stared at her. "Come on, Cam. I know you haven't bought this whole loyalty and duty High Guard brainwashing. You're smarter than that. You must see how much Sean wants to get rid of any threats to his power. Why else would he have picked such an unsecure place for the Solstice Feast?"

"He was attacked, too."

"And yet he got away without a scratch. He pulled guards away from my father and me to ensure his own safety."

"It was close, more than once. If he meant it to happen, then he took a terrible risk."

Armel nodded. "You've seen how he works. He lives on risk."

Ellis had carried out an execution with his own hands, walking into the midst of his enemies to do so. She couldn't argue with this.

"Let's say he knew about the attack and allowed it to happen. That he wanted you and your father to die. But you didn't die, Armel. He can't risk coming after you again without raising suspicion. Except you're telling everyone within hearing that *he* is responsible, and he's driven out anyone who doesn't support him. No one with any power is going to stand with you. If you keep talking this way, he'll have every reason to accuse you of treason." She took a deep breath and prepared to seal her argument. "You know what it means, to lose someone you love. I know you don't want to put Owena through that. Or me."

He absorbed this and the fury lessened. "So, you think I should just sit back and keep my mouth shut?"

"Yes. In the meantime, you can look for proof. Because without that, you aren't going to get anywhere but dead." She edged close to treason herself with a suggestion like that, but she had to stop Armel from his self-destructive path. Her whispered warning to William Harfield hadn't been entirely wise, either, but she had made a promise to Erika. Her loyalties, her promises, and her duties were colliding in potentially dangerous ways.

No more swearing, no more vows.

Armel seemed to understand her, though, and he was nodding. "You're right, of course." He smiled. "You always are."

"Our current search says that I'm not." She punched his very solid shoulder and then leapt away from his retaliatory swing, which got a full grin out of him. She helped him to his feet and they turned back to the hunt for signs of Erika.

On the second day, Cameron found a scrap of fabric snagged in a blackberry bush, which might have matched the scarlet of a Sentinel's uniform a few months earlier but had faded to pink. It was to the south of the manor, the direction from which Erika would have come, so it was no help in determining where she might have gone next.

Armel cheered up somewhat, although every now and then he dropped back into solemn silence. Cameron let him speak as much or as little as he liked. She sensed that he would have liked her to talk more, but did he really need to be coddled?

On the fifth day, in the shade of towering cedar trees, Armel discovered a gleaming pin in the shape of crossed blades. It was half a mile to the northeast of Harfield Manor. Cameron marked its location carefully on the map she had drawn up. When Armel dropped it into her hand, it felt heavy. Somewhere behind her sternum, she felt a pull, like thread snagging in fabric. The pin proved that Erika had burned her childhood home to the ground. It also gave them a vague idea of where she had gone next.

The next morning they rode to the nearest post, a tiny collection of gray block buildings nestled in the foothills of the Crescent Mountains. While Armel called Owena, Cameron made her report to Sean Ellis. When she hung up the phone and could see that Armel would be a while longer, she picked up the receiver again and made a second call.

"Doctor Harfield speaking."

"It's Kardell. I just finished up at your old house yesterday. I'm sure Erika was there and then moved northwest. What have you found?"

His end of the line remained so quiet for such a long time that she wasn't certain he was still there. Then he said, "I got a letter from her."

Cameron felt that tug again in her chest. "Where did she send it from?"

"It's postmarked from Redholme. That's right along the border with Varcove."

"That's a bad area right now."

"There's more," William said. "I had to really work to read her handwriting, and it took a long time to get here; the address was barely legible. But she wrote to say she found something. It's sort of jumbled, but the basic gist is that there's a door in a rock, and there are directions, but they're written from the destination to the town, and it's sort of cryptic."

Cameron turned to a fresh page in her notes. "Tell me."

She copied it down. When William finished, he paused again. "You're going to Redholme, aren't you?"

"You better believe it," she said, and he cursed.

It took most of a month to get to the little town. The first week, they went over small roads in bad repair, dodging potholes. The real trouble struck about sixty miles before Redholme, when a group of secessionists recognized them as Sentinels in spite of their careful attention to the local dress. Their shouted insults were little more than an annoyance until one of the boys recognized Armel. For some reason, sight of the High General's cousin incensed them.

Cameron and Armel left before anyone found a large rock, and they sold the bikes in the next town up. In this part of the country, the vehicles attracted too many stares.

After that, they kept to footpaths that crisscrossed the hills. Cameron made Armel wear a hooded jacket. She took the lead and exchanged greetings with whomever they passed along the way.

They camped at night, every night, and Armel complained bitterly for the first few days about sleeping on the ground. Cameron showed him no sympathy, and he soon gave up. They skirted around towns, only stopping to restock supplies.

One evening, as they scraped the last remains of some tasteless, strangely chewy beans from the bottoms of their bowls, Armel stood, threw his bowl against a tree, and shouted, "If you didn't walk around glaring at everybody like you're imagining their heads on the tops of poles, they would never have noticed us, and we'd be done with this by now! Why the hell did you drag me out here? I haven't talked to Owena in two weeks; she probably thinks we're dead!" Then he stormed off to his sleep-roll, where he hunkered for the rest of the night.

Cameron retrieved his bowl, cleaned up the camp, and banked their fire. By the next morning, he was ready to apologize, but Cameron could see that he was still weary, and she put all her efforts into rallying his spirits for the next few days.

By the time they arrived at Redholme, Cameron was starting to think that Armel might never speak to her again. At least the journey had worn their gear enough that they no longer attracted any attention. They'd refined their story for why they were traveling until it was so uninteresting that people often had the urge to walk away before they'd even finished telling it. No one cared about a couple of kids from the low hills who were on their way to visit cousins in Varcove, and Cameron was familiar enough with their northern neighbor to answer any questions.

Cameron decided to risk letting Armel call her sister. The only phone was at the post office. Cameron carried on a long and painful dialogue with the man at the front desk so he wouldn't notice Armel's distinctive accent. She desperately wanted to ask the man if he had seen Erika drop off the letter, but she didn't dare do anything to make them stand out. A half-hour conversation with Owena, and Armel forgave all.

They stocked up at the market, and then went into the hills west of the town. There, Cameron turned to the directions Harfield had relayed.

" 'A door, a cathedral, a bed of stone, an owl's nest, a rock like a turtle, a field of cows, a town, and the rising sun ahead.' Coordinates would have been easier," Cameron muttered. Erika must have been truly lost to leave instructions like that.

"I don't know what you mean, the cow field is right over there," Armel said.

The field, as it turned out, was expansive. They spent nearly an hour walking its western border before Cameron spotted a rock the next hill over. They scrambled across the valley and up the slope, and then stood over the rock, doubtful. Armel squinted at it.

"From the west side, I guess it kind of looks like a turtle? And that's the way she would have come."

"You're standing to the north of it."

"Oh. Yes, I can see that. So west would be . . . "

"Over here," Cameron said.

"Don't give me that look. Well, from here, if that's the head . . . well, then every rock I've ever seen looks like a turtle."

Cameron scanned the steep-sided hills and the patches of woods scattered between fields. What they were looking for was probably down in a valley, where the trees were dense and the steep terrain meant both man and beast avoided walking there. She picked a likely area, and then narrowed her focus. When she saw the scruffy, gray fledgling owl perched on a dead tree branch, she started toward the ravine, and Armel followed.

The creek that sluiced through the hillside was dry, though this only made walking it easier in that their shoes did not get wet. The rocks along the bottom rolled under their feet, and the sides were slick with fallen oak leaves. Cameron scrambled along until the ravine opened up into a slightly broader valley.

Armel pointed out a grove of trees to their right, a grouping of oaks that had grown in two relatively straight lines. The interwoven branches, the grandeur of their trunks, the light filtering down through their leaves, might suggest a cathedral.

Cameron rushed forward, passing through the avenue of trees, while to the right the hillside steepened and the dirt became a wall of stone. There was a place up ahead where the rock dipped back, creating an alcove.

When she rounded the corner, her heart dropped, and Armel stopped short behind her. She let her pack fall to the ground and went forward. It was impossible to say if there had ever been a door, because all that stood there now was rubble from a rockslide.

Cameron climbed up the sides, looking for any evidence of explosives or a sign that the slide was natural. Armel sat on the ground and watched her. She even tried to move some of the stones aside, but nothing would shift besides pebbles.

Finally, she dropped back down to the grass, sat on the ground next to him. She let her head fall onto her knees. It was now Armel who reached out and rested a hand on her shoulder.

"I'm sorry," she said. "We came all this way."

"It's okay, Cam. We're trying to find one woman, who could be anywhere in Cotarion. Hell, she could be in Varcove, for all we know." He lifted away his hand. "Do you think that there was ever anything here, or do you think it was in Erika's head?"

Cameron looked up. Erika might have imagined things, or she might have misled them. There might have been a door when Erika passed through, and in the meantime, a rockslide had covered it. The fallen stones appeared fresh. On the other hand, someone might have triggered the rockslide to cover up the door. The more she turned it over, the more she thought it might be true. It was all too convenient.

That meant someone knew they were looking and that person didn't want the door found. It meant someone was watching, keeping track of them, and it brought to her mind the tattoo on the beast's ear. Her skin crawled.

"Are you all right?"

Cameron nodded and filed her suspicions away for later. "Let's look around for the rest of the afternoon, just to make sure we don't miss something. We'll camp here tonight, and then start back toward The Ring tomorrow."

"Then what?"

She shrugged. "You know me. I'll come up with something."

025

WILLIAM THREW OPEN the window in his new office. The cool air from outside helped sweep away his frustrations with the last Council Meeting. At least no one had laughed at him this time.

Only because you didn't argue with them today.

Erika would have pointed out that his new office at Gates was thanks to his esteemed position on the High General's Council. He'd finally learned how to make the system work. He had a window, he was less likely to run into Doctor Paige in the halls, and he was even teaching more advanced biology courses.

He just wished he understood how the Council worked. There was so much bickering that progress on their assigned issues seemed impossible. The only part of the job that made any sense to him were the puzzles Sean Ellis put on his desk.

The leaves in the maple just outside his window were tinged with red. In a few more weeks, the trees would all be ablaze with new color. He wondered where Sentinel Kardell and Armel were.

What could Erika be doing? He hoped she'd travelled south.

William pulled a small packet of papers out of his desk drawer. The top sheet was Erika's letter. No matter how often he read it, he didn't recognize his sister in the handwriting or the language. It was only out of habit that he glanced over it now before moving to what lay under it.

William had spent weeks copying out every letter in the fragile, hand-written pamphlet Tristan had brought him. So many times, he'd wanted to read through the crumbling pages, absorb the data within all at once, but he'd held back and handled the book gently. The night before, he'd finished his typed copy. Since then he'd read it four times.

It was called *The Altered Compendium*. It was a guidebook, written for clarity, an instruction manual for identifying and fighting The Altered, which it referred to as absolute fact rather than something of myth and fairytale. It was a note to fellow survivors, recorded by someone who wanted to ensure their continued survival. People like William were the mortal enemy.

Everything was there, perfect descriptions of what he could do, of the horror and destruction he could cause at his very worst, of the things Erika had done when she lost control. Tristan's powers were there, too, and Melanie's. They were separated out in the *Compendium* as series numbers, as if they were products.

The page he turned to was the one he thought might be Cameron's.

Series 24

Simply called 'Twenty-Fours'. The original purpose was to eliminate the dangers of previous Series numbers by altering their genetic structure, removing the ability specific to that series. It now alters genes for its own purpose.

This series requires direct contact with a subject, so distance should be maintained at all times. This can be deceptively difficult because Series 24 is equipped with enhanced physical abilities similar to Series 22, though to a lesser degree.

WARNING! Once a 24 has identified a person as a threat, it will not give up until the threat is eliminated.

He still didn't know how it worked, of course, but it meant something to see his suspicions and theories had been written down in ink so old it had almost faded away. He felt like he was drawing closer to the truth, getting nearer to certainty.

A knock at the door startled him out of his study. He laid the papers back in their drawer and locked it before calling, "Come in." He felt perhaps he was being paranoid until two High Guards filed in with High General Ellis.

The trio filled the office entirely, and William hurriedly swept some of the clutter off his desktop. His resolution to keep his Military Quarter office tidy had not extended to this one since his fellow academics found a clean desk highly suspicious.

Sean Ellis placed a newspaper in front of William.

"Turn to page six. There's an article with the heading 'Lost Village'."

Will turned through to the appointed place, and read.

Early Tuesday morning, Public Safety Officer Samuel Manning of Palisade traveled to the neighboring town of Valance. He was investigating several reports that no one living there had made contact since the evening before. The PSO discovered that Valance was empty of all citizens except those incapable of walking, including the very young and the infirm. No signs of the missing have been found, and no messages were left behind.

"Any information on the location of these people should be reported immediately to my office. In the meantime, the Palisade Safety Office will continue its investigation into these strange disappearances," Officer Manning said in a statement last night.

Sightings of the missing should be reported to the authorities immediately.

William put down the paper when he had finished reading, found an atlas on a shelf behind him, and spread the map of the Low Crescents out on his desk. When he located the town in question, he bit his tongue and struggled not to let his feelings show on his face, though he knew that he was failing. Lines from the *Compendium* filled his vision.

"That's right next to where Sentinel Kardell killed that beast." The monster that had code like theirs. If Erika was up there as he suspected, then she must be looking for answers, too. William felt a rush of foolish hope, offset by the powerful weight of the idea that Erika was responsible for the disappearance of an entire town.

"A matter which I'm increasingly curious about. I spoke with Sentinel Kardell this morning. As you might know, she is out searching for your sister. As soon as I mentioned this article, she was convinced that she should go to Valance. I wondered if you might know why."

William hesitated in the face of a direct question that he definitely didn't want to answer. "I guess she must think that Erika had something to do with it."

Sean Ellis leaned forward, and rested his elbows on the edge of William's desk. "And what do you think, Doctor Harfield?"

"I think it's possible, sir."

The High General nodded. "High Guard Kardell requested that I send you up to assist her in the search. So far I've given her whatever she's asked. However, now she wants me to send the brother of a rogue High Guard to assist in the search for said High Guard. Maybe you can explain her reasoning to me."

William remembered Cameron saying that they would have to work together to stop Erika, that he should want to stop Erika because his sister wouldn't have wanted to hurt people. However, he knew that stopping her meant she would die. He couldn't imagine, at this point, that it would end any other way. He felt the ghost of pain in his side, and wondered if fighting against that end made any sense.

"I went after Erika in Brook's Cove, thinking that I could save her. And Cameron says she wanted me to go looking, because she hoped that I would draw Erika out, which I didn't believe at the time, but, well, I've seen how she works now. She might be hoping that I can draw Erika out again, and that this time she'll be better prepared. Or maybe she thinks I'll be better prepared."

The High General frowned. "I'm not sure I'm willing to lose both a High Guard and a member of my Council. Not to mention the last remaining heir to the Armel line. It seems a heavy price to pay. But, High Guard Kardell believes that if she doesn't strike at Erika in the right way and at the right time, she'll only slip away again."

He studied William carefully. "I told her that you would meet her in the Low Crescents. I already spoke with the appropriate personnel here at the university about it. I hope, Doctor Harfield, that you will continue to prove yourself capable." He stood, and William rose to his feet as well. "The mountains are dangerous right now. Do you need help making the journey?"

"No, sir." His stomach seemed full of butterflies. Whether he was ready for it or not, it seemed that he was going to have to confront Erika again. Assuming, of course, that Cameron was right, and they would find her still in the mountains.

"Good luck."

The High General turned and left, his guards trailing behind him.

As soon as he was gone, William rushed around his office in a panic, gathering up books and papers that suddenly seemed vital. He stuffed as much as he could fit into his bag and went to his cousin's apartment.

Tristan sat at his dining table with an array of shining knives spread before him, a wrinkle in his brow as if he were gazing upon a box of fine chocolates, trying to pick just one. His silver eyes flashed up to William as he approached. Even Tristan looked troubled.

"I need your help getting to the mountains. Cameron wants me to meet her there."

"So it comes to the point," Tristan said. "Are you ready?"

"I don't think I ever will be."

Tristan's eyes went uncharacteristically distant and pensive. "Me either. But here we are. Kardell knows what Erika can do better than anyone, and she's sounded the battle cry." He focused on William again. "You've been practicing your thing, I've noticed. Can I see the lightning stuff?"

William raised his hands and held them out in front of him. He reeled in the available strands of golden light, which glowed bright now whenever he focused.

He balled the haze up tight, let his fear rise up to the surface for a moment, and released it. The sparks and cracks of electricity danced between his fingers for a full ten seconds. They petered out, leaving William feeling a little worn, which always happened when he kept the energy under tight control. The air smelled of burning ozone.

"The best tricks have always been wasted on you, Billy." Tristan's face had paled. "Well, we might have a chance, if you can do that. But just in case, I've asked Melanie to come along."

"That's probably a good idea, I hadn't considered it. I hope Kardell doesn't mind."

Tristan cleared his throat. "I'm sure she won't, since she made the suggestion. She asked me to bring along a few of my more interesting tools, as well. She said something about breaking through some doors. She sounded determined. Either she's going to save us all, or get us killed."

William sighed. "Well, I should go pack, and make sure that I have everything." He cast one last glance over Tristan's extensive collection of daggers and suppressed a shudder. He didn't have much right to judge anymore. His dreams had been full of ringing gunshots, dark blood, and Sentinel Kardell's angry face ever since the Solstice Feast. He tried not to think about it much in the light of day.

"I'll come pick you up tomorrow morning."

Back at his apartment, William looked around and felt once again overwhelmed. As he rubbed Cesar's ears, he realized he didn't know where the retriever would stay while he was gone. Dakota certainly wouldn't want to watch him this time. Maybe his father would be willing, since he was doing work for the High General.

He remembered the wild rage in his sister's eyes the last time he had seen her. Then there was the scar on Kardell's face, strange evidence of how much his sister cared for Cameron. If Erika had not, the Sentinel would have been dead on The Ring along with the rest of the Response Team.

He threw some clothes in a bag before remembering that the weather up in the Crescent Mountains would probably be cold. He dumped everything out and started over. Halfway through, he abandoned the task and went down the hall to the spare room. He pulled out his copy of the *Compendium* again and read.

SERIES 17

Called Readers. The dangers presented by this series are especially dire. Readers can scan the thoughts of others, making them a threat to security of information. Even the most strong-willed individual cannot withstand interrogation.

Can also plant suggestions and impulses, making foes of friends. In the worst reports, Readers can create mind plagues, which spread from one person to another by touch, enslaving all infected to the Reader. A Series 17 can rapidly gather an army of simple-minded followers this way.

Readers are to be destroyed upon identification.

He thought of the empty village as he packed. Had Erika hurt more people? Cameron was right when she said that Erika would not have wanted to be responsible for so much horror and destruction.

William rubbed his hands together, opened them, and watched fire dance between his fingers. He hoped it was enough.

026

THE SKIES SEETHED with dark gray clouds, where an hour before there had been washed-out blue. A chill wind swept leaves down the empty streets of Valance. Detritus piled around the tires of the sturdy vehicles favored up in the mountains.

Armel pulled his coat collar tighter around his neck. "Are you sure they're coming? I don't like the sounds of this Tristan guy."

"They still have fifteen minutes before they're late."

Armel walked back and forth across the road a few times. The set of his jaw suggested that he had more on his mind. Cameron didn't say anything. It would come soon enough.

"How is Melanie Stillwater involved in all this? The last I heard of her, she was the only thing some of the cadets enjoyed about training at Brooks Cove."

"She may have saved Doctor Harfield's life last summer. Hopefully we don't need her help, but if things get rough we'll be glad she's here."

"You must really think she's good, to be okay with her after what happened with Jake."

"That was as much Jake's fault as hers."

Armel made a sound like a bull snorting. "That's quite a forgiving attitude. Especially for you."

Cameron didn't respond. Just on the edge of hearing, she'd caught the sound of a vehicle. "I think I hear Tristan's car."

"I don't hear anything. Nice try changing the subject. You know what I think? I think—damn it, how do you do it?"

Tristan's sleek black car appeared from the east, moving fast. It stopped beside the curb in front of Armel and Cameron. Melanie leapt out first, the bobble on top of her wool hat bouncing as she walked up to them, and the ends of her pale hair fluttering around her shoulders.

"William told us the scientific name of every tree on the way here. I think my brain might have oozed out of my ears at some point." Melanie glanced around, then said in a louder voice, "This place isn't creepy at all, is it?"

William rubbed grime from the general store's window, peered inside, and then stepped quickly away. He and Armel shook hands and struck up their own conversation. Tristan sauntered up behind Melanie, cocked an eyebrow, and said, "So, what's the plan here, Cami?"

"I need you to unlock some doors for me."

Tristan followed Cameron to one of the houses while the other three stayed on the main street. With careless ease he picked the lock on a door. Hinges squealed when he pushed it open.

The inside stank of rotten food and stagnant air. A platter of petrified food sat in the middle of a rough-hewn dining table. Cameron didn't touch anything. Life in the house appeared to have simply stopped, all at once, without warning. Books lay open on tables, their pages winged out, the paper weighed down with dust.

Precious objects sat undisturbed where they had been put for display. Garments hung in closets or lay folded in drawers.

She went through a few houses while Armel, William, and Melanie walked the streets. Tristan followed her, though he cast wistful glances at the others anytime they were in sight.

A few doors were broken in, evidence the people from the neighboring villages had checked on friends and family. There should have been some evidence of theft, but every house had valuable objects sitting in plain sight.

The houses to the north were all still and undisturbed, but as they moved south through the village, some signs of chaos appeared. At first they were small things, a plate broken on the floor, a picture knocked askew; in the last few houses, they found chairs lying on their sides, bowls swiped off tabletops. Cameron made notes about the damage in each house.

When they finished the last house and stood outside the front door, she said, "I didn't see any definite sign that Erika caused this. Did you?"

Tristan grinned. "If that's what you're looking for, I'll find it. Just give me a few minutes."

He left before she could object.

The wind blew harder and colder down the main street as Cameron returned to the others. William and Armel stood close, swapping stories about their adventures. Melanie was in their circle, contributing the occasional comment and standing noticeably nearer Armel than William.

William was fighting to pull up the hoods of both his coat and his jacket when he spotted Cameron. "Did you find anything?"

"No signs of Erika, but Tristan is still looking. Something strange definitely happened here." She flipped to the diagram of the town in her notebook and reviewed her findings in the searched houses.

William's fight continued as the hood of his jacket bunched up at the back of his neck each time he pulled his coat hood up.

"Is there any good reason why all the people here would leave?" Melanie asked. "Maybe they were planning to come back."

Cameron shook her head. "By now, they would have returned and prepared the houses for winter, because buildings up here don't last without a lot of care when the weather gets bad. I don't think they left because they wanted to."

William cursed as once again his jacket hood bunched. Cameron reached over and yanked the hood down over his eyes. Armel laughed as the scientist shoved it back and stared in bewilderment at her grin.

"Doctor Harfield, it will go much better if you pull up the jacket, and then the coat, instead of both at the same time. In the Sentinels, that is called 'Order of Operations'. I believe most people call it 'Common Sense'."

As William's face flushed, Armel attempted to suppress his mirth, and said with just a hint of a chuckle, "Be nice, Cam; he's not used to your sense of humor."

Tristan slipped back into the circle, sooner than Cameron had expected. It took some effort to suppress her surprise at his appearance. "You found something?"

He jerked his head, and they all followed, glad to leave the desolate main avenue. William huffed as he finally arranged his coat to his satisfaction.

Tristan led them through the town and into the wilderness to the north. The wind was even stronger, but it rattled tree branches and dry grass rather than dusty windowpanes. The closest of the High Crescent Mountains were pale, snow-covered outlines in the sky. Tristan led them into a sheltered thicket, taking Melanie's hand when she struggled over the rocky ground.

Cameron's gaze locked onto the tree before Tristan had a chance to point to it. It was an old birch with smooth bark, so the letters were clear. They had been carved with a sharp edge and a steady hand.

Hello Cam

Cameron went up to it and raised her hand, brushing her fingers over the deep-cut message. The hands that had sliced the bark had done the same to her skin. She bunched up one hand into a tight fist, and then let her fingers fall loose again.

William caught up and stood breathlessly next to Cameron. "She knew you would come."

"Yes."

"She didn't do all this just to bring us up here." Poor William. He really wanted it to be true.

"I don't know. She might have been up here in the mountains, and the nights were getting cold. She would have seen the lights, and—she always hated being alone. So she took them with her."

William buried his hands deeper into his pockets, his shoulders pulled up tight, his head low as he stared at the ground in front of his feet. "If *The Compendium* is accurate, then that sounds possible."

Armel said, "Do you think she's still nearby? The town disappeared a whole month ago."

"If she is, it means she's been waiting for us."

Cameron pressed her lips together. "I don't want anyone to go off alone, just to be safe. And try to stay near either Tristan or me." She looked over at him. She wasn't happy about having to rely on him, but she knew that he would hear Erika's approach before she did. He smiled and winked. "We're going to follow The Ring a few miles west of here, to Palisade. I think Erika came this way to look at the doors I found last winter, and I want to go see if we can get them open."

She turned to lead them back to the ghost town.

Samuel Manning was as kind as a man in his position could afford to be. He said that he had flown the Cotarion flag over his building until a few weeks before, when the Safety Office in a nearby town was vandalized by secessionists. Cameron's hope of sleeping under a roof rather than canvas faded as he spoke.

"I know you've done your best, but we are on our own out here." Officer Manning said. He and Cameron stood in his kitchen drinking coffee while Armel made his call to Owena. "We have been for a long time. The secessionists are our neighbors, and when you only see the red uniform fly by every couple of months . . . " He shrugged. "I can never repay you for the help you gave us. I wish I could offer you a place to stay, but I can't put the whole town at risk."

Cameron's smile felt tight. "I appreciate what you've given us, considering the risk. I was only doing my job, and I didn't expect anything for doing it."

"It's a rare person who slays a monster and expects nothing. I imagine that you'll probably find an entire town, this time, and insist it was only your job."

Armel finished his call, and she was spared answering. They all gathered up their things to leave. Cameron shook Manning's hand, thanked him for the coffee, Armel's call, and keeping their vehicles. Then she led them all south of Palisade, into the forest.

The wilderness here was entirely different than it had been near Valance. The trees grew more densely, and the bushes were tall and dark. The mountainside was sluiced by small streams, which meant they had to pick their way up and down ravines.

As they scrambled up a muddy bank, William muttered under his breath, "I should know better by now than to follow you into the woods." Cameron tried to ignore it since he hadn't meant for her to hear it. Still, it stung. Her instinct had been to confront Erika alone, but she didn't have a chance of ending this without help.

Cameron took them to a good campsite she remembered from her last trip. It was sheltered from the weather by large boulders, but not too enclosed if they needed to escape in a hurry.

Cameron and Armel established the camp with efficiency born of too much practice. Tristan and Melanie perched on a rocky outcrop well out of their way, while William did a splendid job putting together his tent in almost twice the time it took the Sentinels to set up the entire camp.

Kardell then turned to Tristan. "Are you ready to give those doors a try?"

He leapt to his feet right away. William, Armel, and Melanie would probably have preferred to remain in camp, but Cameron insisted they should follow. If Erika was near, they couldn't risk separating. She led them through the tangled undergrowth as the light turned gray.

The door in the rock still gaped open, but the room beneath it was clean. Cameron's electric lantern cast light on the pile of photos, flowers, and other objects left in one corner by the people of Palisade who had lost family to the beast. Armel knelt in front of the memorials and inspected them carefully. William stayed by the stairs, and Melanie kept close to Tristan. Cameron's focus was on the doors, but she heard Armel say, "They're almost all little kids."

Tristan rapped the metal surface of the door. He ran his hands over the concrete, then he turned to the bag he had brought, and started working on the wires and charges. He placed a string of explosives on the concrete around the edge of the doorframe, his fingers pressing putty into place. Cameron stood over his shoulder with her arms crossed, watching the procedure.

"Are you sure this won't bring down the whole room?" she said at last. "I've already come across one of these doors hidden under a pile of rocks; I'd rather not end up in the same position again."

He smirked. "I'll be surprised if this does anything at all. I've never seen anything built like this in my life, and I've 'liberated' documents from some very secure places." He stood after placing the last charge. "All right everybody, let's get topside and see what happens."

Armel held them up a little, because he insisted they gather up the pile of memorials and carry them out of danger. Cameron started to object, but he said, "Cam, you've dragged me all over the place for months now, and the only thing I've asked has been the occasional phone call to the woman I love. I'm asking you to give me a few minutes to keep this stuff safe, because it's important, and it's good for you to take care of things that are important to other people." He put a stack of framed photographs in her hands.

Armel didn't just pile the memorials up when they reached the surface. He knelt on the ground and arranged everything just as carefully as it had been placed in the room below. William and

Melanie even joined in, though Will spent an unhelpfully long time staring at the photo of the smallest girl. Cameron let them get on with it and stood to the side with her senses alert for trouble.

Melanie reached over and laid a hand on William's arm. He put the photo down, cleared his throat, and moved on.

Then the ground shook, and a thunderous rumble rattled Cameron's teeth. She spun around, her hand on her hilt. Tristan's laughter rang out over the fading echoes of the blast, the small detonator in his hand.

"You're supposed to warn people before you blow something up!" William shouted.

"What fun would that be?" Tristan peeked around the door, from which a fine dust drifted like a cloud. "I'll check to make sure it's safe." He grinned at Cameron before he vanished. She clenched her teeth together. She'd known his help would come at a price, and she'd asked for it, anyway. He'd already done things that she couldn't have accomplished nearly so quickly on her own.

"He can be such an ass," William said.

Melanie rolled her eyes. "You never say that sort of thing when you need his help, I notice."

Tristan returned after little more than a minute. "We aren't going to get through like that. I don't know what's back there, but someone sure didn't want anybody to find out."

So, it really was important. It had to be, for someone to take all the trouble of constructing something so impenetrable in a place so remote. Cameron was about to say they should stay until they pried the door open, but Armel cut in before she had a chance. "We should probably go have dinner and start fresh tomorrow."

Cameron couldn't really argue when everyone else agreed with him.

Melanie and Armel made dinner with the fresh supplies from Advon, while William, Cameron, and Tristan considered their options for getting through the door. William drew up accurate schematics of the room, and Tristan filled in the details, suggesting his theories on its construction. Cameron watched and listened. They all stayed close to the fire, which provided a pocket of warmth as light faded and the air cooled even more.

When the food was passed around, Cameron and Armel both ate with gusto and appreciation, after months of dried and canned food. William, meanwhile, hardly paid any attention to what he chewed; instead poring over the drawings they had been looking at, frowning and occasionally jotting a note. Melanie sang renditions of the current popular songs in Advon at Armel's request, and William hummed along absently to the ones he knew. Cameron noticed that when William was not studying his notebook he stared at her. She didn't always know how to interpret the expressions on his face.

When they had all eaten their fill and the meal was cleared away, and just before they raised the pack of food up into a tree, Armel passed around a flask of potent apple cider. Cameron glared.

"Come on, Cam; I've been saving this stuff for weeks. Who's taking the first watch?"

"I am."

"And are you having any? Never mind, I know you aren't, because you never do. Try to relax; you're starting to make me nervous." He took a final swig, then he passed it over and she packed it away.

Armel retired to his tent shortly after that, accustomed to falling asleep early.

Cameron sat with William, who stayed awake scribbling notes well after Melanie and Tristan retired to their tent. She knew there were things she needed to say to him, about Erika and the hope he still hadn't let go of. She just didn't know how. Hadn't he seen enough to understand that his sister was gone? In spite of it all, he worked, his eyes lighting up each time he came across some new morsel of encouragement.

When at last the fire had burned so low that he had to squint at his own handwriting, Cameron said, "You should probably get some rest, Harfield."

He blinked at her. "Yes, you're right. It's just—sort of different. Out here, knowing what she's done, what that thing did to those kids."

"I'll put an end to it. Whatever it takes."

"Cameron, I'm not sure I want to find out what's behind those doors."

He would see, she was certain, how necessary it was. "You really need to get some rest."

William shut his notebook. He paused there, looking at her, the shadows on his face deep, but his eyes catching little embers from the fire. Then he went to his tent, leaving Cameron alone.

027

WHEN CAMERON STEPPED out of her tent in the morning, the leaves on the ground were rimmed in frost. Armel and William already stood getting warm over a crackling fire, curls of steam rising from the cups in their hands. Armel handed her a cup of coffee, which gave off a familiar smell. William had brought the beans from Three Sides. The heat of it seeped through her gloves and into her hands.

"We were talking about all this weird stuff that you guys can do," Armel said, always careful to include new arrivals in whatever conversation he had in progress. "It sounds a lot less crazy the way he talks about it, but then I think I've understood maybe half of the words he's using." He looked closely at Cameron. She knew that he was seeing something she could not, the interpersonal intricacies that she missed. "Do you think that there's any chance of saving Erika?"

She shook her head. "Don't you think it's a bit early for questions like that?"

"You roll out of bed sharp as a tack, and Will is two cups of coffee in. You've considered, I assume, the potential trouble when Erika does show up, and he only wants to save her, and you only want to kill her. Sorry, but that's the result we're talking about here. You're working together now because you both want to find her, but for very different reasons. So, we find her, then what?"

Cameron looked over at William, who stared into his coffee. She didn't know what he would do. She didn't think even he knew. He loved Erika, but she had stabbed him, killed so many people. He warred with himself, holding two opposing ideas equally against each other, unable to choose between them, waiting for one of them to win out.

Armel sighed. "When it comes down to it, I'll stand with Cameron. Tristan will stand with you, William, and Melanie will stand with Tristan. But based on what I've heard Erika can do, the most important thing here is that the two of you are on the same side. If you aren't, I think we all might as well pack up and go home right now."

William dragged his eyes up to her. Erika's eyes had never burned like that. Just a few months ago, his hadn't, either. He wasn't who he'd been when his sister fled Advon, and neither was Cameron. She knew that she could not stop Erika alone.

"If I can save her, I will, but it's a big 'if', Harfield."

"That's all I really want. If you'll try, then I'm with you." He smiled, and then hid his expression behind another swig of coffee. Then he walked away entirely, mumbling something about checking one of his books.

Cameron leaned closer to Armel. "Was that really necessary?"

"I trust you in all matters, Cam, except for those that involve feelings. He needed to know that you're on the same page that he is, which ultimately you are, but you have a way of saying things that comes off kind of cold. He's always been on your side, but now he knows it, and that's important for both of you."

"There are no sides. Erika killed people and we need to stop her. She's going to fight and she's going to die. To suggest otherwise is only giving him false hope."

Armel sighed and cast his eyes to the sky.

Cameron studied the damage left around the door by Tristan's explosives. She'd expected something more dramatic. Yes, chunks of concrete had been blown across the room, but the metal underneath was undamaged. The walls were lined in heavy plating, perhaps the ceiling, too. More than ever, she wanted to know what was on the other side. She fought down the urge to kick the door.

She'd seen the second monster standing on the other side. Surely five fairly intelligent people could find a way.

"Do you have anything with more power?" she asked.

"I'm afraid not. It looks impenetrable to me."

"People don't put in doors if they never want anyone to get through. That's what walls are for."

Tristan rapped against the metal surface, his eyebrows high on his forehead. "I know you can hear that. It might as well *be* a wall."

William cleared his throat from behind them, and they both turned. He stood there, an odd look on his face, and he said, "I think— I think that maybe I can open it."

He handed his coffee to Cameron as he stepped past her and put his hands against the concrete by the doorframe.

Tristan rolled his eyes. "What are you going to do, Billy, lecture it open?"

"There's power there—definitely. I'm just not sure how it's supposed to run . . . "

William stood with his hands on the door, his eyes closed, for almost two minutes. Cameron had just decided nothing was going to happen when she heard the gentle grinding of metal shuttling. The door slid into the wall.

William jumped back. Cameron pushed his coffee back into his hands, bringing her flashlight up to light the space beyond. A few strands of her hair lifted on the air that rushed out through the open door. It didn't smell stale.

She saw the shape of a hall and walls, and then she stepped forward through the door. William drew in a breath behind her. She reached out, flipped a switch on the wall, and banks of lights came on, stuttering at first, then growing so bright that she had to squint. The warning William had been about to utter died.

A plain white hall stretched out in front of her. The ceilings, the floors, the walls, the corridors that broke in from the left, were all white. She frowned. It all looked familiar.

She realized that she stood alone and looked back. William, Tristan, Armel, and Melanie all peered through the opening, wearing nearly identical expressions of trepidation.

"Are you all just going to stand there?"

Armel was the one who said, "This isn't exactly what I expected, Cam."

"Life is no fun if things happen the way you expect. Tristan goes in front, I'll be in the back, and you couldn't possibly be any safer."

"It's just—there's no dust on the floor," William said. As if a lack of dust was an obvious indicator that the place was perilous.

Cameron looked to Tristan, but even he appeared a little on edge. "I doubt that there are any people in the world more dangerous than us, and here you are afraid of a well-lit hallway. I'll go in by myself if necessary, but William, I know you want to see what's in here. Armel, I'd think you would know by now that you can trust my judgment. As for you, Tristan, well I shouldn't be surprised that you would be less than helpful when you haven't been paid a small fortune."

She looked to Melanie and there she saw, surprisingly, the person most likely to follow. The girl from the boring little fishing village, who'd heard about Advon all her life and had grasped the first opportunity to go there. She wanted to prove she was brave, which was just as good as tested bravery.

"If you wanted adventure, Mel, then this is it."

Tristan sighed as Melanie tugged him through. Armel was right behind them, and William followed, clutching his coffee.

There were doors, all of them on the left. Like the front door they had no handles, but a black panel gleamed in the wall to the right of each one. Tristan reached out and touched the first one of these black surfaces as he went by. It glowed red and gave a low tone before returning to darkness. He checked two more of them with the same result before they came to the first hallway on the left. The new corridor had a slight backwards curve to it.

William said, "I think—it looks like the arc of this hallway will take it around, and if the other door opens onto a straight hall like this one, then it will connect—what I'm saying is, it makes a semicircle."

Tristan checked another door. "Yes, thank you, very glad for your scientific expertise on the layout." Tristan kept squeezing Melanie's hand as if for reassurance. Cameron hoped he was keeping a good eye on what was in front of them, because most of her attention was on the doors they had passed. She disliked leaving them unchecked, but they didn't have time to break into each one. Armel and William talked as they went, filling in the quiet with a nervous hum.

The curve of the new hall ended in a blank wall, and William frowned. "So, not a semicircle."

They backtracked to the first corridor and followed it farther on to where it ended in another turn to the left. This hall curved back like the last one, although its turn was gentler.

Tristan carried on with his previous procedure, even though every door panel he touched produced the same result. The third door on the left, though, paused an extra moment before it beeped and turned red.

Cameron pressed her hand against it as she passed. The glassy surface turned a golden green.

A female voice drifted out of a speaker overhead, each syllable pronounced with unnatural care. "Subject Seven-Three-Five, do you require entry to Lab Nine?"

William and Armel's conversation halted. The only sound was the whisper of air through vents.

'No' wouldn't get them any farther, so Cameron saw little choice. "Yes."

The door slid back to reveal yet another white hall. This time Cameron didn't go through right away.

"It called you a 'subject'," Armel said. "And a number."

"I did hear that." They all stared at her. "None of you have to follow me if you don't want to."

Armel laughed. "I'm not going to let you go through this door by yourself. I think that's in the Sentinel Code, 'Don't let your best friend go through a door by herself when the door called her a number.' If it's not, then it definitely should be."

Air whispered with disconcerting smoothness over the back of her neck. It would be better to go alone, because she didn't know what to expect beyond the door. She would feel terrible if she led them all to their deaths, but they wouldn't get answers by standing there.

She went through with Armel behind her. The rest followed, although William's fingers drummed on the side of his cup. At the end of the hall was one more door, which she opened with another touch.

"Welcome to Lab Nine, Subject Seven-Three-Five," the words echoed.

Cameron went forward now, each step smooth and careful, as if she expected to step on a tack. It didn't look like a laboratory; not like the ones at Gates University, anyway. Tables ringed the walls; desks formed a circle a few feet in; and in the center stood a column, which supported several rows of flat, black screens. Under the screens sat consoles with angled tops, supporting the same panels that Cameron had used to open the doors.

"Why would it let you in and not me?" Tristan asked, his voice falsely hurt and genuinely worried. He had let go of Melanie's hand and was moving around the room, inspecting it carefully for any signs of danger.

William said, very slowly, "Her ability is the only one that requires activation. None of the rest of us would need to get through the door and into the room where that could be done." He went into the middle of the room and put his hand down on one of the panels. It flashed red, and he looked over to Cameron. Faced with finding out at last what she had done to Erika, she hesitated. Then she removed her blade from her belt and passed it over to Armel, who blinked in confusion.

"The first time I had this power or whatever activated, I changed Erika in a way that I don't even understand. I don't think it's safe for me to hold my weapons if there's any chance that might happen again." He took her pistol as well, but he wasn't happy about it.

"Then why risk it?"

"Because this is what we came here to do."

He shook his head. "We came to find Erika."

"This is part of finding Erika. If there are answers here, then I need to know them. And if there's any hope of helping Erika, then I need to have the ability that changed her in the first place. No matter what, I have to do this." She hoped the smile she gave him was reassuring. "I'll be fine." She made eye contact with Tristan, tried to convey with her expression what she needed from him. He winked.

She went to the same console that William had used without success. "Move back, Harfield," she said. He took one long step away from her. She glared, and he shuffled back maybe another foot.

Cameron let her hand drop down onto the glass, which glowed yellow-green. The upper screen lit up with the words "Lab Nine" before shifting to a pale blue. On it were many rows of tiny symbols. William stepped forward again, so close that his breath fogged the screen.

"It looks like a database, maybe. If all those symbols are files, then we're looking at an awful lot of information." He squinted and studied the characters, as if he might divine their meaning. Cameron reached out and touched one near the center of the screen. It expanded out into a new screen of completely different symbols.

"Um, help," William said, running a hand through his hair, his eyes wide at the shocking amount of data which appeared to be before him.

The disembodied voice spoke again, coming from the edge of the screen. "Do you require assistance, Subject Seven-Three-Five?"

"Yes. What is this place?" She turned to William and growled, "I told you to step back." This time he didn't even react. He just stood there bouncing on the balls of his feet.

"You are standing in Laboratory Nine, part of the Tertiary Center for the Preservation of the Skylark Program." William scribbled all this down, every word.

"There was a creature outside this lab almost a year ago. It was partially human. Can you tell me what it was?"

"That was a subject's unsuccessful attempt to utilize its Alteration."

Exhilarated to have a question answered, Cameron plowed on. "Are there more of them?"

The voice paused for a long time. "I'm sorry; you don't have clearance to access that information."

Cameron stopped so William could catch up, and to think about what they most needed to know. Will finished writing, flipped to a new page, scribbled down a suggestion, and held it in front of her.

Cameron took a breath, and then asked, "What am I?"

"You are Subject Seven-Three-Five in the Genetic Advancement Recovery Program."

"What does that mean?" The sound of William's pen scratching across the paper did nothing to settle her nerves.

"You were created in an attempt to refine and control the genetic enhancements introduced over two thousand years ago. You are a variation of Series 24, which was considered vital in ending the Geno Wars."

Cameron stopped because she wasn't sure she had understood all of that. William looked up to her, ran a hand through his hair, sending it askew. His face was tight.

Tristan had moved in closer. If she should behave in a way that was threatening, he would have time to intercept her before she hurt anyone. She decided to get to the point.

"Is it possible to activate these genetic enhancements here?"

The voice didn't answer right away, as if the question confused it. "Do you wish to engage the activation sequence?"

"Yes."

Cameron expected to hear instructions of some sort, but instead the panel just glowed brighter. Then a jolt ran up her arm, through her shoulder, into the back of her neck, and the inside of her skull lit up.

She pulled her hand away, but the lightness remained. She felt strange. The nervousness and anticipation of a moment before were gone. She felt the air of each breath on the back of her throat, smooth and steady. Her skin tingled slightly.

"Did it work?" William asked, the timbre of his voice now carrying layers of information that she hadn't been able to hear before now. He was impatient, he was worried, he was curious, and a little bit frightened. Cameron didn't know how to answer. There didn't seem any point in trying.

She turned, and the newly opened part of her mind evaluated her surroundings.

She looked to Armel. He was not one of them and that was good. His loyalty was not split; it belonged solely to her. His hands were tight on her weapons, concern for her safety on his face. His faith in her was powerful. He was a friend.

She moved on to Melanie. The young woman had pushed her way to Advon, and yet none of them knew who she was. Master Reese trusted her with William's life, but did that mean Cameron should extend trust as well? Cameron couldn't call her foe, but that did not make her a friend.

Tristan, on the other hand, was not to be trusted. He followed her now, and would continue to do so until the day he finally needed to make his own choices. If he decided to go against her, he could win. He was faster and stronger. She had to keep her distance.

She could also see that Tristan wasn't close enough to stop her anymore, even though he hadn't moved.

William was still speaking. She shut out the meaning in his slow words as she studied him. He was standing quite a bit closer than she'd realized. He wasn't right, somehow. Something was missing, and she knew she could fix that, was certain that she should. If she didn't, he would never reach his full potential. He was friend, perhaps second to Armel, if he could decide to trust her.

She needed her allies to be strong.

Her left hand gripped his right wrist; she placed her right palm against the side of his head, and the new part of her mind opened up. She knew what she needed to do without thinking about it. It only took a moment to access the appropriate part of her brain, a part divested of all emotion.

She felt the spaces in her mind the way she could feel the spaces in her lungs. William appeared to shimmer before her, and she understood that every cell in his body was changing. A part of her told her that she should be frightened that she could do this, but the feeling did not touch her. She looked at her own mind and found it cold and uncaring. She unraveled William's very essence, took out some pieces, then put in new ones. It was simple, and it didn't take long.

Then the bright lights went out, and Cameron stood in front of William. She took her hand away from his head, his wrist. What had she done?

A dagger flashed in front of her, and a hand pushed her away from William. A metal point cut through her jacket and her shirt, came to rest just against the skin over her heart. Tristan's silver eyes were very close to her.

William's knees buckled, and he fell to the ground, slowly enough that Melanie got to him before his head hit the floor.

Armel brought a pistol up to Tristan's head.

Everything remained like that for a moment, and then Tristan reached out, wrested the firearm from Armel's hand, and turned the barrel back at him. The point of the dagger never left Cameron's skin. She swallowed. The extra speed she had a moment before was gone, and she knew she wasn't fast enough to save both herself and Armel from Tristan.

"Please don't hurt him," she said.

Tristan smirked, his grey eyes pitiless. "You'd better pray that Will is okay, Cami." She kept her face still as he increased the pressure on the dagger, but she felt as if she had swallowed ice which had settled, unmelting, in the pit of her stomach. Erika had been an accident, but this was not. She had allowed her pursuit of answers to overwhelm her reasoning. She should have found a way to stop herself.

"He's not hurt," Melanie said softly from the floor, where she sat with William's head in her lap. "Not physically, anyway. All his signs are good."

The speaker on the screen behind Cameron let out a high-pitched tone. "Reserve power is low. Please engage primary power source."

William opened his eyes. Tristan released Cameron and pushed the pistol at her so he could help his cousin. She stayed where she was, waiting.

"What happened?" William asked as Tristan pulled him up. He didn't sway at all once he was on his feet. He raised his clenched fists, concern in the set of his brow.

When he opened his hands, his palms were filled with flames so hot that even Cameron took a step back and bumped against the screen again. Quickly he closed his fingers around the fire, and he looked to her. "What did you do to me?"

"Your code wasn't complete. I repaired it."

He opened his hands again and held them facing each other in front of his face. Flashes of lightning cracked back and forth, splitting the air. William's expression was horrified in the white light.

"Can you change me back?"

Cameron shook her head. "I can't predict what I'll do if I try again. My mind wasn't the same." William dropped his hands.

"I think I—need to go and walk." He pushed past Tristan and muttered, "I want to be alone." Then he found his path out blocked by the door to the lab.

Cameron put her hand back on the panel. "Open all the entrances to Lab Nine, and leave them open." The doors slid back, and William fled.

As soon as he was gone, Tristan, Melanie, and Armel looked to her. Now that he knew William wasn't hurt, Tristan's anger evaporated. Cameron turned away, unable to bear the questions on their faces.

"Who did this to us?" she asked.

The voice was quiet for such a long time that Cameron was not sure it would answer at all, but then it said, "I'm sorry, but you don't have clearance to access that information."

Cameron ground her teeth. "*Why* was this done to us?"

"To re-establish and further the progress made by the Skylark Program before the Geno Wars, and to implement improvements that will prevent a reoccurrence of that destruction."

Cameron stopped, sick of answers. She knew the others were still watching her, and she didn't know what they could possibly want. Mistakes lined up behind her, and yet she didn't see what she might have done differently.

She pulled off one boot, and threw it hard at the wall. The thud was satisfying. She yanked off the second and threw it, too, but then she was out of things. There was the smooth wooden surface of the desk nearby, and she held onto the anger, glad that her mind was not the clear glass it had been a minute ago. She slammed her arms into the surface, until the wood cracked and her arms flared with pain. Then she closed her eyes and lowered her head.

"Reserve power is low. Please engage primary power source."

She had changed him, and she had meant to. She had to accept that. The mind making the choice might have been a little more detached and a little quicker to act, but it had still been her.

If she accepted responsibility for what had happened to William, though, then didn't she need to shoulder the blame for Erika, as well? That was harder to answer, because she couldn't remember what had happened when Erika opened her mind.

Would William spiral out of control as Erika had? That thought rocked her, but she let it pass.

She felt Armel's hand on her shoulder. "Cam?"

"I messed that one up, I think."

His fingers tightened. "Yeah. You know, it happens to the best . . . "

There was a new tone from the lit screen, this one louder and more persistent than the last. "Proximity alert."

Cameron straightened and padded back to the controls on bare feet. She felt the cool glass under her hand again. "Show me."

The screen flickered. Was it dimmer than it had been a minute ago? She was certain that the lights in the walls were. A map flashed up on the screen, marked with topographic lines, and on it was a cluster of bright dots. She studied the terrain, tried to determine where William might be, tried to determine from the movements of the dots on the map what was happening. She remembered the secessionists, the empty village, and Erika. She cursed herself for letting William go alone. "Tristan, go find him."

"Yes, ma'am," he replied with a jaunty salute, and Cameron made another decision that she thought she might regret later. She felt the glass still cool under her palm.

"Is there enough power to run the activation sequence again?"

"Yes."

028

ALL HIS LIFE he'd been living with blinders on, able to see only what was directly in front of him, and believing that was all that existed. Now with his peripheral vision restored, the energy glowed brighter than it ever had before. It was inescapable. He could see the lines of sap trickling from the limbs of trees into the roots, he saw pale orbs where animals burrowed for the winter, and every gust of wind was a stream of light. The entire world was overlaid with golden strands that he could change into whatever form he wished.

Under all these more obvious currents, there were pockets that he had never seen before, places where a nudge would transform potential energy into kinetic action. He could see the fissures running through the ground beneath his feet. A nudge in the right place could set off a rockslide. He could move the earth.

William walked through the woods, hardly cognizant of the snow striking his face or the increasing chill in the air. He felt, urgently, the need to keep walking, to gain distance from what had just happened. No matter how fast he went, he couldn't escape those dark eyes.

The look on her face when she reached out, took his hand, and pressed a palm against the side of his head was the same expression he saw when she defended Sean Ellis, certain and calculating. He had felt his entire body go numb. Was it possible to feel anything when every strand of DNA in his body was unwound?

He walked faster, even though his throat tightened and made breathing more difficult. He felt like she was just over his shoulder, and he needed to escape that presence.

Was this how Erika had felt? Was he now following the same path?

William's feet carried him downhill, away from the lab and their camp, until he broke through the edge of the forest. He stood on the shore of a lake. Wind blew across the water unimpeded by trees and struck him with all its force. The tumultuous gray sky hung low enough to brush the tops of glacier-capped peaks ringing the opposite shore.

Snow swirled across the lake's dark surface. Finally, the rush of his thoughts and feelings coalesced into numbness. As William caught his breath and the heat of his anger wore off, he felt the icy chill of the wind and snow driving into his face. He shivered, pulled up the hood of his coat, and then turned away from the view to stare into the forest behind.

Under a yellow canopy, the tangle of limbs was dark. Caught up in his thoughts, he had not tracked how far he had walked or where he had gone. Could he find his way back through the maze of dark trunks? He remembered a few prominent rock formations, but it would be hard to recognize them from the opposite side.

The next lungful of air felt much colder than those before. He looked at his watch and tried to assign times to events. It was much later in the day than he had expected.

He shouldn't have been so careless about his surroundings. He had to focus.

Don't panic.

He took one last look at the lake, and then reluctantly stepped back into the forest. He was concerned about finding his way, but equally glad to have something to think about, something that pushed everything else into the background.

At first, the moist earth near the lake made retracing his steps easy, since he could see his footprints. Then he could pick out his passage by the snow that had been disturbed, but this sign vanished as more flakes fell. He walked quickly.

The path petered out sooner than he'd hoped. He would have to find landmarks that he hadn't bothered to observe on the way down the mountainside. He told himself once again not to panic, even though his heart fluttered in his chest. He built a pile of rocks so he would at least be able to return to this point if he should go astray.

William kept hiking up the slope. At least he knew he had gone downhill the entire way, although it also meant he now had to trek uphill, and his legs and lungs burned with the effort. The forest was heavy with evergreen rhododendron bushes and stunted pine, which meant that he had to build stacks of rocks frequently to ensure that one stack would be visible from the one before it. Weaving between tree trunks and patches of impenetrable shrubbery meant he wasn't traveling in anything close to a straight line.

The views behind him seemed to blend with what he had seen the last time he checked. So familiar, and yet not familiar enough to give him comfort.

You are getting yourself into more trouble with every step you take.

What choice did he have?

Just wait, someone will come find you.

The thought of hunkering down and waiting for Cameron or Tristan to decide that he was lost, and then find him, was too humiliating for him to contemplate long.

"If I keep going up I'll run into The Ring eventually," he said. That made him feel better.

After a few more minutes, William came across a very large and distinctive rock outcropping, and though he circled the entire thing several times, he finally had to admit that he hadn't seen it before from any angle. He clambered up the side with the shallowest angle and stood at the top, at least able to see above the rhododendrons from there.

He looked out over a thick, dark tangle of bushes punctuated by masses of rock shouldering up out of the mountain. All of it was covered by a mix of pines and brightly leaved deciduous trees, their growth stunted by the high altitude and fierce winds. In every direction, the landscape was just the same, with almost identical creeks running parallel to one another down the slope. He thought he remembered crossing at least one stream, and strongly suspected that it was more than one.

"Okay. So, I'm lost."

He had the impression that Cameron's tracking skills were good. As long as his companions didn't wait too long to start looking for him, and he didn't move any farther, he would probably be found within a couple of hours. He could survive that long, but he didn't think he would fare so well if he had to spend an unsheltered night on the mountainside.

He debated whether he should sit on top of the rock, where he had a good view and was obvious to anyone looking for him, or whether he should go back down on the ground where he had protection from the cold wind. Then heard the rustling of leaves. He turned to the source, expecting to see Cameron or Tristan.

Instead, his eyes landed on a figure that even under the best circumstances would have frozen the blood in his veins. It was a man, so pale and gaunt that William wondered how he was even on his feet, which were almost bare and blue with cold. Clothing hung on his frame in dirty tatters without any sign that repairs had been attempted. His eyes were sunken, blank.

William opened his mouth to ask if the man was lost, if he needed help, but the words stuck in his throat. In one hand the unkempt figure held a large rock. Several things came together all at once: the jagged fingernails and hair left untrimmed for weeks, the empty eyes without a trace of thought, lines from the *Compendium*. William was looking at another one of his sister's victims. This man was from the ghost town he had walked through just the day before, his mind enslaved to Erika's.

William struggled to formulate an offer to help. The man raised the rock high over his head and threw it. William dropped down, a purely instinctive movement. The rock sailed through the space where his head had been before hitting a tree trunk hard enough to make the branches quiver. A few yellow leaves drifted down.

William gathered his scattered thoughts and stared at the patterns the lichen and snow made on the gray rock right at the tip of his nose. He stood, even though he didn't know how he was going to defend himself from a mindless, rock-slinging villager. By the time he got to his feet, the first man had been joined by five more figures, all of them just as thin and ragged, all of them clutching rocks or large sticks.

He raised his hands out in front of him, trying to ignore the way they shook, and called up a rush of flames and heat. None of them flinched. When a second projectile flew at him, he managed to catch it, though such coordination was rare for him. Without giving it much thought—he was far beyond taking time to consider what he was doing in response to the current situation—he threw it back. It thudded against a skull. One assailant slumped to the ground. William's stomach rolled. Had he had just killed a person who might have been saved and returned home?

He lowered his hands, and the next projectile struck his shoulder. He stumbled back, and one foot landed on empty air. He panicked and threw himself forward. Even as his senses sparked with adrenaline and he tumbled down the rock, he knew that he had made a fatal error. Death waited for him at the bottom of his fall. When his back thudded against snow layered on top of cold, wet leaves, he stared up into the thoughtless faces of the lost villagers.

The sound that escaped from his throat was unfamiliar and inhuman, one brief burst of abject terror as he looked up at his fate. One pair of hands reached down for him. As he was pulled up, he tried to pry away the wasted fingers grasping his coat. It was his fear that brought the jolt of electricity coursing through his hands and drove the attacker to the ground in a twitching heap.

A heavy branch swung at him. He raised his arm, caught the rotting wood near his elbow. As he stumbled, he fought back with flames. He wound in every golden streamer near him, and energy swirled.

He lashed out at the closest pale face with another burst of electricity, because the smell and the screams of the burned villager were unbearable, but that pulled more of the energy than he could afford to use. Fortunately, the figures stood very close together and the sparks jumped to two others, felling them, but so many more still stood.

A rock struck the back of his head, and he dropped to his knees again, stunned. More rocks pounded his back. He lashed out with the fire that he knew so well, throwing it along the ground at the unshod feet in long streamers, keeping his eyes turned from the result.

The air around him had gone from cold to hot, and now the villagers withdrew from the flames. He pushed up to his feet and stumbled forward with fire dancing in his hands, making a path out of the smoke and ash filling the air. He heard their footsteps behind him, and then he heard the thud of a body striking the ground. He wheeled around.

A blade flashed, and he thought at first it might be Cameron. But no, the figure now cutting through the villagers was taller, thinner. Her long, light auburn braid swung around her shoulders as she moved.

William leaned against the closest tree and caught his breath while Erika made short work of his remaining attackers. When the last one fell, she turned to him and grinned, her green eyes bright. His arms and legs shook with exhaustion.

Erika stepped closer, her smile the one he remembered. "Little brother. I see you've learned a few things." She looked around at the villagers lying on the ground the same way she used to look when he caught a prize fish out of the stream behind their house. "I am sorry about that; they got away from me, but you nearly finished them off. I'm guessing that Cameron might have helped you a bit?"

"I wouldn't call it 'help', exactly." He stood straighter, pushed away from the tree. This was the moment he'd been fretting over for months now, and here he was, spent, unprepared, and apparently out of energy to worry. "Now what?"

She hitched up one shoulder, returned her sword to its scabbard. "I don't know anymore. I don't want to keep going on this way, but I can't seem to stop. What else is there for me? Either I'm alone, or I'm killing everyone I come in contact with, and as far as options go, those aren't great." She took a deep breath, and then let it out in a hiss. "Your brain is the worst. You just cannot stop thinking."

She looked at him, her smile never faltering. She was so close. The urge to go to her was just as strong as the urge to run away. "You've always liked fire best. Why is that?"

"I don't know," he said. If she went poking around in his head, would he know?

"Don't you? Well, allow me to suggest an answer. Your science, in its purest form, is as dispassionate and dry as anything gets. But you, William, you love, and yearn, and fear. Fire is physics, and it is the chaos of emotion, united. It is dangerous, and powerful, yet delicate. You must feed it to keep it going, and never let it get too close." Her face was suffused with all the love she had ever felt for him. Without thinking, he stepped nearer. "The fire, Will, is in your soul."

Stay with me. His head filled with images of their childhood, when they lived in the woods all summer. *You can help me.* She reached her hand to him, her fingers outstretched.

She almost touched him before he had the sense to stumble back. He called on the fire, held the flames between them. He feared her touch, certain that she needed contact to plant the most devastating suggestions in his mind. Otherwise, she would have already done so.

"I won't come with you. And I can't let you go."

Her laughter was a harsh, ringing thing. *Then stop me, please. It would be a relief.*

She vanished. William blinked at the empty space, then spun around. He saw her again, a little farther away, and again under the trees. She scattered her presence across his vision. It was impossible to say what was real and what was not. She must be multiplying the image of herself as *he* saw her, because every figure glowed with energy.

He pushed at the bright fissures running through the earth. The ground pitched, and cracks split the soil. Erika lost her footing and resolved into a single figure. She drew her sword and rushed at him as the earth stopped shifting.

William picked up a rock, and threw it with extra force behind it. She dodged, but it still struck her hard enough to spin her around and drive her to the ground.

He saw the pain on her face as she rose, and his heart twisted. She shook her head, a sneer on her lips. "You always lacked what it really took to fight," she said as she approached him again. "Even with your life at stake, you hesitate."

Her eyes held his, and he saw the shadows in the forest darken and stretch toward him, felt fear rise up. *Run, little brother.* He didn't move.

When she was close enough to touch, he pulled in a great ball of the golden glow. He sent a shock at her, bolstered by the fear she fed him.

The impact threw her to the ground. At first, he was afraid that he had killed her, but then he frowned. She should have known what he was going to do. She must have seen him thinking it.

"Of course I did." Erika's voice was hushed in his ear, and he turned, but not fast enough. One of her hands rested on top of his head, and he felt her mind falling over his, like shadows creeping over a landscape at dusk. His thoughts gave way before hers just as the light drew back when the sun sank.

William fought. He saw the ancient forest that was the inside of his mind. He willed it to stand firm. But darkness encroached.

At least Erika wouldn't be alone.

She gasped and let go of him. The mountainside reappeared. William reeled back, the invading darkness lifting much more slowly than it had fallen.

Erika pulled a dagger out of her shoulder. Tristan flitted through the trees, knives spinning from his hands and glinting in the air. A second struck Erika in the side, and she cried out in rage as Tristan moved closer.

Erika's eyes narrowed, and Tristan doubled over, his face pale, agony sharp in his features. He did not scream. William didn't think he could. Erika dragged Tristan by his wrist to a fallen tree.

There she drove a dagger down through their cousin's hand, sinking it deep into the tree trunk. William's courage wavered, and failed entirely when she pinned Tristan's other hand the same way. When her green eyes turned back to him, shining with fury, he backed away.

He would have to kill her if he wanted to live. He saw no other way. He gathered up all the energy around him, though there was little left nearby. The golden ribbons swirled, and he held onto the fear, wondered if he could send the shock out to hit her no matter where she was. Then he remembered the haze that surrounded her, the energy he had forbidden himself from touching because it was the very essence of life.

She reached out and moved her hands towards his head. He pulled desperately at that light. He couldn't see any other way. He reeled in the glow around her as quickly as he could.

Then her hands jerked; she screamed and stumbled. Erika wheeled around to tear the blade from Armel's hands, her back bleeding, and her rage palpable. Cameron was there, and in William's eyes, the Sentinel shone with energy, like a beacon in the dark. How long had she waited for the right moment to move in?

Cameron gripped Erika's wrist, her face showing nothing but an intense watchfulness. Erika's lips turned up in a slight smile.

"I've been waiting for you."

"You haven't been very patient." Cameron's voice was absolutely dispassionate, yet it vibrated with power. She was shining with the potential energy coiled tightly within her.

Erika twisted her wrist in Cameron's grip. "It will kill me," she whispered.

"The power is part of you now." The dark eyes flicked to William briefly. "When I take it, you will die. There is no other way."

Then she applied the energy to Erika as she had to William. His sister shimmered like a mirage. He remembered how it felt to waver between realities with Cameron the only anchor. In less than a second it was done. Cameron blinked, a few layers of ice sheeting away, the radiant power gone.

Erika's breath left her in a rush. William wasn't quick enough to catch her before she collapsed to the snow. He stumbled and fell to his knees by her side. It took all his remaining strength to gather her into his arms. Snow fell on her face, and her eyes stared up unseeing.

Cameron knelt across from him, reached out with a tenderness he hadn't known she possessed, and closed Erika's eyelids. He looked up to the Sentinel, a quake running through him. Something sharp had lodged in his chest. Cameron's expression was soft, even sad.

"I'm sorry, William." She reached out to place a hand on his shoulder, but he jerked away.

"Please don't touch me." His voice snapped out of him, laced with rage. Then he wept, the tears as cold on his face as the snow, the frigid air burning in his lungs as he gasped. Cameron stayed where she was for a moment, her hand hovering between them. Then she stood and walked away, leaving him alone with Erika.

029

THE LAB WAS dark by the time Cameron returned. She walked down the halls, put her hand against some of the door panels. They didn't even flicker. The last activation sequence must have drained the reserves, and she didn't know how to restore power, if it was even possible. All those answers William had been hoping to find were lost. She put her boots back on, picked up the notebook he had left on the floor of Lab Nine. Hopefully it would be enough.

Back at the camp, Melanie had finished healing Tristan's hands. He and William sat side by side in front of a new fire, looking equally exhausted. Armel packed up their equipment, with some help from Melanie. Cameron didn't say anything about the lab, certain that no one cared anymore.

Tristan raised his hands up. "Look, Erika gave me some amazing scars, too. We're special, you and I." She smiled, but she cast a quick glance at William to see how he bore it. The scientist appeared not to understand most of what was happening around him. He was a mess of cuts and bruises, and he hadn't attempted to brush away any of the dirt on his face or hands.

As she looked at him, she realized that she saw him differently than she had before. He stood out sharply from everything around him, as if a film had fallen over the rest of her vision. Like the world was just background. When she looked away, nothing appeared out of the ordinary. She looked over to Tristan, and she saw him the same way.

"Melanie, could you stand next to Armel for a minute?" Melanie did as she asked, though both she and Armel gave her very strange looks as she circled them, staring hard. No matter what angle Cameron looked from, Melanie was sharp, obvious, her presence impossible to ignore. Armel, meanwhile, looked just as he always had.

"I can see what you are," Cameron said at last. "I can tell when someone is Altered."

William spoke, his voice tired and flat. "It makes sense. Series 24 was made to hunt down and remove the abilities of other Altered. You would have to know when you were looking at one, wouldn't you?"

"But why now? I've never been able to see it before."

She looked back to him, but his head was turned away from her. "Your ability was never fully activated before. Erika broke through to where it was in your head, she accessed it without turning it on. That's the best that I can guess. We'll probably never know exactly what happened." He frowned, his eyebrows drawn together. Then he stood and looked down at Tristan. "Can we please go back to Advon now? I want to go home."

Cameron helped Armel carry supplies back to Tristan's car, and then the three of them left, Melanie in the driver's seat. Cameron took advantage of Samuel Manning's goodwill one more time to call to Sean Ellis and inform him that the task had been completed. The High General sounded pleased.

When she hung up, Officer Manning looked up from staring out the window at the falling snow. He said, "Secessionists or not, you can stay here tonight."

Advon was surprisingly warm on the day of their return, the sun bright, though its light was definitely the glow of autumn and not the blaze of summer. Cameron and Armel stopped first at the Military Quarter, where they turned in their written reports. Sean Ellis was too busy to hear the full debrief. Then they walked through the city to Cameron's parents' house.

Owena must have been watching by the window, because she flew out the front door when they were still halfway up the block. She hit Armel with enough force that he stumbled back a little. He buried his face in the top of Owena's head, and Cameron wondered if she would have to pry them apart. She couldn't help smiling. How she could have resented the happiness of people who so clearly loved one another?

Owena caught sight of her watching, and she let go of Armel. With joyous tears in her eyes, she bounded over to Cameron, too, and squeezed her.

"I'm really sorry about Erika, and everything."

Cameron did her best to return the hug. It was strange to her that everyone else was mourning Erika now, when in her eyes her friend had been lost months ago. She was trying to understand, had even asked Armel to explain it, but differentiating between 'hope' and 'foolishness' had become a point of contention, so she had let it drop.

Only her dad had taken enough time off work to welcome them back to Advon, so he made Cam promise to see her mom later in the week. She agreed to make room in her schedule so readily that he smiled. She was trying, as much as she could, to be human.

Cameron, Armel, and Owena all left after dinner, the couple walking with their hands intertwined and their heads close together. When Cameron turned to go to her apartment, Armel disentangled himself from Owena's embrace and ran up to punch her on the shoulder. He said, "It's not a bad thing that you're trying to spend more time with your family, but I know why you're doing it. Forget all that stuff about monsters and experiments and labs. I know you, Cam, and you're a person. Weird, yes, but I like you that way." He shrugged and smiled, and she punched him back. He and Owena went home, and so did she.

Her uniform was crisp and fresh, her boots clean, her hair a smooth, dark knot. She had not been this tidy in months, and it felt strange. She held all the pages of information she needed in her hands, and all the details in her head.

High Guard Vincent opened the door to the High General's office, and Cameron froze when she saw Sean Ellis.

His office and the High Guards at either shoulder appeared unfocused and inconsequential around him. He stood out, sharp and impossibly real from everything else, just like William, Melanie, and Tristan.

"Kardell!" he said. "I did not make room in my schedule for this so you could stand and stare at me. Sit, and tell me what you've been doing the last few months."

She moved again, although every sentence she had carefully arranged fled. She placed the packet of papers on his desk, and then struggled to bring her mind back to the task, but it was all scattered. When she spoke, she knew she sounded uncertain, the explanations disjointed. She had only uttered a few sentences when Sean Ellis raised his hand to stop her.

"Please stop speaking. Again, I 'm glad I didn't pick you for your verbal skills, because it would seem they are nonexistent. What is in your written reports will suffice for my purposes. You eliminated the threat, passed through the fire and so on." He paused, his angular eyebrows raised. "Is there something on my face?"

She averted her gaze. "No, sir."

"You've spent too much time out in the field, I think. Well, you performed so well, Kardell, that I believe you have earned a reward. As much as it pains me to release you from my personal service, I have arranged a very good slot for you in the Intelligence Corps." He slid a pile of paper across the desk at her, and then folded his hands, a knowing smile on his lips as he watched her.

Cameron's heart leapt as she turned through the pages of the transfer packet. It was what she had always wanted, exactly the kind of position she had hoped for. Field work and investigations, infiltrations and travel, unwinding secrets, tasks that would test every skill she possessed.

Very slowly, she let the edges of the papers slide against her fingers so the top page fell flat. She looked back up at the High General, and saw the way the world went hazy around him. Someone had given them these abilities: William to make fire, Melanie to erase wounds, Tristan to climb buildings, Erika to read minds. Cameron to change them all. They hadn't asked for this, and that wasn't right. This was the mystery that needed solved, more than any other, and Sean Ellis might have some kind of answer.

"High General Ellis, I would like to make a request, if you don't mind." He nodded. "I am honored by this offer. But I would prefer to remain in the High Guard. I don't think there is any better use of my skills than here."

He pulled the Intelligence Corps packet back, reached into the drawer next to him, and slid another packet of papers in front of her, with a pen resting on top. "You'll be a full member of the High Guard. It means some additional responsibilities and stipulations, but you've already proven you are capable."

She read every paragraph carefully then signed the bottom of the last page. He stood, and she rose as well. He grasped her hand tightly.

He commanded her now, even more than before. It was probably exactly what he wanted. William was his as well, and hiring Doctor Harfield had not really made a lot of sense. Yes, he knew what they were, and he was drawing them in, keeping them close.

If he was responsible for their powers, she would find out.

She woke early the next day, even though she had it off. She had grown accustomed to rising with the sun, and it was a difficult habit to break. A day stretched ahead of her, with no vitally important tasks to fill it.

She met Owena for breakfast. It was the first time in a long time they had spent any amount of time together without their parents around. They talked about Owena's plans for her occupation. She had settled into the idea of counseling, which Cameron did her best to encourage. They talked a little about Armel, although that was a strange topic because they each knew him from such different perspectives. Talking seemed to make Owena happy, so Cameron considered the breakfast a success.

When Owena had gone to class, Cameron was free again. It was past time she visited Doctor Harfield. She wouldn't tell him yet what she knew about Sean Ellis, but she needed to know if he was still pursuing answers about the origins of their abilities. Besides, her promise to Erika that she would watch out for him was still valid. The walk was not far.

She knocked on the door and waited. She heard the clacking of a dog's nails on hardwood, then the gentle padding of socked feet, and the door opened.

William stared at her for such a long time, scarcely breathing. Cesar gently pushed by and licked her hand. For just a moment, his lack of expression gave her hope. He had grown leaner in the last two weeks, but otherwise looked well, his clothing neat, his face shaved, and what she could see of his apartment was tidier than it had been the last time she had visited.

Finally, he said, "What do you want?"

"I wanted to say sorry for what I did to you."

"It's not so bad, actually. I have better control than I did before. It would have been nice to know in advance, but . . . " He shrugged. He hadn't yet met her eyes for more than a second, and was gazing into the space over her shoulder, a strange smile on his lips. "You know—I keep having this dream where you carve out my heart, and you don't even hold me down when you do it. I just lie there and let it happen. And I don't know what it means."

The air felt much colder than it had a moment before. She was starting to think that smile didn't mean what she thought it did. "Harfield . . . "

"Don't! Don't call me that. It's what you called Erika." He swallowed, "I can't stand to hear it. I can barely stand to look at you!" His knuckles were white as he gripped the doorframe, and his nostrils flared. "You killed her. You killed my sister, and I will never forget it. Please leave."

She backed away, trying to think of something to say, but he slammed the door before anything came to mind. There were no words that could undo what had been done, and his anger was not entirely unreasonable. Maybe with time, it would lessen.

And then what? she thought. What was she looking for from him? A friend to replace the one she had lost?

She went home and played a strategy game against herself, several times. She was looking at the books on her shelf for something to read when the doorbell rang. A young man stood there, dressed all in black, his hair streaked with blue dye. He did his best to look like he belonged in a hallway that smelled like cat urine. He held a large, flat box.

"Good morning, Sentinel Kardell. I am from The Cloth. One of our regular customers, Tristan Rush, requested we deliver this to you." He opened the lid, and Cameron peered cautiously inside, half-expecting venomous snakes. Instead, what she saw was a leather jacket. She was certain at least two months of her pay lay in that box.

"Did Tristan touch this at any point?"

One of the young man's eyebrows twitched up. "He said you would ask something like that. No, he gave us measurements and made certain requests. We took care of the rest."

Cameron reached out and took the box, thanked the young man for the delivery, then watched him leave. Only when he was gone did she close the door and open the box.

A note lay on top of warm, dark brown leather. She picked up the paper and unfolded it.

"Let's have more adventures sometime. But promise not to kill any more of my cousins. T."

The jacket beneath was soft in her hands, lined with scarlet. She ran her fingers over every fold and seam, checking for any signs of sabotage, but she found nothing. Finally, she pulled it on. The fit was perfect. Pockets sat in all the right places, and the cut allowed for full range of motion. She had never worn anything made just for her, and she was tempted, but taking such a gift from Tristan seemed foolhardy.

Her doorbell rang again. She'd expected the mischievous grin of the jacket-giver, but instead it was Harfield who stood in front of her, looking small. He glanced up when she opened the door, then quickly looked away to the carpet.

She held back her greeting, and anything else she might have to say to him. The silence was so deep that they could hear the mice skittering around behind the walls. Cameron was just starting to feel the itch to do something when he looked up at her again.

"We have to figure out who did this," he said.

"Yes."

"I can't do it without help. Can you?"

"No."

His eyes widened, but otherwise he hid his surprise. "Then—do you want to go to Three Sides? I have theories we can discuss." And the thought of this brought a light into his eyes, and wiped the remnants of anger off his face. Cameron kept her own expression blank as she nodded.

She tied on her sword, ensured that it was well positioned, and went out onto the streets of Advon with William.

He went along as he always did, slightly distracted by his own thoughts. Cameron walked carefully, giving room to the people wrapped in their hats and scarves. No human wanted to share space with monsters.

ACKNOWLEDGMENTS

To Mom and Dad, for loving a girl even when you didn't quite understand her, and for believing in her, even when you couldn't see what she saw.

To Matthew, for sharing my love of books, and letting me read Harry Potter to you.

To Molly, for standing up for me against all sorts of foes, and for being my friend even when I was a twerp.

To Sarah B. and Angela H., for diving into my first stories and embracing them. Never has a high school writer had a better audience.

To Sarah F. for all the writing sessions, the coffee walks, the shopping trips, the new mom commiseration, and unceasing support.

To Sarah V. for providing much-needed critique of the second draft, and embracing Cameron Kardell. I don't have to wish for our daughters to grow up in a world with powerful examples, because they already do.

To Madigan. You shaped me more than I can hope to shape you, and incredibly, this never would have happened without you. I hope that what you see in what I write is possibility.

To Sullivan. For all the smiles, and consistent naps.

To Josh. Without you, I would never have valued my dreams the way I do. Thank you for demonstrating the utmost importance of refusing to give up, no matter the obstacle.

To Erik. For finding an ember, and providing the kindling it needed to ignite. I'm serious. Shut up.

Many thanks to Kelly, for providing copy-editing skills.

The cover art for this book is everything I could have hoped, and for that I thank Josef Richardson.

WANT MORE?

Megan Morgan lives in Baltimore. She enjoys tweeting about what she had for lunch and how she writes between a job and two kids as @M3writes. On Facebook you can find her on her author page, Bright Ink Writes. She blogs advice and philosophy at brightinkblog.wordpress.com. She would love to hear from you.

Meanwhile, she's finishing *The Altered Rise*, the sequel to *The Altered Wake*, and contemplating what to call the third installment.

MORE GREAT TITLES FROM CLICKWORKS PRESS

www.clickworkspress.com

Death's Dream Kingdom

Gabriel Blanchard

A young woman of Victorian London has been transformed into a vampire. Can she survive the world of the immortal dead—or, perhaps, escape it?

"The wit and humor are as Victorian as the setting . . . a winsomely vulnerable and tremendously crafted work of art."

"a dramatic, engaging novel which explores themes of death, love, damnation, and redemption."

Learn more at clickworkspress.com/ddk.

The Dream World Collective

Ben Y. Faroe

Five friends quit their jobs to chase what they love. Rent looms. Hilarity ensues.

"if you like interesting personalities, hidden depths . . . and hilarious dialog, this is the book for you."

"a fun, inspiring read—perfect for a sunny summer day."

"a heartwarming, feel-good story"

Learn more at clickworkspress.com/dwc.